PRAISE FOR SPEAK NO EVIL & TELL NO LIES

[Speak No Evil is] dangerously addicting.

— SHERRILYN KENYON #1 NEW YORK
TIMES BESTSELLING AUTHOR

Crosby serves up suspense, secrets and Southern scandal like no one else!

— HARLAN COBEN #1 NEW YORK
TIMES BESTSELLING AUTHOR

Well written, almost Southern Gothic type, romantic suspense with nonstop thrills, chills, and mystery.

— AMAZON READER

Crosby easily paints an eerie setting that on the outside seems beautiful, but lurking beneath the shadows is something sinister. Reminiscent of an old Hitchcock film, Crosby

is able to give the reader the shadowy figure in
the background, always close, but unseen by
the hero and heroine.

— AMAZON READER

TELL NO LIES

TANYA ANNE CROSBY

PROLOGUE

There is no place within the human body where the soul can be found and carved out. It does not sit on an altar in the cavern of the heart. Nor does it linger in a decomposing corpse. It cannot be extinguished like a lamp.

Energy; it is said the human body produces about two hundred and fifty BTU while sleeping, up to twenty-four hundred with heavy labor.

How much does fear produce?

Everything we do is controlled by electrical pulses running through our bodies—even those crucial signals telling our hearts to beat faster when we're in danger. Our blood pumps more oxygen to our muscles and brains. Pupils enlarge to better see. The digestive and urinary systems slow. Lungs expand to take in more air ... so we can focus and fight until our final breaths.

All things become crystal clear during the moment of death ...

"But I am her mother," I said, and felt it was my duty to intervene, to set the course for my wayward child ... because like me, she would make too many mistakes before stumbling onto the right path ... and if she strayed too long in the darkness, she might go too far ... and never turn back ...

1

Sunday, August 16, 7:15 p.m.

The sun was going down, filling the woods ahead with long, slithery shadows.

Cody Simmons imagined there were copperheads under every rotting log he leapt over. He knew a kid once who got bit just by sitting down on a log, so he kept his eyes wide and his jumps high, watching for signs of snakes in the tall grass.

TC, who was thirteen and a full year older than Cody, would make fun if he thought Cody was scared, so Cody kept his mouth shut and kept pace behind TC as they raced toward the old abandoned church.

TC was his best friend, but sometimes he got Cody into trouble and Cody's grandma Rose didn't like TC's family too much. She said they were "puttin' on airs" and that "you couldn't make a silk purse out of a sow's ear no matter how hard you tried," but Cody didn't exactly know what that meant. Sometimes his grandma said things that didn't make sense and Cody's mom said it was 'cause Grandma Rose was still living in the past—whatever. Cody didn't care as long as he could still play with TC.

He heard Grandma Rose's voice in the distance, calling his name for supper. There was a roast simmering in the pressure cooker and sweet creamed corn waiting, but he didn't stop. They had at least thirty minutes before she got serious about finding him, and TC said he was pretty sure they could make it to the church and back without anyone realizing they were gone.

Maybe he was a little scared, but the anticipation that was bubbling up over seeing something he'd never seen before, except in TV shows, was way more thrilling—a real-life crime scene! TC swore on a Bible that he'd seen blood on the altar at the old church and even though Cody didn't believe him, that didn't make it any less exciting.

His new sneakers were muddy now because they ran through the marsh, skirting the woods until they had to go in. They spotted the little white broken-down church as the huge ball of orange sun at their backs plunged into the creek, extinguishing most of the light from the woods.

Skidding to a halt, TC waited for Cody to catch up.

"We shoulda brought a flashlight," Cody lamented. "Scared!"

"Am not! Bet you just didn't bring one so I couldn't tell if it's blood or something else! Probably it's just oil or something."

"No, it's blood," TC assured, shooting him a keen-eyed glance.

The church building was no more than thirty feet away now, the front door ripped off so you could see right into the black interior. It looked like a yawning mouth in a mean face. Two darkened windows sat on either side of the door. The windowpanes had long ago been smashed out and not much remained now, except for a sliver of jagged glass wedged in the bottom sill of the right pane. The orange glow from the setting sun reflected off it like a glint in someone's eye.

The two boys walked slowly toward the building, past old tombstones and rotten wooden crosses that marked the church's ancient graveyard.

TC's dad had told them stories about long-ago secret meetings right here in the woods. He'd said they'd found a man hanging right inside the old church. Supposedly, he committed suicide—something about doing bad stuff with kids and feeling guilty about it—or maybe someone just did him in to make him pay for his sins. Cody guessed that was why they didn't use the church anymore—that, and because they went and built a Harris Teeter grocery store right over the dirt road that led to the old church, cutting off the way for anyone who might have been brave enough to face the ghost of a hanged man. In the five or so years since the road had been blocked, the forest had already reclaimed the dirt road.

"Whattaya think the blood's from?" Cody asked, fighting the urge to bolt back in the direction they'd come. He was starting to feel weird—like maybe somebody was watching—someone they couldn't see. It was a bad feeling he couldn't shake.

"I heard tell of people killin' and skinnin' cats 'n' things, could be something like that," TC said, in that same know-it-all tone his dad used.

Cody wrung his shirt. One of his fists balled at his side. "That ain't right."

"Well, sometimes people ain't right, my dad says."

"I bet someone slashed themselves on that glass, maybe. Looks awful sharp to me."

TC glanced at the jagged bit of window and shrugged noncommittally. "Maybe."

They stopped at the door and peered inside. Cobwebs stretched across the top of the door frame, into the interior. It was nested with insects, all waiting to be sucked dry.

"Check this out," TC said.

He fingered the remains of a dried-up cicada carcass, trying to pry it loose from the exposed wood on the door frame. When it wouldn't come off, he smashed it with his fist. The *whack* reverberated within the dark interior of the church and somewhere within the shadows something squealed.

Cody swallowed the lump that rose in his throat.

A barely visible altar rested on a stage inside. The pews were all gone but you could still see the path where people had scuffled down the center aisle, the wood worn by hundreds of Sunday-best shoes. The path was obscured three-quarters of the way down, disappearing into shadows.

They slid wary looks at each other.

"Go on in," TC ordered him. "I've already seen it."

"I'm not going in alone!" Cody protested.

"Why? You scared?"

"No!"

"Chicken!"

"No, you just have to show me where is all— maybe it ain't really there."

"No, I swear—look." He pointed toward the right of the altar. "See where all those rags are hanging? They're dripping with blood."

Cody squinted to see in the darkness. "I just see a bunch of dirty old rags hanging like maybe someone's been cleanin' the place."

TC made a disgusted face. "Why would anyone

clean this old dump?" he argued. "Ain't nobody used it in a hundred years."

Cody lifted a dubious brow. "Yeah, well, your dad said he used to come here to church when he was little."

"My dad was born in the sixties. That's a long time ago."

"Yeah," Cody relented.

"Yeah," TC said.

Both boys had completely lost their nerve. Neither wanted to go in, but neither wanted to admit they might be too scared, so they stood there, each clutching a frame of the doorway. At their backs, the last traces of sunlight were barely visible through the tree line. But right where they stood, it seemed pitch-black and growing darker by the second.

The sounds of the marsh were intensifying. Crickets chirped louder and bullfrogs croaked from their hiding places. In the heat of August the time was ripe for frog gigging. Cody thought maybe those frogs were better off keeping their mouths shut unless they wanted to end up on someone's dinner plate—not his, of course. He'd never tried one and since his mom was scared of frogs, he guessed he never would—not that he cared to since everyone said it tasted just like chicken. He'd rather just eat chicken. His stomach grumbled.

"I think I heard your grandma calling," TC offered.

"Yeah. I think she's worried."

"Probably."

The sound of a shuffle came from the dark interior of the building. Cody's heart beat a little faster. "Hear that?" he whispered.

TC shook his head no, but his wide eyes said yes.

They froze, listening for more sounds.

"Probably just a rat ... or a snake," Cody whispered, but it didn't sound like either one of those things. It sounded more like the way a smooth-soled shoe did when it brushed over a rough floor, a soft scuffle like the one he could make when he slid his Sunday-best shoes over Grandma Rose's old wood floor.

Cody didn't have the guts to peer inside again, and TC's eyes were fixed on Cody's face. Both boys were frozen with indecision.

Deep inside, something crashed to the floor and both boys bolted.

Cody ran for his life, but TC was faster and Cody struggled to keep up, not quite as sure-footed in his new sneakers. He was too scared even to watch for snakes or logs and tripped in a hole in the ground, tumbling into the darkness knees-first.

"TC!" he yelled as he went down, but TC was racing toward the disappearing sunset and he didn't stop to look back even after he broke through the trees. The last thing Cody saw was the back of his friend's bright yellow T-shirt.

Cody's head hit the soft dirt on the other side of the hole, a wall of wet mud that oozed with stinking water. It was another confused instant before he realized he had fallen into a deep hole—a grave—and he choked on fear as he felt something squishy beneath him. It was a person— a dead person—but he couldn't scream, 'cause his voice stuck in his throat. His ankle hurt like maybe it was broken. Pain shot through his leg when he tried to stand.

Cody began to cry—softly, so that whoever might be inside that busted-up old church couldn't hear him. He was alone in a hole in the woods and couldn't see anything except for a splinter of dusky sky above the canopy of trees. There wasn't even enough light to be able to see what he was kneeling on, but he tried again to stand, despite the pain, and found the ground uneven and mushy and fell back to his knees, clutching what felt like a bare butt cheek. Horrified, he shrieked and lurched to his feet, but more pain shot through his ankle and he crumpled to his knees, choking on a sob.

As his vision adjusted to the growing darkness, he could see the faintest outline of a pale breast and a distorted face beneath him.

Or maybe it was his imagination.

God! He was pretty sure he was kneeling on a cold dead body.

Hot tears poured from his eyes, but he stifled his sob. What if someone was out there? He didn't want them to know where he was. Maybe TC would come back with help. What kind of a friend left you to die in a hole in the woods? Maybe his grandma was right and TC wasn't right in the head! Even old as Grandma Rose was, she would never have left him alone to die. He thought about his grandma getting worried about him and felt another wave of welling hysteria.

A shadow loomed up and towered above him, a form with pale eyes and he felt something warm trickle down the inside of his leg.

Cody froze, looking straight into those eyes, unable to move, unable to cry.

For the longest moment, the inky shadow stared down into the grave, saying nothing, and Cody's mouth quivered.

God, what was he going to do? He swore he would never again leave his house without telling someone if he could just go home. He would never listen to TC— never again!

"You hurt?"

It was a man's voice, not a monster's, but Cody couldn't see a mouth moving and he realized there was something covering the man's face, except for the eyes. Cody nodded, unable to speak.

The man fell silent again, staring down at him, and Cody felt fear rush through him like a freight train. His whole body started to quake. And then the man leaned over the grave, reaching toward Cody.

2

———

Pam Baker was officially a murder victim.

Her body lay twisted beside an open grave while the medical examiner wrapped up the initial exam. Later, when all the evidence had been collected, they would bag her and haul her in.

Only recently had the Lowcountry recovered from the epidemic of terror that had propelled Charleston out of the age of innocence it had stubbornly clung to. The possibility of a copycat killer was unthinkable.

Detective Jack Shaw was beginning to see spots before his eyes from the insistent flash of the assistant's camera. Photos of the body, in and out of the grave, the hands, the mouth, the church, the perimeter, and anyone milling about the scene—thankfully, at 2 A.M. there weren't many onlookers. Realizing what they were facing, they'd purposely kept silent on the police band.

He stared down at the bagged hands. Samples from beneath her nails would be taken later in the lab. The tape over the girl's mouth was undisturbed, though he had a hunch he knew exactly what they would find once they removed it—or more importantly, what they wouldn't find. If the MO was the same, the tongue would be gone and the inside of her mouth would be painted blue. The problem was... he could see this one didn't exactly follow the previous patterns, and there was a growing sense of unease in the pit of his stomach while he waited for an estimated time of death.

"Dual lividity ... present."

Which meant that the body had been moved since death. The perp had probably killed her somewhere else and then dumped her here. The obvious place to look would be inside the abandoned church, but the place was clean as far as he could tell. The only discernible footprints they'd found along the dirty wood floor were those belonging to kids. A few oily black rags had been hanging inside, but they appeared to be covered by a coating of wax or grime. Still, the lab would test them thoroughly.

"No presence of larvae—ants, check, flies check. Exposure to elements ... brief." The examiner's assistant stood behind her, scribbling down every word uttered onto a notepad. Somehow, the toneless oration seemed an insult to a girl who, only weeks before, had been full of life. Jack had met her only once, but he'd talked to her on several occasions whenever he'd called the *Tribune*'s offices. Pamela Baker had disappeared while investigating the Secessionville murders for the newspaper. He sighed. She was a wannabe reporter who never got to finish her first case.

"Rigor mortis ... on the decline. Hand me the thermometer."

The assistant scrambled to produce the desired

instrument. After a moment, the examiner continued, "Body temp matches environmental temp, currently eighty-seven degrees. Initial guess, time of death, judging by the lack of blood decomposition, somewhere between twenty-four and thirty-six hours."

Although he was expecting it, Jack felt bile rise in his throat at the announcement. The girl's skin was pale, bloodless, no marbling yet, very little bloating. Her eyes were sightless, covered with a thin film, but you could still see the dark spidery web of broken vessels in the bulging whites of her eyes. Inserting a thermometer into her liver had been easy since, unlike the other victims, this one had been sliced from her pelvic cavity up past her navel.

Maybe the killer was evolving?

Whatever the case, the team would leave no stone unturned tonight, because if the medical examiner was correct—and she had seen more than enough dead bodies to know—Pamela Baker had only been a corpse for less than thirty-six hours while suspected murderer Ian Patterson had been sitting in a jail cell for more than three weeks. There was a dead girl lying near an open grave in an abandoned graveyard and a missing kid—a twelve-year-old boy—and it was entirely possible they had the wrong man behind bars.

He stared down at the body, unblinking.

From the beginning, Patterson had insisted on his innocence. Only now it seemed the man might be telling the truth. But if Patterson didn't kill Pamela Baker ... who did? That was what Jack had to figure out before the case against Patterson collapsed.

Before Cody Simmons turned up dead, as well.

Talk about shitty Mondays. He glanced at his watch. It was 2:20 A.M. He wondered how Rose Simmons was doing. The kid's grandma had been rushed to the emergency room after the news of his disappearance—heart attack. He knew the old lady personally and hoped she would make it.

The medical examiner gave him a glance over her shoulder. "Well, Jack," she said. "It's official. This makes number three. *Now* you've got yourself a serial case."

With the discovery of the first body, a college student, Jack's gut had told him they were dealing with a serial killer, and he had nearly lost his job trying to get the higher-ups to listen. Now it was the last thing he wanted to hear. "You sure?"

She peeled off her gloves as she faced him, grimacing. "As sure as I am that Baker is dead."

They both turned to look at the body that had been hauled out of the grave. Sliced from pelvis to breastbone with the blade of a sharp instrument, she lay sprawled under the trees, her body tinted blue-green under the moonlight that sliced through the canopy of green. Her hands were posed prayerfully and taped together. Her mouth also was taped shut, her eyes bulging and sightless.

"Obviously, we'll want to be certain of her identity before we release the news," she added. "I'll be able to tell you for sure once we get her into the lab."

After a month of looking at her picture day in and day out, Jack didn't need a lab report to know who it was. Unfortunately, Baker's time had run out.

Cody's clock was ticking now, and if Ian Patterson wasn't guilty, then they didn't have a clue where to begin. "Thanks," he said, and walked away.

Tuesday, August 17, 2:15 a.m.

Augusta pressed her eyes shut, trying to block out the images taunting her.

After two weeks, a good night's sleep still eluded her. She took pride in the fact that she didn't have any hang-ups, and wasn't the type to sleep around, but something about Ian Patterson had made her throw all caution to the wind—not that she could add that particular virtue to her list, mind you. She was stubborn, impetuous and nonconforming, but caution was not really a strong point. This time she might have really screwed up.

The night they'd discovered Kelly Banks's body, she had, in fact, been with Ian at the Windjammer, a beachside bar on the Isle of Palms. By now she had fully expected to be brought in for questioning, but so far Ian had remained silent about their time together. Why, she couldn't fathom, but she guessed everything would come out once they proceeded with a trial.

She could see the papers now: *Aldridge Heir Steps Forward with Alibi for Murder.*

Her sister Caroline was going to flip.

As publisher of the *Tribune,* Caroline would take heat over it and Channel 11 would seize the opportunity to excoriate her.

But Augusta had gone over it again and again in her head.

Alibi or not, it wasn't as though Ian couldn't have committed that particular murder. Still, he hadn't seemed like a killer. Augusta had been so certain he was being persecuted by her sister and by the media that she had jumped to his defense.

"You're pushing all my buttons," he'd warned with

that slow smile and Southern drawl that somehow managed to confuse her. "You don't want to go there."

"You're not a priest any longer," she'd countered, pressing the cold, damp bottle of beer to her lips. She could almost taste the sweat from his body as she stared at him across the table and crossed her legs, gasping softly at the physical sensations that rushed through her.

"No," he said, his expression dark.

A warning maybe? Augusta ignored it.

"I'm not."

She was baiting him. "So then you've sworn off women?"

"No."

His pale blue eyes glinted like ice in the dim light of the bar, and the single word made Augusta's heart jump a little. "Only those related to the ones hell-bent on putting me behind bars."

He was talking about her sister, of course. Caroline had worked tirelessly to keep Ian's sins in the public eye. She'd dug up every last offense Ian had ever been accused of and had published it without mercy, putting questions out there for everyone, including the police, to consider. Thanks to Caroline, they all knew he'd had sex for the first time at the age of eleven and spent a summer in juvy.

Augusta didn't believe any of those stories were relevant—not a single one—especially since they had been tainted by her sister's efforts to pull their family's legacy—an ailing newspaper—out of the gutter. Augusta truly believed Ian was the victim of a witch hunt, not a criminal, and the only danger she faced seemed quite carnal in nature.

Her gaze never left his eyes. They were like deep,

clear blue pools beckoning her into his soul. Somewhere in those depths she saw his vulnerability, and it spoke to her in a seductive whisper. "Guilt by association?"

He shrugged noncommittally. Augusta took a long pull of her beer, tearing her gaze away from his face with some effort, concealing the shudder of her breath behind a long exhale.

Every nerve in her body was taut and alive.

He arched a dark blond brow. "Why are you here, Augusta?"

Despite the fact that the Windjammer was full of sweating bodies and buzzing with chatter, all Augusta could hear was the sound of his voice and her own heartbeat ticking at her temples. Her palms felt sweaty, and she wrapped the bottle in her left hand and brushed the cool dampness of it with her right, wondering if the taste of him was as intoxicating as the brew in her hand. She shrugged. "Maybe I'm here because I don't believe you're guilty?"

The arch of his brow deepened. "Are you asking... or telling?"

Augusta was much more adamant this time. "No, I *don't* believe you're guilty!"

He sat back and assessed her a moment. "That would make you the only person in this city who doesn't," he suggested.

Augusta eyed the girl on stage, inclining her head. She smiled knowingly. "Apparently, not the only one."

In her early twenties, the dark-haired girl was obviously smitten with Ian. Absently strumming her guitar, she hadn't taken her eyes off them all night, but Ian didn't seem to notice. His attention was focused on Augusta, and she knew he was feeling exactly the way she was feeling at the moment. The air between them felt as tightly wound as the strings of his "girlfriend's" guitar. Augusta tipped her chin toward the girl on stage. "She believes in you enough to give you an alibi."

"She told the truth," he said. "I was here that night, watching her play—right here at this table, in fact—waiting for her brother to join me." He tapped the table.

"So I hear." Augusta tilted her head, eyeing him coyly, and then she asked, "She your girlfriend?"

"*Friend.*"

Her heart leapt a little over the way he emphasized the single word, making it clear there was nothing more between them.

"With benefits?"

"Without."

Augusta tilted him another questioning look. "Her choice or yours?"

He lifted a brow. "Does it really matter, Augusta?"

Augusta shrugged, feigning indifference though she felt anything but.

"Alright ... so you don't believe I'm guilty," he conceded. "But why are you *really* here, Miz Aldridge?"

Augusta blinked at him. The truth was that she didn't know.

She sat forward in her chair, uncertain how to answer. "I ... I want to help ... if I can," she said and met his gaze directly, willing him to see her sincerity. "I suppose I feel guilty about the way my sister is harassing you."

He brought his glass of water to his lips. No beer—straight up H2O. "I'm a big boy," he said. "I can take care of myself. What you need to worry about," he added darkly, "is your sister ... and yourself. You're in over your heads," he told her.

Augusta's face flushed. It was the truth. Whether or not he was innocent or guilty, she was a danger to herself right now. She suddenly felt crowded and stifled and stood abruptly, not really certain if she meant to go.

He peered up at her with a look of concern. "You alright?"

"Yeah. I just need some air."

That moment sealed her fate.

They shared a long look, one that said nothing and everything at once.

"I'll walk with you," he offered. "We could both use a little breathing room."

Augusta set her beer down on the table, glad that she hadn't ordered a second, pretending to herself that she still had her wits about her and her sensibilities intact.

It was the second lie she'd told herself. The first was that she didn't know why she was here, because deep down, she knew exactly what she was doing.

He followed her out back, where, even in the thick heat of summer, there was a serious crowd—some spillover from the performance inside, others who simply wanted an excuse to drink a bottled beer out on the beach and still others whose youths had been spent loitering around the volleyball nets that were strung outside the Windjammer and who couldn't see their way through a summer without reliving a moment from their past. Although the façade had changed somewhat, the Windjammer was an Isle of Palms institution. She made her way toward the beach, wholly aware of the man who silently followed.

She could barely hear his footfalls along the boardwalk.

Augusta tried to clear her head.

What made her so certain Ian wasn't the killer everyone was trying to make him out to be? And why was she leading him onto a dark beach on a nearly moonless night? Her sisters would be out of their minds with worry if they had an inkling where she was and whom she was with. "You don't have to come with me," she offered belatedly, though she hoped he wouldn't stop.

"And miss the chance to find out what makes Augusta Aldridge tick? Fat chance," he said, and chuckled low.

They walked down the boardwalk, through the shifting dunes and down onto the beach, which stretched nearly to mid-pier with the tide at its lowest point. A slash of moonlight reflected on the wet sand. There was just enough light to see that there was no one else on the beach, despite the sounds of revelry that filtered over the dunes. Her heart beating fiercely, Augusta made a left toward the pier, where it was darker and a little more private. She wasn't in control right now. Some primeval part of her brain took over. All she could think about was kissing Ian ... for starters.

He didn't fail to note the direction she led him and laughed huskily. "You're a real puzzle, Augusta."

Augusta reached down, plucking off her sandals as they reached the pier, flashing him a mischievous grin. She threw the shoes up toward the dunes on a drier stretch of beach and leaned back against one of the piles, lifting her chin.

He stood a few feet away, reluctant to come to her, studying her, his gaze traveling the length of her despite his resolve not to flirt with her. "Feeling better, I take it?"

Augusta nodded, her smile as flirty as she knew how.

His blue eyes were pale, glittering dangerously under the moonlight. "You really enjoy playing with fire, don't you?" he whispered hoarsely.

Augusta's gaze fell to the bulge in his jeans. He was aroused ... and she had never in her life been more turned on by a man. Her body craved him. Her nipples ached. She shrugged, her breath hitching on a sigh. "Looks to me like you're the one who's scared," she taunted.

He ventured closer, seeming to wage a war with whatever thoughts were going through his head, and Augusta felt the moisture between her thighs. She dug her toes into the cool water and sand beneath her feet and beckoned him nearer. She'd worn a white V-neck T-shirt over an ankle-length skirt the color of ripe berries. Her breasts strained at the material, aching for his long fingers. Somewhere in the fog of her brain she realized how reckless this was, but she couldn't bring herself to care. She shuddered as he stared, hunger in his eyes.

He didn't say anything as he approached and less when he reached her. There was no need to pretend coyness. It wasn't Augusta's style. She wanted him to kiss her—needed him to touch her—and she slid her arm around his neck as he bent to her mouth, welcoming the feel of his soft, warm lips over hers. He didn't hold back. He gave her his tongue, sliding the fevered warmth of it into her mouth, tasting every corner greedily, nipping her tongue, kissing her hungrily, and they locked into a carnal embrace right there on the beach, under the cover of darkness.

Augusta met every exploration of his hands with her own hungry inspection of his body. She had lived thirty-one years and never experienced this aching need to be filled so deeply by a man's body.

"Is this why you came to see me, Augusta?" he whispered, his voice raw against her cheek. He pressed his groin against her so she could feel the full evidence of his arousal, and her breath caught. She tasted the sweat from his upper lip and lapped it greedily from her lips. She was vaguely aware that one breast had escaped the confines of her T-shirt and her bare flesh was being caressed by cool night air. She wanted his mouth to warm her skin.

His eyes impaled her, those clear blue eyes that made her want to say anything to keep him right here in her arms. "Yes," she said with a shivery sigh, and reached up to nip his lip.

"You sure?"

Would a killer ask permission to make love to her? *She didn't think so.*

Augusta nodded.

He was innocent, she decided, but right now she felt anything but. Her lips were bruised by their kiss. Her heart pounded against her ribs. He leaned to kiss her nipple, taking it into his mouth and suckling hard, seeming to read her thoughts.

Augusta moaned deep in her throat.

Her head fell back against the pile as he slid a hand beneath her skirt, into her panties ... between her thighs. He dipped his finger inside her and his eyes met hers over the rise of her breast. His mouth left her nipple long enough for him to whisper with a devious smile, "Looks like I found your sweet spot."

Don't stop, she begged silently.

Don't stop.

Augusta spread her legs, and he slid his finger deeper inside her body. She adjusted to accommodate him, her head falling back, whatever will she might have summoned completely lost. He brought those fingers without shame to his lips to taste her as she watched.

"Sweet as honey," he said huskily.

Augusta's heart hammered. "I want you inside me," she said desperately.

It wasn't like her. She was not *that* girl, but she felt completely carnal and open in his presence, unjudged, uninhibited.

She didn't have to ask again.

He dragged her under the pier where it was darkest—where they would be shielded from prying eyes—passing her shoes in the sand. Somehow he unzipped his pants before he had her on the ground. And he covered her, shoving himself inside her.

At the time it had felt so right.

She had never experienced such an overwhelming desire in all her life—never. Her body was like a puppet dancing to his every look, his every touch. She could no more have walked away in that moment than she could have said no.

Only right now it seemed so wrong.

Ian Patterson was behind bars for the attempted murder of her sister. He was suspected of having murdered two more women and was possibly responsible for the disappearances of at least three others, including a young reporter who worked for her sister.

Augusta struggled with her guilt.

How could she have been so wrong?

After his arrest and her initial shock, she had fully expected them to let him go, saying it was a mistake. Her soul was dying a little with every day that passed without his release—not so much because she needed to see him, needed to confront him, or even because she had been so very, very wrong about him, but because she had been so willing to do battle with her own flesh and blood in defense of a stranger.

And because she craved his tongue between her legs ... even now.

The memory of it made her yearn to slide her hand beneath the covers. Was it any wonder she couldn't sleep? She felt like a traitor and a hussy.

With a miserable groan, she tugged the covers over her head to block the blinking red numbers on her alarm clock. Hopefully, everything would look better in morning.

MORNING SUN GLINTED off the metallic roof in the distance.

Feeling the strength of his surroundings, he anchored his small boat, glad for the day off and the quiet sunrise. Later, the marsh would be a steam bath, but right now it was serene and beautiful. Birds swooped around him, plucking insects and tiny shrimp from the surrounding waters. For all anyone knew, he was just an ordinary fisherman poling his boat along the flooded spartina flats in search of tailing redfish ... and the blood at the bottom of his boat, beneath the blade of his knife, was from his last stringer of fish.

There was time to do this right.

He wasn't in a hurry.

Encroached upon by the sea, this place was just another cast off of humanity, abandoned, forgotten, picked away by the beaks of birds and visited by creatures whose only purposes included eating, sleeping and defecating.

Like the Morris Island Lighthouse, you couldn't reach

it except by boat. Even then, access to the inside of the building was available only to the most agile and intrepid. The walls were high, the doors and windows long boarded up, and the trestle beside it was a huge steel skeleton, rusty and ready to come down if the winds blew just right.

A boat whizzed by, rippling the water in its wake. Annoyed, he pulled in his line, watching the wavelets travel as far as the building's pylons.

Inside the decaying carcass of the building itself, nothing remained of value. Like the rest of Charleston's ruins, it was slowly returning to nature. But the roof was intact, concealing what lay within from an aerial view, and at most, the flame-scarred brick, like the multitude of stranded boats along the shoreline, drew curious glances, but nothing more. Local fishermen turned a blind eye to it. Weekend warriors were more interested in having a beer behind the wheel of their ski boats, and the possibility of water moccasins or gators kept even the most curious in their boats.

It made a fitting way station—until he could determine how best to reclaim his sacred ground.

He waited for the water to calm, and the wake to pass.

Redfish were opportunistic feeders. They lived along the edges of a channel, where the tidal currents were concentrated, positioning themselves to take advantage of the current. The trick was to know where to fish and to keep your bait on the bottom along the edge of a structure situated in the middle of a changing current. The building made a great obstructer, giving the fish a perfect spot to take advantage of the changing flow.

That was the key. Knowing when and where to fish ... unless you were willing to make do with trash fish.

He wasn't.

He hadn't cared too much about entombing Pamela Baker in his special place. She was trash fish. Part of a game, no more—a game he'd won too easily. A game that had left him disgusted and unfulfilled—ungrounded. He would have left her there to rot in the cemetery and fully intended to cover her and go ... until the kids showed up.

He'd heard their little voices approaching in the distance, and had hidden, fully prepared to put two more bodies into the grave if necessary. One got scared and left ... then there was one ... a perfect little specimen that had made everything worthwhile.

For a moment he'd considered letting the boy go.

He knew better than to act on impulse. And yet, except for the unexpected interruption, he'd planned the disposal with utmost care. There was nothing to be traced back to him.

Snakes molted from their skins.

Butterflies emerged from cocoons.

Cicadas shimmied out of exoskeletons.

Plans, like tides, were meant to change.

No, he needed the kid.

If he could have this one ... there might be peace ... for a while.

He eyed the old rail station. He'd kept the Baker girl alive in that building and no one had found her. She was hidden in plain sight ... invisible ... like old people. Even when they looked you straight in the eyes, their tired old eyes seeking acknowledgment, most people walked right on by, looking through them ... because no one saw anything except what they wanted to see.

He'd tied the kid up good and tight.

He took his time baiting a new hook, savoring the early morning quiet, waiting to make sure the sound of pipes rapping against the stone wall would be lost amidst more peaceful sounds. Seagulls squealed above him. A distant boat horn caught his attention. But all sounds coming from within the little building, like the creaking of the old rail bridge, were lost in the morning breeze. Wrapped in cloth, those old pipes were more than sturdy enough, he decided. He smiled and kicked his feet off the side of the boat, leaning back to enjoy the scent of pluff mud on the morning breeze.

3

———

Exhausted and cranky from a restless night, Augusta sat on the bed, drying her hair with a towel, staring at the woodpecker that was perched on her windowsill.

Three months into their sentence—as she'd come to regard the terms of their mother's Last Will and Testament—she was more confused than ever. She hadn't actually expected to inherit a dime of Flo's money—especially since they had been estranged for years before her death. Sadly, she couldn't even remember the last time she'd had a real conversation with her mother, and in fact, could no longer picture her face. She tried to determine how that made her feel, but couldn't pin down a particular emotion. Behind the numbness, there was something distressing, but she pushed it away.

Although she wasn't quite as unemotional as Caroline and Savannah seemed to believe, she also wasn't given to fits of sentimentality. She came by that trait honestly; their mother had been a bit of a brick wall with very few chinks. Still it had surprised Augusta to learn that Caroline and Savannah had discovered box after box of mementos in the attic—all apparently tucked away by Flo. Evidently, their mom had a paper-thin sentimental streak that had never been evident.

Take the room Augusta was sleeping in, for example. It had been Augusta's room growing up, but nothing in it resembled the place where she had suffered through teen angst. The walls were patched now and repainted in a pristine satin khaki. Her eclectic and haphazardly hung magazine covers and posters had been replaced with respectable paintings. Flo had remade this as her *guest room*. But if you were looking for the nostalgia, it was there—a single collection of photos that occupied the walnut dresser—appropriately, all of Augusta with her sisters and Josh Childres, who had been Augusta's best friend and coconspirator throughout their childhood.

Throwing the damp towel on the carpet, she wandered to the dresser, lifting up a photo of her and Josh. In this one, they were both probably about ten, wielding sledgehammers. Flo had ordered the demolition of the slave quarters. Knowing how much it meant to Augusta to destroy the relics of their Confederate sins, she'd let both Augusta and Josh hurl the first blows. Her sister Caroline hadn't approved and had refused to participate. Her eldest sister felt that, right or wrong, the remnants of Charleston's slave culture were part of their history and should be respected. Her sister, Savannah, on the other hand, had been too young to be able to lift the heavy sledgehammers or to have an opinion. But Augusta and Josh had had a field day destroying anything and everything in sight—except that Augusta had limited herself to inanimate objects. Josh had gotten distracted by mosquitoes and flies, wielding his sledgehammer like a Viking murder weapon.

Their housekeeper Sadie's only son had been a

cocky little kid, full of piss and vinegar. Cherished by both Sadie and by Flo, he was probably the only male Florence Willodean Aldridge hadn't despised—aside from Sammy, of course. Sammy she had worshipped above all. If not before his death, most especially after.

Her baby brother's disappearance had been the turning point in their lives, changing everyone, and not for the better. Caroline had assumed the role of pleaser, taking it upon herself to try to make their morose mother happy and failing at every turn. Savannah had withdrawn into her head while their father had abandoned them less than two months later. He'd gotten himself a new girlfriend and died, all within six months of Sam's death. And Augusta ... well, she had become a bit of a hellion—angry and defiant.

She liked to think she had changed, but the truth was simmering somewhere beneath the surface, threatening to erupt at any moment. She was *still* angry, but defiance wasn't an easy act to play these days. She was supposed to be an adult, not a rebellious teen.

Who the hell was she defying anyway? Flo had never given a crap about any of her daughters. If they all simply stayed out of her way and out of the press, their mother was a happy little clam buried deep in her palace by the sea.

With a sigh, Augusta set the photograph of her and Josh down on the dresser, scanning the rest. To look at all the pictures sitting there in a place of honor it was easy to believe Flo gave a damn. But they were probably all for show—so Flo's guests would praise her undying devotion to her wayward, unappreciative children.

Or maybe Flo had truly wished to preserve a trace of Augusta here somewhere, as a memorial to the daughter who'd forsaken her. Who knew? All those answers were long gone now, buried along with their mother.

She eyed the photo of Josh.

Augusta hadn't seen him much since Caroline had managed to piss him off by implicating him as a source in her article about the Secessionville murders —an article that, incidentally, also nearly got her own fiancé fired from the police force. Much as Flo might have done, her sister had gone after Ian Patterson like a pit bull and Augusta couldn't help but wonder how much her persistence had had to do with Ian's arrest. She couldn't shake the feeling that he was innocent. It clung to her more stubbornly than their retriever Tango's dog hair.

Disgusted, she turned away from the dresser.

There were too many things on her mind right now—not the least of which had to do with the renovation of the house. Upon her mother's death, Flo had left her daughters each with a task—a final distasteful chore to earn one last allowance. With Flo, nothing could ever be given freely. No hugs. No smiles. Everything had to be *earned*, and the price usually included a piece of one's soul.

Caroline's *job* was to revive the *Tribune*—one of Charleston's oldest newspapers—from its painful death throes. Savannah—her youngest sister and their mother's favorite—if indeed Flo had a favorite—had to face her writing demons and pen a new book. No doubt, Flo was hoping Savannah would immortalize her in ink. And Augusta, well, she got to restore the house they'd grown up in—this Civil War-era monstrosity she had come to hate. And the kicker... they had to do it all while living together under the same roof, without killing each other.

Whatever that was supposed to accomplish, Augusta didn't know, but Flo had one helluva sense of humor and the joke was on them.

So far, Augusta had been living out of a single drawer, reluctant to get too comfortable, but she opened the dresser drawer now and stared at the empty bottom. A glance at the closet floor confirmed that her entire wardrobe was lying there waiting to be laundered, and a wry smile curved her lips. Apparently, a limited wardrobe only worked if you were willing to do laundry often.

Retrieving a pair of shorts from the dirty pile and plucking up the cleanest of the T-shirts, she decided another trip to New York was in order. Augusta had kept her apartment there, fully intending to return after their year's sentence was over. She had brought only the most basic necessities. Caroline was going to flip out over her leaving again, she knew, but it couldn't be helped. Although at this point, Caroline's fits were the least of her worries, and even the house lagged far behind the situation with Ian.

What had she been thinking?

Whether he was guilty or not, sleeping with him might have been the stupidest thing she had ever done in all her life. Not daring to explore last night's dreams too closely, she made her way downstairs, passing the loose board that had sent her mother tumbling to her death. For the hundredth time, she stopped to inspect it, examining the warped wood. It looked a little like water damage, but a glance up revealed no telltale stain in the ceiling. Toeing the raised board, she resolved to begin the renovations of this mausoleum—this tribute to Southern aristocracy—as soon as possible. Christ, but if her mother thought she was going to leave the place as it was, she was dead wrong. If she was going to be forced to handle the restoration of this relic of the Old South, it was going to end up as something Augusta could look at and not feel shame over.

It was no secret to anyone that Augusta hated this house. For that matter, she hated Charleston and its genteel façade that hid a putrid soul—melodramatic perhaps, but the description suited her feelings just the same. Nope, give her New York and honest, straightforward people any day of the week.

At the bottom of the stairs, she checked the massive old mirror that had been hanging in the hall for literally a century and frowned at the dark circles forming under her eyes. The mirror had at one point belonged to Charles Pinckney, one of the signers of the Declaration of Independence. But that distinction hadn't saved Pinckney's plantation and he'd sold the estate—and the mirror—due to mismanagement. His loss was apparently the Aldridges' gain, or rather her great-great-grandmother's gain.

When they were younger, Sadie had had them all convinced the mirror bore the souls of the dead, and dead was exactly what she looked like this morning. The original silvered glass was hardly flattering, but her mother had gladly sacrificed her reflection for the cachet of owning a gilded glass that had once hung at Snee Farm.

All of it was straight-up bung as far as Augusta was concerned. She didn't much care to stare at herself in any mirror, but if you were going to do it, it was better to actually be able to see yourself clearly.

Voices came from the direction of the kitchen. "Lordy, Caroline! You didn't have to do this, eah!"

Augusta walked in as Sadie was inspecting a gift, apparently from Caroline, pulling the little dipper out and twirling the wand in her hand. Painted yellow, the small bowl was seated atop a base shaped like a minia-ture sunflower. Augusta walked over to inspect it, too, and then realizing what it was, her cheeks flamed and abruptly, she turned away, saying only, "Pretty."

She settled at the kitchen bar, listening to her sister and their longtime housemaid and mother's friend chatter away while she tried to block out all memories of last night's dreams.

"Sweet as honey ..."

"Where on earth did you find it?" Sadie asked.

"A great little shop in Mount Pleasant. Jack and I had lunch on Shem Creek last week while we were shopping for a wedding dress."

"Love it!" Sadie announced.

"Have you two set the date yet?"

"Not yet," Caroline said.

Augusta was betting they never would. Caroline's fear of commitment bordered on paranoia. To her dis-may, Sadie set the honey pot down on the island in front of her. Augusta eyed the ceramic gewgaw with no small amount of chagrin and tried not to think about Ian.

It wasn't as though she didn't have enough on her plate.

And today, before she even got started with the final inventory of the relics they were getting rid of at the auction she'd organized, she was going to have to call her office in New York and make her leave of ab-sence permanent. She'd been kidding herself that none of them would last here more than three months, because here they were, each of them buried deep in her own task, and the truth was that, no matter how much she liked to think she was above bribery—because that's all this inheritance really was

—she wasn't. There was no way she was going to walk away from her share of twenty-seven million dollars.

Neither would her sisters.

Maybe she would buy a calendar and hang it in her room so she could tick off the days like a forgotten prisoner in a stone cell. The thought made her smirk. Pinning up a calendar would infuriate her mother's ghost—tacks in the walls—just like old times.

"I have just the thing to put into it!" Sadie said. "I bought some local honey from Bee City. But you girls will have to come over to my place to try it out 'cause I'm taking this lovely thing home with me."

"I hoped you would," Caroline said. "You do so much for us, Sadie. I just wanted you to know how much we appreciate you." She pointed to the base of the object. "See, it's signed."

Sadie gasped with delight and gave Caroline a swift kiss on the cheek. "You know what I appreciate? I appreciate you did the dishes last night, baby girl."

Caroline peered over at Augusta. "Actually... it was Augie's idea. We figured if you can cook for us, we can pull together to clean up after."

Sadie hurried to Augusta's side and planted an unexpected kiss on her cheek.

Augusta's face heated. "Cripes!" she said. "All this saccharine crap is making me ill." But she smiled, warmed by Sadie's heartfelt kiss.

Her heart gave a little kick of protest when Sadie pulled away. Hers was the only bit of warmth Augusta could really recall from their youth. She missed those loving arms.

As usual, the kitchen smelled delightful, with the aroma of freshly baked bread competing with apple-smoked bacon. The best she had ever managed in

New York was the lingering scent from a box of H&H bagels or freshly roasted coffee—free trade, of course.

Okay, so maybe there were *some* things about Charleston that were better than up north. At least this prison sentence gave her the opportunity to get reacquainted with her sisters and Sadie, though it galled her that even from the grave their mother was still controlling their lives.

"Coffee, Augusta?"

Augusta gave Sadie a wide-eyed, exaggerated nod. "Please!" But she got up and went for a mug herself, hardly expecting Sadie to wait on her. She was just a little distracted this morning.

"Here you go," Sadie said, bringing her a clean spoon as Caroline's phone rang.

As she always did these days, Caroline dove for her cell phone, probably hoping it was Jack. The two of them had become inseparable after their reconciliation. Augusta was happy for her sister, even if, in her opinion, it was impossible to go back. Once something was broken, it was broken for good. Like a shattered teacup, you could piece it all back together, but the glue stains remained. Her mother had been right about that much.

A flash of memory accosted her, of handing Flo a repaired porcelain cup—a fine white teacup with hand-painted azaleas. Her mother had handed it back and told her to throw it away. It was ruined. Unusable. Worthless. Augusta shut out the memory.

Really, she hoped the best for Jack and Caroline.

"Hello?" Caroline's smile curved into a slow grin— a clear indication that the caller was, in fact, Jack Shaw. But then her smile faded and she rushed into the hall to talk. "Oh, no!" she said.

Augusta and Sadie shared a knowing glance.

"Trouble in paradise already?"

Augusta shrugged. It wasn't really her business. She picked up her spoon and stirred the cream into her coffee, trying not to listen to the conversation out in the hall.

Sadie fingered the little wand on her gift. "Augusta, dear, did you see my honey pot?"

Augusta nodded, her face warming. She wished the damned pot were anywhere but in front of her face. It was a sweet gesture from her sister, but the last thing in the world she wanted to be reminded of was the man she'd lost her mind over.

"Oh God!" she heard Caroline exclaim from the hall. "Oh ... dear God ... Jack." Caroline choked out the last few words and a chill skittered down Augusta's spine. Her sister wasn't the sort for melodrama—none of them were—but Caroline least of all. As the eldest child of Florence Willodean Aldridge, she had often been the one left to pick up the pieces. At times, Caroline seemed as much a stone fortress as their mother.

Obviously eavesdropping, as well, Sadie slid Augusta a curious glance, and Augusta sipped at her coffee while she waited for Caroline to walk back into the kitchen. What in the world would have her so upset already this morning?

Maybe Jack was backing out of the wedding?

But Augusta didn't think so. She had never seen a man with bigger goo-goo eyes than her prospective brother-in-law. After ten years apart, she didn't think those two could be separated with a crowbar at this point in time. But Jack was a police officer, so maybe it had something to do with his job ...

There was a weighted silence from the hall. When Caroline walked back into the kitchen, her face was pale as paper, her eyes glassy.

"What on God's green earth?" Sadie asked, her black eyes full of dread.

Blinking back tears, Caroline walked into the kitchen, her gaze zeroing in on Augusta. She swallowed hard, clutching the kitchen island, and said, "They found Pam Baker's body."

"Oh no!" Sadie exclaimed.

Caroline looked as though she were about to faint. "There's more," she said, and a prickle raced down Augusta's spine.

IAN HAD LEARNED to tune out most of the sounds of prison, but the small things still got through somehow. The constant running of his toilet, the distant *ting, ting, ting* of someone tapping impatiently on a metal bed and the low-grade scratching of what sounded like fingernails on cement walls.

Lying on his cot, he stared at the yellow stains on the mattress above him, wondering how the hell he had become so deeply embroiled in someone else's affairs.

As always, everything had begun innocently enough. He'd been asked to search for a missing girl—a member of his parish. Sixteen-year-old Jennifer Williams had accused him of improper conduct, but she had been in pain at the time, and his rejection had sent her reeling. The girl had regretted her accusation almost at once and fessed up—too late to save his affiliation with the Church. But it was just as well. Ian wasn't cut out to be a priest.

He obviously wasn't cut out to be anyone's savior either, because he was doing a piss-poor job of helping anyone—including himself. Somehow he'd managed to dive headfirst into legal piles of shit. First, Williams's accusations. And now he was being held on not one but two counts of capital murder, neither of which he'd committed.

Scheduled in exactly thirty minutes, his preliminary hearing would establish once and for all whether the evidence was solid enough to go to trial.

He knew it wasn't. Ninety percent of the evidence had been planted. But by whom and why? That he didn't know. All he could figure was that someone knew he was getting close to the truth and wanted him out of the way. Somehow, he felt in his gut that it all came back to the Aldridges. There was a connection there; he just didn't know what it was yet.

"Enjoying your vacation?"

Recognizing the voice, Ian tensed. He didn't bother to get up. "Sure," he said, sliding a look at the face peering in through his bars. "The accommodations are great. Always wanted a bird's-eye view of men getting fucked up the ass, both literally and figuratively."

Jack Shaw stood outside his cell, assessing him, and Ian sat up.

"You'd look great in pink," Shaw suggested, referring to the color of the jumpsuits issued by the state to sexual offenders. "But I'd personally love to see you in green."

The color issued to inmates on death row.

Despite the fact that Ian was innocent, Jack's comment hit the mark.

Once upon a time, he'd believed all good people went to heaven; all the bad ones went to hell. Now he suspected there was no heaven or hell except for the one that existed right here on earth—more specifically right here in this cell. He never would have imagined an innocent man could be convicted of a crime—

not even after Jennifer Williams had accused him of wrongful conduct. In the end, justice had prevailed. But right now he was facing the possibility of a death sentence, because South Carolina was one of thirty-three states that still kept a death row.

Struggling with his anger, he peered down at his prison-issue shoes. "What do you want, Shaw?"

"To see your reaction, I suppose."

Ian leaned forward, interested despite his anger. He crossed his fingers into a fist—never again would he bend his hands in prayer.

There was no justice.

There was no God.

No one was innocent anymore.

Not even him.

Shaw's canny eyes watched him.

"Reaction to what, exactly?"

"You're going to find out soon enough," he suggested. "So I wanted to be the one to break the news. Seems they found Pamela Baker's body."

Ian's stomach plummeted. It didn't matter that they thought he was guilty. He wasn't. And now another girl was dead; he braced himself for the rest of the news. He might as well know exactly what it was they were going to attempt to pin on him. "And?"

Shaw hitched his shoulders. "Looks like you're off the hook for this one."

Ian surged to his feet. "Why?"

"Doesn't seem the sort of question an innocent man would ask."

"My innocence hasn't stopped you from trying to prosecute me thus far—or from harassing the girl who's my alibi."

"People lie," Shaw suggested.

The two of them stared hard at one another, un-flinching.

"Baker has been dead for less than a week," Shaw finally offered.

Blinking, Ian found himself drawn toward the bars, staring Jack directly in the eyes. Something like hope took seed in his gut. "I didn't kill anyone," he swore for the hundredth time.

"So you've said."

"It's the truth." He reached a hand toward the bar, wrapping his fist around the cold metal.

Shaw didn't bother to move away. "So you say."

The two locked gazes, and in a moment of weakness, Ian came close to pleading. "I'm *not* guilty," he insisted, his jaw working.

Shaw seemed to study him harder. "Maybe not," he conceded after a long moment, and then he took a step backward, and turned and walked away, down the hall toward the security doors, leaving Ian securely locked behind bars.

"I want to see my attorney!" Ian shouted at his back.

"He's on the way," Shaw offered without turning, and God help him, Ian felt a bolt of relief. More than love or human compassion—or even sorrow for the girl who had lost her life—he felt relief for himself.

As he stood there watching Shaw disappear behind the security doors, he knew beyond a shadow of doubt that every last trace of the man he used to be— the man he was trying to be—was gone.

Who was he now?

Someone he didn't know.

Someone he didn't want to know.

AFTER THE PHONE call from Jack, Caroline went right to the hospital to see Rose Simmons. Augusta declined to go, mainly because she couldn't bear the thought of facing Rose or her family right now ... not knowing what she was about to do ...

A memory of Cody Simmons—tiny and premature, with shining black hair, emerged in her thoughts as she sat in her mother's car, staring at the King Street building that housed Greene & Ashe Law Offices, their family attorney. There were bars on the windows —a necessity in this part of town. While Augusta had defended Daniel's decision to remain here in this area of urban reconstruction—because she admired his resolve to stand firmly by the people who needed him most—after being mugged last month, she no longer felt comfortable coming here alone. Her car doors remained locked and her windows were up despite that the car's vintage air-conditioning was sputtering a little.

Beads of sweat trickled between her breasts as she waited. Her gaze shifted anxiously between the newspaper on the passenger seat and the black-painted door of the law office.

The sound of ringing suddenly erupted from her purse. She fished the phone out with some trepidation. It was Josh. She grimaced at the sight of his name on her caller ID. Of all the people who might have called, he was the one person Augusta couldn't bring herself to avoid. Unlike with her sisters, she felt obligated to pick up his phone calls, even though she didn't want to talk to him—maybe out of some lingering sense of loyalty? As kids, her mother had claimed they were "tight as ticks" and they had been, but things changed. She had changed. She tapped the answer button and tried to keep the chagrin from her tone. "Hello."

"Hey, you. I heard about Cody. Where are you?"

Augusta frowned at his question. For a guy who seemed to get his way without fail, he was strangely lacking in social graces. Augusta didn't want to tell him where she was. "Downtown," she offered.

"You okay?"

"Fine," she reassured, but refused to offer more. The days of confiding all to Josh were done. Besides, he of all people wouldn't understand.

There was a long pause on the other end of the line. She had the sense that her answer disappointed him—as though somehow Josh had expected her to handle the news of Cody's disappearance with the same outrage of her youth. More than that, she had the feeling he *needed* her to lean on him.

Unbidden, the memory of the two of them out behind the boathouse accosted her. They had been sixteen that day when he'd kissed her. Augusta had immediately regretted it and their relationship had suffered afterward, although Josh seemed bound and determined to pretend everything was exactly as it had once been.

Well, it wasn't.

"I just wanted to be sure," he said. "Are you on your way to the hospital now?"

Guilt pricked at her. "Caroline's there," she said. "You know I'm not really all that great with words."

"If it'll make you feel better, I'm not sure anyone really knows what to say. Gruesome shit. Promise me you'll be careful."

Why did everything he say seem to annoy her these days? She smacked the steering wheel with the butt of her hand, eyeing Daniel Greene's office door. "I will, Josh. But you don't have to worry about me, you know. I'm a big girl. I can take care of myself."

But that wasn't exactly true. They could all use a watchful eye these days, including Josh. So far, three bodies had been discovered—all found naked, hands posed in prayer, the tongues cut out. As much as the police tried to keep the details quiet, there wasn't much chance Augusta wouldn't know some of the more gruesome details when her sister was both a potential victim and publisher of the *Tribune*—not to mention the fact that Caroline's fiancé was, at least initially, the detective in charge of the investigations.

Josh was trying to help, she reminded herself. He wasn't Caroline. Her sister's micromanaging eclipsed everyone else's. So what was she really reacting to? Maybe her own sense of guilt for the kiss behind the boathouse? In fact, she had never kissed anyone before that day and had actually egged him on, eager for the experience. The fact that it had left her with a sick feeling in her belly afterward had little to do with Josh, or anything he had done, and everything to do with herself.

Across the street, Daniel Greene pulled into a parking space in front of his building and got out of his car. "Look, Josh, I've got to go."

He sighed, but Augusta just couldn't change the way she felt. She wanted him to move on and let go. "Bye," he said.

Augusta hung up as Greene walked into his office. Her eyes returned to the morning's edition of the *Tribune* on the passenger seat beside her.

Ian was innocent, she was sure of it.

Cannibalizing the inside of her lip, she stared at the paper. Jack hadn't given Caroline all that many details, but she'd overheard enough to know Pamela had still been alive a week ago. Now she wasn't, and there was no way Ian could have killed her sitting behind bars. No, someone else was doing this, and she felt guiltier now for not having come forward sooner. One more alibi might have gotten Ian out of jail. Apparently, despite all her talk, she was just a chicken at heart ... but she could make up for it now ...

Considering the potential aftermath of her decision, she sat rooted to the seat of her car—not ambivalent exactly, just full of dread.

Caroline would go out of her mind. Savannah would say nothing, but privately think she was insane. Who knew what Jack would do, considering the crimes Ian Patterson stood accused of—two counts of murder, and at least one count of attempted murder, with her sister Caroline being a potential victim ...

The thing was... Augusta hadn't believed in Ian's guilt from the beginning—and even though she had been there the afternoon they had cuffed him and hauled him away from the ruins on their property, she had had a difficult time believing any of it was true.

That wounded look in his eyes—she couldn't forget it. His gaze had been fixed upon her, unwavering, those blue eyes laced with anger... and something else ...

Disappointment?

Now another child was missing, and deep down in her gut, Augusta felt Ian was the best chance Cody Simmons had. She felt it down in her bones—maybe not quite the same way Savannah *knew* things, but she felt it nevertheless, without any ambivalence... despite the fact that it seemed to go against all rational thought. Ian *knew* something ... even if he didn't know what he knew ... and someone was willing to frame him for it.

A hearing had been scheduled for this morning. The news was already plastered across every headline. In a very emotional, controversial decision, they had set bail rather than hold Ian without. Set at one point five million, all he had to come up with was 10 percent. It was money she knew he probably didn't have.

But Augusta did.

Their attorney would balk, but he would do exactly as she asked. After all, it was Augusta's money and she had a right to use it however she wished. This time, it wasn't simply about siding with the underdog. It was about a deep and abiding desire for justice. And Ian Patterson was at the heart of that justice. Having spent the last six months searching for Jennifer Williams, he knew as much as the police did about this investigation.

Maybe he would find Cody? It was a long shot, but she was willing to risk it. Let the cards fall where they may...

Even if it meant adding her name to the witch hunt.

Even if it meant severing the fragile bond she was finally forming with her sisters.

Even if it meant risking the chance that she might be wrong.

Taking a deep breath, she opened the car door and slid out from behind the wheel of her mother's Town Car. Locking the door and dropping the keys into her purse, she headed straight into Daniel Greene's office, with the intention of paying Ian's bail.

4

———

Apparently, Lady Justice had a name; it was Augusta Aldridge.

Less than two hours after Ian's hearing, with his exit procedure completed, he made a beeline for the door, half-expecting to find Augusta waiting outside. She had paid his bail but not in person—she had sent her attorney instead. He didn't exactly know how to feel about that. He did know he felt both relief and disappointment that he didn't spy her strawberry-blond head outside the station, though he wasn't sure what to say to her, aside from *thank you.*

He hadn't been able to get her off his mind.

With three weeks spent for the most part in his own head, Augusta's face had been a constant ghost before his eyes. The look on her face as they'd hand-cuffed him and hauled him away after her sister's or-deal had cut him deeper than he might have expected, especially considering that he really didn't know her. He'd spent one night with her. One night.

But one helluva night.

Augusta was not the sort of girl you easily forgot. Brash. Honest. Beautiful. She spoke her mind and wore her heart on her sleeve. Exactly the sort of woman he could go for ... if he were free. But he wasn't free.

What was worse, he was lost.

He still hadn't quite processed his excommunication from the Church—not that celibacy had ever been a welcome requisite, though he had been fully prepared to do what he had to do. But that wasn't his problem right now.

Right now, as much as he would like to walk away and forget everything he knew—forget there was a murderer out there snuffing out innocent lives—he couldn't. Bottom line: Someone was willing to derail his life to get him out of the way. Someone was watching him. And if they were watching him, it meant he was getting close, even if he didn't know what it was he was getting close to. But he was no longer moving under the radar—possibly never had been. If he let Augusta Aldridge anywhere near him, he'd be placing her in danger, too. Because now more than ever, Ian was determined to find out who was at the bottom of Jennifer Williams's disappearance. He had a hunch that person was also responsible for the deaths of at least three other women and possibly more. In fact, he was sure of it. Though there was as yet no body for Jennifer, he knew in his gut that the disappearances and murders were all connected—including the disappearance of Amanda Hutto, a six-year old girl from Folly Beach who didn't fit the profile of the known victims.

He hailed a cab and went straight to the nearest rental car dealer, renting the cheapest vehicle they had—a red Ford Focus that would unfortunately make it real easy for everyone to spot him. His Acura had been impounded so they could go over it for evidence. Hopefully, they hadn't destroyed it during the process. Maybe he'd get the damned thing back soon, but in the meantime, he had to have something to drive and he needed a little more time to consider what to do about his poor little rich girl.

With some luck, her sister Caroline would keep her nose—and her fish-wrap paper—out of his business, although he was pretty sure that wasn't her style. Well, he would tear down that bridge when he got to it. First things first. He resolved to get home and see if there was anything at all the cops had missed when they had searched his house. Someone had planted evidence to incriminate him and Ian intended to find out who. He had never seen that bag before, nor its contents, but whoever had put the hit bag together had known precisely what to put inside, including the same roll of tape used to tape the victims' mouth shut and a vial of blue dye, along with various other items.

Pulling onto the expressway, he headed over the Ashley River, toward James Island, shoving thoughts of Augusta Aldridge out of his head.

For her own good.

For his own good.

FOR BETTER OR WORSE, the deed was done, and now Augusta braced herself for the worst. She drove her mother's old lemon-yellow vintage Lincoln Town Car onto the gravel drive and stopped in front of their house, cutting off the engine, considering the house.

Right in front, inside a circular garden, a massive oak stood surrounded by shivering azaleas. Through the windshield, Augusta peered up at the ancient tree, which now stood humpbacked and burdened on one side with limbs that stretched toward the ground like a mother swooping up her children. On the other side, where the branches had threatened the roof, they had been lopped off, amputated like the legs and arms of Confederate soldiers.

That was the trouble here, Augusta mused. What most people saw on the outside—the storybook gables peeking through majestic oaks liberally painted with Spanish moss, the gracious wraparound piazza—none of it spoke to the dark secrets tucked inside those old walls.

While some kids might have visions of sugarplums dancing through their skulls, Augusta had entertained images of malaria-stricken women and slave babies laboring in rice fields. That was what growing up around rows of slave quarters did for a child's imagination. She had never been able to comprehend how Sadie could make her home in that damned overseer's house. But that was Sadie's problem, not Augusta's. She had long ago resigned herself to the fact that it was Sadie's right to sleep wherever she wished to sleep —and if she happened to want to lay her head where men once slept who had tortured her ancestors ... then so be it. It wasn't as though the "big house" didn't have its own share of troubles—not the least of which had been introduced by the present generation of Aldridges—herself included.

She sighed—an expulsion of breath that was part wistful, part relief and part trepidation.

When she was a kid, magazines like *Southern Living* and *House Beautiful* had come to photograph the aging memorial of days gone by, snapping shots of the colorful drifts of azaleas that surrounded the whitewashed wooden façade ... the high dormer windows that, to Augusta, had always looked like sinister eyes peering out at the world. Her eyes were drawn upward to the widow's walk. Its highest point rose nearly forty feet into the trees, its copper weather vane nearly invisible in the blanket of limbs and moss that surrounded it. No one ever went up there anymore, but it was a true widow's walk, not for show. Access was only available through the attic now, but she and her sisters had used the walk to maintain their suntans. She wondered—not for the first time—how many widows had waited up there for husbands and sons to come hobbling home from the war, with sawed-off limbs and the shadow of death in their eyes.

Tapping her fingers on the steering wheel, she let her thoughts return to Ian.

Had they released him yet?

She inhaled a shaky breath, wondering whether he would call.

What the hell would she say?

For that matter, what would her sisters say when they discovered she'd paid his bail?

Really, she was no different from this house. She offered a façade to the world, and behind that façade were secrets that, if ever shown the light of day, would color everyone's perception of her. And despite all of Augusta's best intentions, she seemed to be adding to those secrets day by day. For her sake, she had to believe all those sins could be washed away.

Shoving Ian resolutely out of her thoughts, she studied the house she had come to despise, wondering what part of the renovation to tackle first. Somehow, even with all the drama surrounding them, she was going to *have* to make time to do it—sometime between funerals and aiding and abetting accused murderers. Jesus, what a mess she was! And pretty soon, if she didn't get to work on the house, she was going to be a broke-ass mess, as well.

Maybe she would call in a contractor tomorrow? She had a few recommendations, but that was as far as she had gotten.

When she'd first considered the task of restoring the old house, she'd approached it resentfully and without any real purpose. In fact, the only thing that had even remotely excited her was the prospect of gutting the sucker—literally—and getting rid of every stick of furniture. Absolutely nothing would have given her greater pleasure than to toss those old Civil War muskets hanging in her mother's office and the family portraits of people she didn't really want to be related to into a raging bonfire. But here she was, and after three months of whining over the task her mother had set before her, it was beginning to become important to her to believe this old place could somehow be redeemed ...

Maybe her mother had known something after all?

Nah, she decided, refusing to give her mother any credit. Florence W. Aldridge had remained completely absent from their life; she didn't get to start parenting from the grave.

Plucking her keys out of the ignition, Augusta got out of the car. She slammed the door, locking it. It used to be that you didn't even think about having to lock your car outside your own front door, but after all that had transpired you couldn't be too careful.

She paused at the top of the porch steps, looking out over the marsh. There was always a slight breeze this close to the water, and the marsh grasses bowed submissively under the oppressive afternoon sun.

Where will Ian go first? Will he come here? Back to the ruins? He was searching for something, but what?

She'd kept her cell phone near, even though she wasn't even sure whether she planned to answer. Poor

Cody had disappeared from the old abandoned church where she and her sisters had played as kids. Even then the place had seemed sinister. Why were kids drawn to danger?

The same reason adults are, a little voice in her head pointed out. *What the hell is Ian if not dangerous?*

Damn, but she didn't relish having to explain her actions to her sisters.

She was so lost in her own thoughts, wondering what to say to them, that she didn't hear the raised voices until Sadie was near the front door.

"Of all people, Savannah! I wouldn't have expected this from you!"

The door opened abruptly, and Sadie, purse in hand, gave Augusta an angry glare, then, muttering something unintelligible, tried to close the door before Savannah could follow her out.

Savannah stepped out before Sadie could shut it, and Sadie turned and marched down the stairs without waiting for the door to close. Taken by surprise, Augusta moved out of her way and Savannah came out of the house to plead a little desperately, "Sadie, I didn't go behind your back—please! Listen to me!"

Sadie kept walking, shoulders straight, making her way down the drive toward her house. "If you girls get hungry," she said without turning, "you know exactly where the fridge is!"

Augusta was pretty sure that was meant for her, since clearly, Sadie wasn't pleased with Savannah and didn't give a damn whether she ate or not.

Savannah's hand went to her hip. The left hand, which was still in a cast after a nasty fall from a kitchen stool, hung helplessly at her side. "Sadie!" she shouted.

Sadie kept walking, ignoring her.

"What the hell was that about?"

Savannah gave Augusta a disgruntled look and turned to open the door, stepping aside so Augusta could precede her into the house. "Obviously, I pissed her off."

"You?"

"Don't sound so damned smug!" Savannah chafed.

Her youngest sister was probably the least likely of them to piss anyone off, and Sadie was not the easiest woman to rile. "How the hell did you manage that?"

As the door slammed behind them, Savannah marched by Augusta, straight toward the kitchen. The scent of food made Augusta's belly grumble. It was only then she realized she hadn't eaten all day because she had been so stressed out about Ian.

"Hungry?" Savannah asked, ignoring Augusta's question.

"A little."

"Sadie was in the middle of cooking. I guess we can finish what she started. Do you feel like opening a bottle of Mom's good wine?"

Augusta laughed. "Hell, yes!" she declared. "It must have been a doozy of an argument for you to dive into Mom's stash."

Savannah peered back at her. "I like wine. I just don't like drinking," she said, and gave her a little smile.

In principle, Augusta shared that opinion. She was a long way from being the lush her mother was, but wine did relax her and she wasn't quite principled enough to say no to a great bottle of vino. In that way, she was a lot like her mother, and if it weren't for Augusta's intense dedication to being nothing like Flo, she might have ended up a pill-popping alky like their mother. But it would be a cold day in hell before she took on any of her mother's traits. Plus, her taste in wine was far too expensive to really indulge it often. Her practical nature wouldn't allow it.

"I'll get the wine," she offered, and set her purse and keys down on the counter, then made her way to the wine fridge her mother had had installed sometime before she died. Although it was new, Augusta knew exactly what was in it and didn't waste much time making her choice. She grabbed a 2007 Gaja Barbaresco, an Italian red that probably cost her mother about two hundred and some change, but Augusta wasn't paying for it, so what the hell. This one would be perfect for commiserating. She brought the bottle to the counter and then ferreted out two wineglasses. "Is Caroline home yet?"

Savannah stood at the stove, assessing their abandoned, half-cooked dinner. "Not yet. Do you know anything about making a roux?"

Augusta took out a third wine goblet, but set it on the counter out of the way, eyeing Savannah. "Nope. Caroline does."

"Well, we can't wait for her. I'll have to give it a try."

Augusta poured wine into one glass and then lifted it, tasting. "It's just fat and flour, right? Fry the flour in the butter until it looks brown and goopy. We'll live if it's not exactly right. We've got worse shit to worry about."

Savannah sighed. "Yeah." She turned to watch Augusta top off her glass, then pour a second. "I don't think I've ever seen Sadie that angry," she worried.

Augusta lifted up Savannah's glass from the counter and brought it to her. "I have," she confessed with a slight turn of her lips. In fact, there weren't many people Augusta hadn't pissed off at one point or another, including Sadie.

Savannah laughed, and then sighed as she took a small sip of her wine. "Here's to pissing people off," she said, and raised her glass high.

Augusta choked on her laughter. "Now you're talking," she said. "So tell me, what did you do to earn Sadie's wrath?"

THE PAIN in Cody's ankle helped to keep him awake.

His head hurt and he felt a little like he had the time he'd snuck into his pop's liquor cabinet, woozy and sick to his belly. Trying to focus, he fixed his gaze on the railroad trestle outside the window. He could see part of it from where he lay, handcuffed to a bunch of old pipes, enough to recognize that it was an old rail bridge like the one his dad had taken him to near Bushy Park. His pop told him that when he and his friends were little they used to jump off the trestle into the river until one of his friends dove into a moccasin bed and died from hundreds of snakebites. It seemed to Cody that his dad had been trying to scare him, but Cody always thought he heard a note of wistfulness in his voice whenever he told that story. It didn't matter; it worked. Cody wasn't just afraid of heights; he was terrified of snakes and he used to think that was the most awful way to die—surrounded by fangs in muddy black water.

But he had another nightmare now.

One he couldn't wake up from.

Dying right here, right now, would be the most awful thing—wet, cold and alone.

His missed his dad so bad, the ache was a massive

lump in his throat. And his mom and grandma were probably sick with worry over him. His jeans were wet, maybe from the river, but he'd peed his pants and maybe other stuff, too. He was too groggy to figure it out. He couldn't even wipe the snot that was drying beneath his nose because he couldn't reach it with his shoulder.

He'd woken up here in the pitch-black, with no memory of getting here. The man in the mask had pressed something sweet over his face and now he was handcuffed to these pipes, his feet tied way too tight with ropes. There was something soft and bunchy shoved deep inside his mouth, beneath the tape—the way they did in those old cartoons when they tied some lady across a railroad track in front of an on-coming train.

But there was no train coming.

Outside, there was only silence, except for the chirping of crickets and croaking of frogs.

Cody stared at the trestle. The tracks were rusted, maybe broken, but he couldn't sit up to get a better look. All the windows were boarded up, except one. On that one the slats were only nailed partway up and jutting above the boards were shards of glass that looked like gnarly icicles wrong side up.

Never in his life had he wanted his mama more—he didn't care if that made him a baby. That idiot TC had left him there to die in the woods. The muscles in his throat hurt from trying to swallow around the cloth in his mouth, and he was thirsty. He laid his head back against the brick wall, taking it all in before the last of the daylight was gone.

He'd never seen this place before—had no idea where he might be—but he smelled water. And stinky mud. There was no mistaking the smell of pluff mud.

It was strong here—like he was surrounded by it. The inside of the building was empty and appeared as though it had been abandoned a long time ago. It seemed maybe there had been a fire here, because the brick looked like the inside of their fireplace at home, burnt and ashy. A great big rusty metal door sat at the opposite end of the room. It was open and he could see what looked like lockers in the other room—not a single row like at school, but smaller ones stacked high—like maybe at a gym.

Peering up at the pipes above his head, he thought maybe they were from a bathroom ... or something... but he couldn't tell that either. The only thing he knew for sure was that they were firmly attached to the wall with cloth wrapped around them, and they wouldn't budge far enough for him to bang them. Both his hands were restrained in a single handcuff hole, racked above his head and tied again with the same rough rope that was secured around his ankles. Trying to squirm out of them only made his skin raw and almost ready to bleed.

Outside, the sun was setting fast. The trilling of crickets and croaking of bullfrogs climbed higher and higher. A black crow landed on the inside of the window-sill, perching on the water-stained board. It cocked its head curiously, peering at him. Across the cement floor, something scurried across a dark corner —a mouse, maybe a rat.

Maybe a snake.

Fear slithered up Cody's spine.

And then he heard it and his heart danced against his ribs.

The sound of a boat engine.

He waited patiently for it to come near and then when he thought it was close enough, he opened his mouth to scream. All that came out was a choked sound that scared the bird away... and then the engine slowly faded ... leaving Cody alone in the deepening shadows.

He began to cry.

REPLETE FROM DINNER, Augusta lay sprawled on one couch, Savannah on the other. Nearly empty, the bottle of wine sat on the table between them. Both of them had tried calling Caroline, but without much luck.

Rose Simmons had died, the news announced. The woman who had been the closest thing to a grandparent Augusta had ever had had slipped away without ever having awakened—a small mercy that she didn't know her grandson was still missing.

On the muted television, the image of reporter Sandra Rivers paraded through the abandoned cemetery where the body of Pamela Baker had been discovered late last evening. Instead of the news, it looked more like an episode of *Cold Case Files*. Rivers seemed to know exactly where to direct her cameraman for the greatest impact, and somehow the lens always ended up right back on the reporter's perfect lipstick and lovely green eyes. The woman had sensationalism down to a science. Augusta's name suddenly scrolled across the screen and her heart leapt a little. She sat up, peering anxiously at Savannah to see if she had seen it, as well, but her sister had begun to yawn, no longer paying attention to the news.

The banner shifted. *Ian Patterson Free on Bail,* the screen said, and next to it the disclosed sum of one hundred and fifty thousand dollars. But Augusta's name was gone.

Soon everyone would know—especially now that Rivers had gotten wind of the fact. But the only person Augusta dreaded having to tell was Caroline. She glanced at the clock on the wall again, her heart pounding like a fist against her lungs. It was 10 P.M.

What were the chances Caroline had already heard by now?

Pretty good, she decided.

Caroline had stepped neatly into her mother's shoes as publisher of the *Tribune*. There wasn't much that escaped her these days. The thing was ... if Caroline knew, she probably would have come storming home by now with Augusta in her crosshairs.

Briefly, she considered telling Savannah on the off chance that she might gain an ally, but Savannah probably wasn't going to approve either, so she'd rather save it and tell them both at once.

Chickenshit.

Most people thought Augusta was full of pluck, but God's truth, she was trembling on the inside. Why, she didn't know. Caroline wasn't her mother. Nor had she committed any sin here. She had simply made an honest decision based on a strong gut feeling.

On the other couch, Savannah was blissfully unaware of the message on the screen, sipping her wine, eyes closed. Augusta settled back onto the sofa.

The den hadn't changed much in the years since Augusta had left home. The same cherrywood raised paneled walls, the same portraits on the walls. Only the carpet and couches were new, probably because her mother had been a Type-A germaphobe. Anything organic had been recycled religiously and a single spot on the carpet started the end clock ticking.

Kids with chocolate fingers were generally not welcome anywhere within Flo's house. And yet, despite that fact, the den was the one room in the house that had always felt welcoming.

For one thing, it was the only room with a television, which gave it a certain normalcy, though Augusta couldn't imagine her mother watching TV.

Then again... she wouldn't really know, would she?

Only Savannah had spent much time with her at the end. For all Augusta knew, Flo had sat here alone night after night, with their grandmother's quilt strewn over her legs, alone and forgotten, watching reruns of *Jeopardy*.

But that wasn't the image that thrived in Augusta's head. Her mother had never been one to sit still long enough to watch a single show and certainly not long enough to feel sorry for herself. No, Florence W. Aldridge had led a full life... it just so happened that it didn't include her daughters. And if she ever slowed down for five minutes, and feelings crept in, she'd medicate them with alcohol or drugs.

Unfortunately, that was the Florence Aldridge Augusta recalled.

"Have you started writing your new book?" Augusta asked Savannah.

Savannah opened her eyes and shook her head. Taking the last swallow of her wine, she leaned forward to set her goblet down on the table, then snuggled deeper into the sofa, pulling their grandmother's quilt down off the back of the couch.

She was facing away from the TV now, which gave Augusta a bit of relief. The banner at the bottom seemed to permanently read: PATTERSON FREE ON BAIL.

"Maybe once I get this cast off," Savannah said,

lifting her arm and inspecting the frayed edges around her fingers.

Augusta was trying hard not to be distracted by the newscast. "When will that be?"

"Next week—thank God!"

"I'm really sorry about the hand, Sav."

"Augie, you need to stop apologizing. You elbowed me. I dropped the bacon. Tango went after it. He tipped my stool. Accidents happen. I'm over it."

Augusta sighed. "So why do you think Mom left you with that particular task anyway?"

"Writing a new book?" Savannah shrugged. "Who knows." She met Augusta's gaze squarely, looking much as though she wanted to say something, but then she hesitated and said, "It's not as easy as it seems, you know."

Augusta knew she was referring to the comment she had flung at Savannah in anger—that her task was a no-brainer and that it wasn't fair—but she couldn't apologize for believing Flo was playing favorites. Augusta still believed it was true. Savannah's task had absolutely nothing to do with the house or the newspaper. In fact, their mother was asking Savannah to do exactly what she had chosen to do with her life. There seemed to be nothing punishing about that. In contrast, neither Caroline nor Augusta had wanted anything to do with the *Tribune* or the house. The fact that Caroline suddenly seemed to embrace her role at the paper was beside the point. Augusta couldn't get past the feeling that, in fact, Flo had meant to teach each of them a lesson ... or reel them in at the very least.

Helpless to ignore it, she returned her gaze to the television, watching as Sandra Rivers paused in front of the darkened entry of the little broken-down church, her white-tipped nails perfectly manicured. Looking more like Marilyn Monroe than a news reporter, she gripped the microphone with slender fingers. Augusta could almost hear her break out in a breathy strain of "Happy birthday, Mr. President." Bright yellow tape stretched across the church door, barring humanity from its shadowy interior. The broken window behind her was a dramatic backdrop, and her blond hair was perfectly in place. If she had sweat glands, they clearly weren't working.

"That woman makes me ill," Caroline said, walking into the room.

Tango, their mother's black lab, who seemed to have taken to Caroline more than anyone else, had probably been waiting for her by the front door. He sauntered in behind her, his collar jingling as he walked.

Savannah sat up. "You're home!" she said. "I didn't hear you come in. Are you hungry?"

Caroline shook her head, dropping her purse on the French marble-topped console their mother would have cut off their fingers for touching. She chose a seat on the end of Savannah's couch and Savannah pulled back her legs to give her room. Tango sat on the floor at Caroline's feet. "Rose Simmons died tonight," she said solemnly, and then reached down to stroke the top of Tango's head.

"We heard," Augusta said, glancing anxiously at the television screen. She reached forward to pick up the remote, switching the TV off.

Savannah's feet returned to their previous spot, her toes touching Caroline's thigh and Caroline glanced down. "We tried calling," Savannah offered.

Caroline nodded, and tugged a corner of Savannah's quilt onto her lap, covering Savannah's toes. She dabbed at her eye. "I've been with the family."

Sensing her distress, Tango sat upright and stared at her, and Caroline automatically reached out to reassure the canny beast.

Savannah's eyes misted, too, and Augusta wondered why she couldn't feel what they felt. Rose Simmons had been one of their mother's dearest friends, and Augusta hadn't even said hello to her at Flo's funeral. But that wasn't nearly as disturbing to her as the simple fact that she had yet to shed a single tear for her own mother. All her life she had been driven to do for others because her heart bled indiscriminately. Only now it seemed that wellspring of emotion had completely dried up. Yet she couldn't get Cody Simmons out of her head. If her heart bled, it was for him right now.

"We figured," Augusta said. "How are they?"

Caroline shrugged. "Upset."

"Understandably."

"Man, you've gotta feel for them," Savannah said. "Cody's missing. Rose is gone. How the hell do you grieve when you're dealing with a missing child?"

"I can't imagine," Augusta said, her thoughts honing in on Cody.

Where could he be?

Amanda Hutto had never been found—despite the reward money that had been offered for information—money Augusta had donated and the *Tribune* had sponsored. Tons of calls, but no one ever came forward with reliable information. Still, she thought about offering another reward for Cody anyway, despite the fact that his family had more than enough money of their own to do so if they wished. It probably wasn't appropriate, she decided. What was appropriate had been getting Ian out of jail so he could pursue whatever leads he might have. She couldn't find it in herself to feel bad about that.

Caroline sighed. "Poor Janet."

"What about Claire?" Savannah asked.

Caroline shook her head. "I didn't see her. I guess she's due in tomorrow."

Janet was Rose Simmons's youngest daughter. Her oldest daughter, Claire, had been Caroline's best friend—before life happened to them all—before a big to-do over Jack that had led to Caroline and Jack's ten-year breakup. Their older brother Nick Simmons had been everyone's crush in school, including Augusta's, but Augusta had no idea where he was these days. She was sure they would run into him at his mother's funeral. As much as Augusta might hope to avoid that, she wasn't so far removed from her sense of propriety that she could ignore a funeral obligation. If she could have, it would have been her mother's.

For a long moment, they sat together, all three of them, contemplating the circumstances, the only sound in the room the nervous tapping of Augusta's nails on her crystal goblet and the soft jingling of Tango's collar when he adjusted his position at Caroline's feet.

"Did Sadie go home?" Caroline asked finally, sounding surprised by the prospect—for good reason. Since their mother's death, Sadie had spent more time in their house than she had in her own home.

"Yeah ... well ... about that." Savannah grimaced. "I hate to break it to you after a day like today, but there's more drama, so brace yourself."

Before Savannah could begin her story, Augusta grabbed the wine bottle from the table and poured the remainder into her own glass, taking a deep breath.

She felt only slightly guilty for not offering it to Caroline, but after this conversation, if Caroline wanted wine, Augusta would gladly open a new bottle.

"I don't think Sadie's coming back for a while," Savannah said, and she proceeded to tell Caroline about the afternoon's argument. Augusta had already heard the story, so she said nothing, hoping to remain inconspicuous.

A few weeks ago Savannah had discovered a codicil intended for their mother's will—an amendment that, although signed and dated, had somehow never made it into the attorney's version. While the original will had bequeathed Sadie the carriage house along with all its surrounding property, the new codicil would have seized the house from her and willed it, along with the surrounding property, to the County of Charleston. Although Sadie had always claimed she didn't care about the land, she damned well did care about the house. And evidently, Savannah had taken her discovery to their family attorney without talking to Sadie first, and he in turn had confided in Sadie. Clearly, Daniel Greene's and Sadie's relationship had become a conflict of interest and Daniel should be held accountable for the breach of ethics, except that he was obviously too close to their family—and to Sadie—to believe any of them would report him. He was right.

As Augusta had earlier when Savannah told her the story, Caroline screwed up her face in confusion. "What do you mean a codicil?" She shook her head. "And *why* is this the first I'm hearing about it?"

"Well..." Savannah sat up straighter, nervously tossing away the quilt. Augusta noticed and couldn't help but wonder why they both seemed to fear Caroline's wrath so much. She was their eldest sister, so what? "It's not an official document," Savannah explained. "I just wanted to see what Daniel had to say about it. Honestly, I didn't expect him to tell Sadie."

Caroline looked even more confused. "I don't understand. What do you mean, it's not an official document?"

"Yeah, so this is where it gets really confusing," Augusta added, swallowing the last of her wine and setting her goblet down on the table.

Savannah sighed. "Okay, from the beginning... I found this pad of paper in Mom's office. I noticed the indentations were well-defined, so, out of curiosity, I used a pencil to do a rubbing. So I don't have the original—the one with the actual signature and writing on it—I didn't think the damned thing would hold up in a court of law anyway. I just wanted to find out *why* a codicil Mom went so far as to sign and notarize never ended up in the final version of the will. I figured Daniel must have been aware of it, so I asked him. It's that simple."

"Mom is—was—a notary, right?"

Savannah shrugged.

Caroline placed a hand to her forehead, as though the conversation threatened to give her a headache. "Well, it doesn't sound simple to me."

Savannah continued, "Bottom line: Daniel says he's never seen the thing. He suggested Mom must have written the codicil, then changed her mind and threw it away."

"Which is entirely possible," Augusta agreed.

"Since it was written the day before she died— that's what the date says, right?—maybe the original never made it out of this house?" Caroline suggested. "Maybe it's somewhere in Mother's things and we just haven't found it yet?"

Savannah shrugged again.

Caroline drew her brows together. "So Sadie's pissed now because you brought the document to Daniel?"

Savannah shook her head solemnly. "No, Sadie's pissed because I asked her whether she'd seen the codicil, which she felt implied maybe she'd kept it from us. And because I asked Daniel if there was any legal recourse to investigate honoring Mother's wishes —if that's indeed what the codicil is."

"And the answer is?"

"No. There's no original document, and even if it wasn't just a pencil shading, it's our word against..."

"Sadie would *never* lie!" Caroline assured them both. "Not even to save her house!"

A sense of gloom entered Savannah's gray eyes. "I only asked her if she came across it in Mother's things, Caroline. I never accused her."

They sat there in silence for a few moments, and then Savannah added, "But you have to wonder about the break-in we had a few months ago. It's awfully convenient that Mom apparently wrote this thing and then died the very next day."

It was true. Augusta had nearly forgotten about the break-in with all the other drama that had happened since. The night after the first Secessionville murder, someone had broken into their mother's office, shattering one of the expensive lead-glass panes in the double doors that led to the back veranda. No prints had been discovered, and nothing had been left out of place. Caroline had been alone that night, with Jack, in the kitchen. Augusta had been in New York, where she'd gone to pick up a few necessities for an extended stay in Charleston. Savannah had been with Sadie. But clearly that meant Sadie couldn't have been the thief... unless it had been done much earlier in the day and made to look like a break-in... but why would she bother when she had free access to the house all the time? It didn't make sense.

"Don't forget the break-in at Daniel's office the day of the reading," Augusta interjected, remembering suddenly.

Caroline stood, apparently having heard enough. "Christ—no wonder Sadie's pissed! Especially if you brought all this shit up to Daniel!"

Savannah sat back on the couch, looking defeated. "What would you have had me do? Ignore it?"

Caroline shot Savannah a glare. "You could have brought it to us, Savannah. Pissing off Sadie is the last thing any of us needs right now! We can't manage without her." Shaking her head, she walked out of the room, snagging her purse on the way out. Tango skulked after her without looking back. The sound of her footsteps receded down the hall.

"She's had a hard day," Augusta offered, when Caroline was out of earshot. "It's not your fault, Sav. And it's not your fault Sadie and Daniel are bumping uglies either."

Savannah laughed at the image that presented and tilted her a curious glance. "You know that for sure?"

"Well, I haven't stalked their bedrooms, but don't you think it's obvious?" The two of them had been spending an inordinate amount of time together.

Savannah shrugged.

"Anyway, Daniel should have kept his mouth shut."

"All I was doing was asking questions," Savannah explained. "Isn't that what attorneys are for? I just wanted to be sure it was something before I got everyone all riled up over it. Turns out it was nothing and everyone's all riled up anyway. I just wish he hadn't told Sadie. But I do have to wonder why Mom was suddenly planning to give Sadie's house to the city. It's a huge departure from the original will and the break-ins are at least weirdly coincidental—don't you think?"

Augusta shook her head. "There's no telling what Mother was thinking, though I do know Sadie would have accepted Mom's decree without any question. She's loyal."

"And give up the house?"

"Not happily, but yes."

"Well, she's pissed about it now," Savannah observed.

"Yeah, well, I might be, too, if you didn't come straight to me, and besides, didn't you imply there might be something shady about the whole thing?"

"Indirectly."

"No judgment here, Sav. Out of all of us, you've got the biggest heart, and you did what you thought was right. But Sadie is family. If you questioned my loyalty, I'd be pissed, too."

Savannah's eyes grew moist, and she averted her gaze to the dead television screen. "God, we're all a mess, aren't we?"

Augusta laughed softly. "Some of us more than others, and I'll accept the greatest share of dysfunction." She raised her wineglass. "At least I know you guys think so anyway."

Savannah laughed, though her eyes remained glassy. "So how the hell do I fix this? You've had more practice at this sort of thing."

Sadly, it was true. "Don't worry. I'll go by Sadie's in the morning and talk to her."

Savannah tilted her a look of surprise. "You?"

Augusta lifted a shoulder. "Yeah, why not?"

"Augusta, you haven't been to Sadie's in more than fifteen years!"

Augusta smiled ruefully, knowing that it was hardly an exaggeration. Although Sadie's house was literally a stone's throw away, Augusta could barely stomach the place and hadn't gone there since she was a teenager with a bad attitude.

Some would say she still had a bad attitude, she supposed. "I guess it's about time, huh?"

Savannah smiled. "I owe you one," she said.

Augusta gave her a conspiratorial wink. "Nah. We're sisters. We're all in this together, right? Just remember this next time I piss you off."

Which would be precisely tomorrow, Augusta thought.

Savannah laughed again. "You don't exactly piss me off," she countered.

Augusta gave her a wry smile, and for once, her barb was meant sincerely and without any sarcasm—at least not much of it. "Only because you were born with a degree of sainthood, Sav—something Caroline and I, unfortunately, don't share."

Savannah gave her a knowing look, one that Augusta recognized. It was a look that made Augusta feel as though Savannah could read her thoughts—as though somehow her sister knew all her darkest secrets. "Maybe I'm just better at keeping the devil on my shoulder muzzled?" she suggested with a bit of a grin.

"Right. Well..." Augusta stood, afraid of where the conversation might lead now. Tomorrow was soon enough to spill her guts about Ian. "I'm off to bed."

Savannah gave her another look that made her feel as though she was waiting for her to speak up, but there was no way Savannah knew about Ian or she'd have said something by now, and for the moment that was how Augusta meant to keep it.

"Good night, Sav."

"Night, Augie."

"Night, John-Boy," Augusta added and Savannah's laughter followed her out of the den.

5

―――――

Some secrets were harder than others to keep.

Sadie Childres stared down at the trio of graves at her feet, feeling old and tired. Only through sheer tenacity did the morning sun permeate the canopy of green above, but the grass beneath the huddle of old oaks was thankful for the respite, verdant green even in this hellacious heat. New patches were already beginning to spread over Florence's grave.

Florence had been dead four months now, and nothing would ever be the same.

Sammy's empty grave lay between both of his parents', a change decreed by Robert and Florence's expedient and very discreet divorce. Neither of them had been able to stomach the thought of their bones lying beside each other through eternity. Robert, who, with those smiling blue eyes, could convince anyone of anything. And Florence, whose friendship had meant the world to Sadie—a friendship that had spanned their entire lifetimes.

Swiping at the moistness gathering beneath her

eyes, she blinked at the fresh roses she'd placed upon their graves. Roses for both Florence and Sammy.

Robert got nothing—the same as he always gave. How anyone had ever loved him was beyond her—how *she* had loved him was inconceivable.

So many secrets.

So many lies.

So many regrets.

Staring at the roses, Sadie blinked back the assault of painful memories.

She had been coming here in secret for years now —ever since Sam's death. Florence, God rest her soul, had never been able to bear it, but someone had to honor that poor child.

Devastated over his death, Flo had gone completely to pieces afterward, refusing to give him up, refusing to admit that he was gone. Once the authorities stopped searching for his body—long after there was a chance he might be found alive—she paid to have the shoreline dredged—more to prove he wasn't dead than to prove he was. With the powerful currents in the channel, his body was never found. But as far as Florence had been concerned, no body meant no proof, and although she went through the motions of burying a child, she had always believed her Sammy was still alive.

But he was gone forever; Sadie knew that.

All these years later, she couldn't forget his sweet smile and his father's blue eyes—his chubby little fingers as he'd tugged at her skirts. Losing Sam had been devastating for all of them, not just for Florence. But despite Florence's grief, after his funeral she had never, ever come here to his grave. It was Sadie who kept his flowers fresh.

And now she would keep Flo's, too... in spite of everything.

Lord, could Florence truly have meant to put her out of her home?

Sadie had a hard time believing it—and yet... what if she had discovered the secret Sadie had kept all these years? Even twenty-nine years of praying hadn't given her any peace. And it was probably why she couldn't detach herself from the girls, even now.

Guilt.

The truth was that she wasn't so much angry at Savannah for taking that stupid piece of paper to Daniel. She understood why Savannah needed answers. But Sadie was heartbroken over the question of her loyalty —and her honesty—heartbroken but not indignant ...

Because she *had* lied.

She was *still* lying.

And she would continue lying until her final breath, because telling this particular truth would serve no purpose other than to destroy lives.

No, this was her burden to bear. And if her secret was a one-way ticket to hell, so be it. She wouldn't be the only one there. She glanced at Robert's grave and frowned.

"Find me, Sadie!" she heard Sam's little voice call out from the distant past.

"I'm doing laundry, child. Unless you're inside the hamper, I won't be doing any looking today, eah!"

His little face peered around the corner, looking neglected, his pink cheeks so unlike those of Sadie's dark-skinned son, though his eyes were as vivid a blue.

"Please, please!" he pleaded.

Sadie dropped a pair of red pajama bottoms on the hall floor. *"There you go now, eah. Why don't you come help Sadie instead?"*

His gaze fell upon the pajamas. He was too smart for a four-and-a-half-year-old. *"After you do laundry, can I have a Popsicle then?"*

Sadie smiled at him. *"'Why yes, sir!"* She nodded down at the pajamas. *"Grab them for me. You want peach or blackberry?"*

"Peach!" he shouted gleefully, and hopped forward to grab the red pajamas from the hallway floor. *"I love peach, Sadie!"*

"I know, dear. And just 'cause you do, I went and bought another box. But now who's gonna eat all that blackberry, eah?"

He strutted beside her down the hall, peering up at her with a sweet smile. *"Josh?"*

Sadie had laughed at that.

Josh indeed.

Josh had been the only male example the boy had had to look up to. His father had never been present, even when he was in the same room. God's truth, even when Robert Aldridge was standing right in front of your face, he was gone missing someplace.

"You're my best friend," Sam announced sweetly.

"Really?"

"Yes'm."

Now Sadie stared down at his empty grave, tears blurring her vision. "I love you, little boy," she whispered.

A fat tear swept down her nose as she bent to straighten a long-stemmed peach rose in Sammy's urn, adjusting it so the baby's breath would keep the flower upright. The heat would soon wither it, but for now, she wanted the bud to stand lovely and tall. When Sammy's was adjusted to her liking, she adjusted Florence's roses, as well, and without a backward glance at the unadorned grave beside it, she turned and walked away.

No one was home at Sadie's house so Augusta left her mother's Town Car in the driveway and ventured toward the ruins with her cell phone in hand. Her shoes crunched over the gravel as she made her way down the drive and into the charred grass.

It had been three weeks now since the fire that had nearly claimed her sister's life... three weeks since Ian was arrested. The woodlands were devastated. Only Hugo had wreaked this much havoc, pulling up trees, like the outcome of a sisterly cat fight where gobs of hair were ripped out by the roots.

Except that Hugo had been an act of God.

This was an act of human violence.

Were it not for recent rains, the fire might have actually engulfed Sadie's home, as well, and then there would have been no house to fight over, Augusta mused. She looked toward Sadie's house. Her blue porch was faded now to a dull blue gray. Haint blue, she called it. It was an old Charleston custom that had come straight from Geechee folklore. The blue was supposed to keep spirits out and the occupants of the house safe. But now it was a popular thing to do and most folks painted their porches blue around here. Even the main house's porch was painted a pale sky blue to match the blue of a clear summer sky.

Augusta stood there, scrutinizing the landscape.

Before the fire, you couldn't see Sadie's house at all. Even in winter, it was completely hidden from view. But the once-thick underbrush was burned away now, and many of the trees had been lost besides. The ones that remained were scarred black. Peering around at the burnt trunks, she wondered how many of the old oaks had survived the first fire—the one that had destroyed the original house—only to succumb to this one.

The old slave quarters had once stood on this side of Sadie's place, away from the main house—close to the marsh—where the mosquitoes were worst. The shacks were gone now, but Augusta always had a general feeling of malaise whenever she walked this part of the property. Today, the gloom was palpable.

She might have grown up here, but there was something not quite right about Oyster Point—something that she had never been able to put her finger on ... but it was there just the same.

Had Ian sensed it, as well? What was he looking for? Obviously, he was stalking these woods, but to what end?

The first time she had set eyes upon him, he had been right here, in these woods, holding their mother's running shoe like a football. He had been contemplating them from a distance—Caroline and her as they walked Tango. The expression on his face had been one of curiosity, not one of malice.

What was he searching for that day?

She tried to see the place through his eyes.

Certainly not the stupid tennis shoe, although finding their mother's shoe out in the woods was certainly weird. At the time, Augusta had downplayed the fact when Caroline made such a big deal out of it, but she had to admit it was creepy. Florence W. Aldridge would never have stepped foot in the woods. She might have torn her skirts on blackberry brambles. And hell, she'd bought running shoes, but Augusta would lay bets that she had never used them for their intended purpose. So what was her shoe doing in the woods—one, not both?

The idea that Ian would break into their house and steal their mother's shoe and then hand it back as some kind of warning was ludicrous. First of all, their mother's death had been an accident. Flo fell down those stairs; no intrigue there. And while Caroline had been targeted by a killer, it was most likely because of her role at the *Tribune*. Caroline was high profile now, and she had made a big deal out of searching for the Secessionville killer. Of course he would notice her. *Everyone* in the city had noticed her. And despite the shit they all said—and felt—about their mother, Caroline seemed so ready to step into Flo's shoes. It seemed Caroline's principles had more dents than an Eggo waffle.

Admittedly, Augusta had a hard time with that fact. Maybe she wasn't always in the right, and maybe sometimes she was a bit of a bitch about it, but at least when Augusta said something, she didn't vacillate. Come what may, she was single-minded, decided.

She didn't know her sister anymore and that fact made her sad.

She turned and walked a few yards deeper into the brush until she reached the burnt carcass of the old Georgian house. The original main house had burned down during a kitchen fire the year after the Civil War ended. All that was left of it now was a pile of twice-charred bricks with the remains of a chimney at one end. The wooden columns had burned completely the first time around, but pilings still remained to show where they had once stood, along with a few of the brick steps that led up to the porch. You could still see —but barely—where Jack had carved his and Caroline's initials into the brick during their senior year together. Hopefully, their relationship would last at least as long as his artwork, she mused, and stopped in front of the steps to reexamine the surroundings.

Whoever had lured Caroline here that night had done so using Augusta's cell phone. She tried to recall the kid who had taken her purse that day after she'd left Daniel Greene's office, but all she could remember was that he had short brown hair and big feet. She couldn't even give a proper description for a police sketch because it had been so late in the afternoon and she'd really only seen the back of his head as he ran away. By the time she'd realized her purse had been nabbed, along with her car keys and cell phone, the kid had darted into an alley. Augusta didn't go in after him, chiefly because of something Savannah had said to her.

A few nights before the mugging, she'd said, *"There might come a moment when you will ask yourself, 'What should I do?' Do what Augusta Aldridge would never do."* Although it had pissed Augusta off at the time, Savannah seemed to have this uncanny ability to know things.

Without her car keys, she'd called Savannah to come get her. And somehow their mom's Town Car had weathered a night on the street in one of the worst parts of downtown without a single scratch. Later, police searched the area to no avail. In retrospect, Augusta wished she had paid more attention to details, but who could have predicted the events that had transpired that night? Not even Savannah could have truly known.

Crossing her arms, she wondered ... if they found the kid who'd stolen her purse... would they find a link to the real killer? Ian—she was more certain than ever —was innocent.

Balancing on her arches on the top step of the ruins, she peered out toward the marsh. At low tide, the shallows seemed to stretch on forever. With so many of the trees decimated, all you could see now was spartina flats for miles. From where Augusta stood, it was easy to see where the water had risen the night of the fire because the singed grass stopped abruptly and fresh grass rose high beyond that threshold, golden tips swaying softly in the breeze.

The cemetery where Cody Simmons had disappeared was just down the road a bit—close enough to raise the tiny hairs on Augusta's arms.

Was there something about the ruins themselves? Or was it simply a coincidence that both Jennifer and Pamela had visited this place—and that Caroline had been lured here, as well? It seemed to Augusta that Ian believed there might be a connection.

She turned to reexamine the charred bricks. Right now, they were laid bare—the moss and vines scorched away. Behind the ruins, she could see Fort Lamar Road. At this end of the street, there weren't many cars passing by—for the most part only those coming to Oyster Point because the road dead-ended into their property. For all intents and purposes, the ruins were simply ruins ... pretty much exactly the same as any of the ruins in these parts—random piles of bricks that nature had begun to reclaim.

Augusta had come across an old tintype once that showed the old house in all its former glory. With two wings that spread out like arms off the main house, its proudest moment was in its service as a Confederate division field hospital. Just down the road, commemorating the battle of Secessionville, there were nearly three hundred unmarked graves where she and her sisters had played as children. These days it was illegal to trample over the embankments, but there was something about old graveyards that drew kids ... like moths to a porch lamp.

Poor Cody.

Her cell phone rang, startling her, and she glanced down at the number. *Caroline.* Her sister had been calling from the moment she'd got into the office this morning and Augusta knew why: By now Caroline knew Augusta had paid Ian's bail, but she wasn't in the mood for one of Caroline's lectures. She waited for the ringing to stop to be sure she wouldn't accidentally answer and shoved the phone into her back pocket.

Really, she should simply turn it off, because she was getting texts by the dozens—mostly from pissed-off folks who didn't agree that she should have paid Ian's bail. It was none of anyone's business, and it had been a grievous mistake to give out her personal phone number as a contact for the reward money for Amanda Hutto. All of Charleston seemed to be calling her. Right or wrong, she was never going to hear the end of it now.

"What are you doing out here?"

Augusta started at the sound of Josh's voice. "Shit!" she exclaimed. "You scared the hell out of me!"

She put a hand to her breast, settling her heartbeat. She hadn't realized how spooked she was to be out here alone where her sister had nearly been murdered, and where two more women had vanished. "Looking around, I guess. What the hell are *you* doing here?"

"I saw the Town Car at Mom's."

With his hands in his pockets and dressed in his usual politician's uniform, Josh seemed like a stranger to her—hardly the little boy she had grown up with. Unlike Josh these days, that kid hadn't always had an agenda. "She wasn't home," Augusta offered. "So I came out here to poke around. You know where she is?"

"Yep," he said, but offered nothing more, simply gave her a very patient, somewhat condescending look.

Augusta took offense. Irritation prickled up her spine. "Well?" Whatever fight Sadie had with Savannah, it wasn't Augusta's fault. She didn't appreciate his attitude.

He took his hands out of his pockets but stood right where he had appeared—probably worried he would get his Armani suit dirty. Augusta peered down at the hem of her jeans, noticing for the first time that hers were covered in black ash.

"Damn," she said, brushing her pants.

"Mom doesn't want to talk to you right now. Just give her time."

"You know Savannah didn't mean to upset her," Augusta offered, feeling helpless and a little disconnected without Sadie in their lives. As long as she could recall, Sadie had been the one to clean up their scrapes. She'd been the one to hand Augusta orange juice when she came in sweaty and hot after playing outside. Their own mother had never been around for that.

"Doesn't matter what she intended, Augie. The fact is, Mom's feelings are hurt."

"None of us believe she had anything to do with the missing codicil, Josh—not even Savannah."

Josh shrugged, apparently unconvinced.

"For God's sake, she's a writer!" Augusta reasoned. "She's got to ask questions, no matter what she believes!"

"Yeah? So I'm an attorney," he countered. "Questions are my business, too, but I'd defend you without hesitation, because I just *know*. Seems to me you should have just known."

Never mind that Augusta had had nothing to do with any of it. The self-righteous look on Josh's face pissed her off. "People make mistakes, Josh," Augusta argued. "In this case, *Savannah* made a mistake. Is Sadie really going to punish all of us because of something one of us did? I mean, come on!"

Josh shook his head. "Like I said ... give her time. Anyway, it's not like you and Mom had any real relationship, did you? If you're worried your socks won't get folded, hire a maid."

Augusta rocked back on her heels, feeling as though he'd slapped her across the face. Josh more than anyone knew how she felt about Sadie's employment at Oyster Point. It was Augusta who had taken offense over the incestuous relationship his mother had with this relic of slavery. She couldn't even find her voice to speak to defend herself. "Are you angry at me, too, for some reason?" she asked him directly. "It seems you've kept your distance, and I told myself it was because of Caroline, but I feel like you have a bone to pick with me."

He shook his head again. "Nope. Not angry. I learned a long time ago that everything in life took a backseat to your crusades, and it seems you've made Ian Patterson your latest campaign."

Augusta moved toward him, the ruins forgotten now. "So that's what this is about?" she asked angrily. "Ian Patterson?"

He shrugged again.

"Who I help—who I care about—is none of your concern, Josh!"

He stood his ground, his look dark. "So you care about him now? Is that right?"

The question took her by surprise, and she halted in her step. "I didn't say that!"

His hands went back into his pockets and he gave her that "attorney look" he had mastered so well. "I would argue that you did."

Jesus, she had, hadn't she?

That simple fact stilled her tongue faster than anything else could have. Her hands shook. She might consider herself a woman of the world, able to sleep with a man without consequence, but that obviously wasn't the truth.

She did care about Ian. But it couldn't be love. It was too soon for love! Wasn't it?

Her head spun. There was too damned much going on. Tears stung her eyes.

Josh's dark brows narrowed over bright blue eyes. "The math is pretty simple. You don't pay one hundred and fifty thousand dollars for some guy you don't give a shit about, Augusta." He was angry now and apparently wanted her to know it. "Donating ten grand to help find a missing kid is one thing, shelling out one hundred and fifty Gs for a suspected murderer is another matter entirely. You can't explain that one away without a little exchange of body fluids. Fuck me! Did you ever consider Caroline in this? Or Jack?"

He'd left himself out, she realized. She knew he didn't give a damn about Caroline or Jack. Josh had always been Josh's greatest concern. Augusta's chest constricted with anger. She wanted to rail at him, tell him it was none of his business *whom* she slept with.

He made it sound so clinical, sordid and ugly.

He made her sound selfish and uncaring—things she strove hard not to be. On the day she finally closed her eyes, all she really wanted to be remembered for was giving.

She wanted to tell Josh that she could never love him—ever—no matter what their history. She wanted to say that she had run away from him—from his expectations and hurt puppy dog looks—as much as she had from her mother and this dysfunctional house. She couldn't help that her heart didn't feel what his did.

"Go to hell!" she said, and stormed past him, hurrying toward her car. She knew he wasn't following, but she couldn't get away fast enough.

Josh simply stood and watched her go, the wedge between them deepened to what seemed an irreparable rift. Sadie drove up as Augusta reached her car, but Augusta couldn't find her voice to speak, much less reason with her about Savannah. She pulled open the car door as Sadie got out of her vehicle and stood there staring at her, mouth agape while Augusta started her mother's Town Car and peeled out in front of her.

"What was that about?"

Josh shrugged. "She can dish out the truth," he said. "Apparently she can't take it herself."

IAN SPENT the greater part of the day putting his place back in order—literally. It wasn't as though he had all that much to his name, but everything he owned had either been rifled through then discarded once it was determined to be useless to the investigation, or confiscated. The only real loss here was the notebook he had kept to chronicle his investigation. Far from incriminating him, that one piece of evidence would have served to validate his story.

Unfortunately, he was going to have to put his life into the hands of a jury who, after following Caroline Aldridge's witch hunt in the papers, couldn't possibly be objective. He hadn't been lucky enough to have had the charges dismissed; for the time being, the court was moving forward with a trial, though his attorney was filing a motion to suppress evidence. The police claimed his door had been left ajar and that suspicious articles had been left in plain sight. But that was impossible. Ian didn't have anything to hide, but he wasn't stupid enough to leave his house unlocked— nor did any of the "evidence" found in his home belong to him. If the house was open, it was left open by whomever had planted the hit bag. The police had probably dusted the entire house for prints, so he was certain that hadn't yielded anything, or he would have heard by now. Despite the fact that they had gone after the wrong man, they were thorough and diligent.

So where exactly did that leave him?

He sat on his bed—because that was the only true piece of furniture in the house—a fact that probably hadn't helped his case much. He was a transient as far as everyone was concerned—an ex-priest with a record. He fell neatly into their profiling net. He got that. In retrospect he supposed most of his decisions were suspect.

He'd chosen this rental house because it was near the ruins, because that was the last place he could track Jennifer to. The fact that now at least two of the possible victims had visited that site, as well, and Caroline Aldridge had been lured there, too... led him to believe there was some significance to the place. But what it was exactly, he didn't know.

There was such a thing as being in the right place at the wrong time. Maybe the fact that all three women had been there previously was a coincidence? Until the fire, it had been a private place, concealed from view. It had taken him more than a few forays into the surrounding area to locate the spot he'd seen only in a photo.

The shot had been taken close up, with only a blurry view of the ruins of a chimney at her back. Judging by the smile on Jennifer's face, she had not only been familiar enough with the photographer to hand him her cell phone, but she obviously admired him. There was that look in her eyes—the same one she had given Ian—the same look that had compelled him to send her home with a lecture and a note for her mother, a plea for her mom to seek help for Jennifer.

He pulled out a new notebook and made a list of people connected to the Aldridges. He wrote the names of all three sisters, stopping to underline Augusta's—not because he suspected she was involved, but because he couldn't stop thinking about that look on her face as they'd cuffed him and shoved him into the police car.

Confusion. Anger. Hurt.

She wasn't alone.

He added Joshua and Sadie Childres to the list— the Aldridge housekeeper and her only son, an ambitious attorney with his sights set on both the solicitor's office as well as a mayoral desk if James Island managed to keep its newest incorporation status. Josh had an impeccable reputation—graduated *egregia cum laude*—a distinction he'd earned by pursuing a rigorous political science curriculum along with his law degree.

As for Jack Shaw, Caroline's fiancé, apparently the investigation had brought those two back together. Awfully convenient—especially considering that one of the dead girls was Jack's ex-girlfriend ... the other was an employee of the *Tribune*. It was feeling like a very incestuous crime, except that at least half the supposed victims had no connection with the Aldridges at all: Amanda, Jennifer, Amy.

He stared at the notebook, mulling that over.

At the bottom of his list were Florence and Robert Aldridge, both dead. Then there was Sam—the son who drowned back in 1989. Not much to go on there. As far as Ian could tell, the kid had gotten into his little inflatable boat and sailed away into the great unknown. These things happened—especially around Charleston, where the currents were strong.

The father apparently died the same year—heart attack; the mom four months ago—accident. She fell down her stairs. According to the paper, the housekeeper found her the following morning. Nothing out of the ordinary there. For all intents and purposes, the Aldridges seemed to be a decent family, if maybe a little too far up their own asses. If one of them tripped, the world read about it—and now the oldest sister was at the helm of the nation's eighth oldest paper. He really felt sorry for Jack Shaw. That woman could be a ballbuster.

He put question marks by Jennifer and Amanda Hutto's names. Like Jennifer, Amanda was still missing.

Amy Jones was the first victim. The girl had been a senior at the College of Charleston, and as far as Ian knew, no known connection to the Aldridges. He had helped her put gas into her car the night of her death and what he got for his trouble was a murder charge—even though he had an alibi that was sticking.

Unlike Pamela Baker and Kelly Banks, she had no connection to the Aldridges. There seemed to be no pattern there ... but somehow, Ian knew in his gut the deaths were all connected.

What did a seventeen-year-old runaway, a twenty-two-year-old college kid, a thirty-year-old police dispatcher, a six-year-old girl and a twenty-three-year-old reporter have in common?

Then there was Cody Simmons—still another connection to the Aldridges, although with a history in the city older than God, who wouldn't know the Aldridges? Cody had nothing in common with the rest of the list of possible victims. Maybe the kid was just unlucky enough to have seen the murderer?

He jotted down Cody's name, tapping his pencil. He knew exactly which cemetery the kid was nabbed from, because he'd been there a few times while scouring the area. At least for a while, getting in there would be impossible, because the police would have the place cordoned off. The paper claimed Cody hadn't been alone, but they wouldn't disclose the name of his friend. Smart move, but good luck keeping that one a secret. Twelve-year-old boys liked to talk. So did angry mothers.

The doorbell rang, an annoying chime that thankfully didn't go off often.

Frustrated, Ian tossed down his pencil. He had few acquaintances in Charleston—mainly his old high school buddy who owned the Wash 'N' Shine out in Mount Pleasant. It was his sister-in-law who had given Ian his alibi—the same girl he'd gone to watch perform the night Augusta showed up in his life.

The house he was renting was a throwback to the

seventies—a ranch house that butted up to the water. The only thing that saved him from having to pay a high-dollar rent was the simple fact that this property hadn't been maintained. Despite the fact that the owner didn't live there, he apparently didn't want to give up his land to another of those million-dollar homes. All Ian cared about was having a clean place to lay his head—especially after having spent three weeks on a cum-stained cot in a jail cell.

In the living room, there was a folded beach chair in one corner and a few books stacked beside it. The walls were bare and still looked freshly painted, aside from a few scuffs.

Ian unlocked the dead bolt and pulled open the door, fully expecting to find another reporter lurking outside. They were like roaches congregating around a crumb.

Her face pale, Augusta Aldridge stood on his porch, clutching her purse, looking too much like an innocent girl, not like the temptress he knew she could be.

His eye was drawn to the car parked about thirty feet behind her vintage Lincoln Town Car—a dark black sedan with tinted windows that could be police issue. "Hi," she said, and the greeting was tentative, as though she thought he might send her packing.

Despite his earlier resolve to keep her out of his life, he opened the door wider, letting her in. "You shouldn't be here, Augusta."

Those stark blue eyes appealed to him.

She looked as though she'd been crying. He turned away, letting her close the door, leaving it open wide in case she felt like running. He half-hoped she would, half-hoped she would come in and stay.

"Wow," she said, peering around. "Talk about living sparse!"

"I never planned to stay this long," Ian admitted, throwing a glance over his shoulder. "Want a glass of water?" She was dressed in one of those long skirts that fell around her calves and a simple white tank top. The top hugged her breasts, revealing the texture of the lace border of her bra. After weeks without seeing a woman, he felt his cock stir like an errant child intent on defying his wishes.

She threw her purse down on the floor since there wasn't any place else to put it. "Please."

Ian tore his gaze away from her breasts. He couldn't forget the way it felt to be inside her, that sweet velvet heat of her body. Simply knowing she was within arm's reach, he could feel the tension building inside him.

The house was uncomfortably silent as he retreated to the kitchen and grabbed a clean glass from the kitchen shelf. He turned on the tap water, and felt guilty as he watched the glass fill. The water here tasted like shit, but he hadn't had a chance to get to the store, and everything that had been in the fridge had had to be tossed out. But, hell, the woman lived here so she must be used to the water by now and he hadn't invited her. He took the glass to her, handing it over as he inspected her again.

Fucking gorgeous.

He shook his head, an errant gesture. He hadn't been able to resist her that day on the beach and didn't think he could do it now.

He willed her to keep her distance.

She took the glass and their fingers touched for the briefest instant. The beast inside his pants stirred again.

Christ.

She had some kind of power over his body. If she said the word right now, he'd carry her to his bed and strip every piece of clothing from her body. That was how much he wanted her.

"Why are you here, Augusta?"

Straight and to the point.

People who had things to hide skirted issues, Augusta thought, and she had never met someone more straightforward than Ian Patterson. It was part of the reason she believed in him so resolutely. It had nothing to do with the need to justify the fact that she'd slept with him, she reassured herself. Right now, there were far more important matters to worry about —like a missing child and the fact that her sisters were probably going to disown her forever for everything she had done.

He deserved honesty, she decided. "I didn't know where else to go." Hungry for the sight of him, she inspected him over the rim of her glass as she took a tiny sip, glad to have something solid between them, even if it was simply a glass of water.

He made her dizzy.

His gaze assessed her, from her toes to the top of her head and back down, but it was something more than sexual, Augusta sensed, and she fought a wave of unexpected emotion that seemed to throttle her words. She took another sip of water and cleared her throat.

"You shouldn't have come," he said.

Tears pricked at Augusta's eyes, but thankfully, she held them back. "Like I said, I didn't know where else to turn. I told you I didn't believe you were guilty, Ian ... I still don't."

His blue eyes pierced her. "You sure about that?"

She didn't blame him for doubting her. She had stood by without a word while they had arrested him the night of the fire and she still hadn't even told her sisters—or the police—that she'd been with him the night Kelly Banks's body was discovered. Though she fully intended to once the opportunity presented itself. "Dead sure."

His lips curved a little ruefully. "Nice choice of words."

"Unintended," Augusta assured him, smiling wanly. "Will they drop the charges?"

Ian shook his head. "Not at this point. For all they know—for all *you* know, Augusta—I'm working with an accomplice. In their shoes, I would play it the same way." His blue eyes studied her.

"So ... are you?"

His brows lifted. "Do you think I would tell you if I were?"

Augusta lifted a shoulder. "I suppose not."

"Then why bother asking, Augusta? Either you believe I'm capable of cold-blooded murder, or you don't. It's that simple."

"I paid your bail," she reminded him. "Would I do that if I didn't believe in you?"

Their gazes locked and held. He narrowed his eyes at her and that sexy mouth thinned as he regarded her. Augusta had the impression they were playing some mental game of chicken, and if she passed... well, maybe then he would believe her?

"Coming here was stupid," he told her suddenly. "Even if you believe I'm innocent, you have to also believe someone framed me, and if that's the case, do you honestly think I'm just suddenly going to drop off their radar? If anything, my being out on bail simply means they have their scapegoat back."

"I need your help to find Cody," she said.

He gave her an incredulous look. "You've got to be kidding! Who the hell put you in charge of saving the world?"

He'd hit a nerve. Augusta handed him the water glass back, uncertain what else to do except to empty it in his face. Anger surged through her. "He's a family friend," she explained.

"That's too bad." He shrugged, as though he couldn't care less and took the glass from her, then turned and walked into the kitchen. "I'm done," he told her as he walked away. "My involvement in this case has only brought me a load of grief."

Augusta followed him. "What about Jennifer?"

He set the water glass down on the counter and turned to stare at her, expressionless, though his eyes revealed something different. "What about her?"

After everything, he couldn't possibly just be *done*. The simple fact that someone out there might still be ready to use him as scapegoat seemed a good enough reason in itself to pursue the truth. But more importantly, a little boy's life was at stake.

"I thought you had a commitment to Jennifer's family—to her mother. And now a child is missing, too—he's just a kid, Ian. Between us, I know we can help—"

"Help what?" he interrupted. "I've been searching for Jennifer for nearly six months. She's gone, Augusta! I have to accept that fact and so does her mother. I'm sick of being hounded by the papers—by your sister—I'm fucking done!"

Augusta's shoulders tensed.

He was lying.

He must be.

His words didn't match the emotion she spied in

the depth of his eyes. Nor did it sound anything like the man she had gotten to know ... but, really, how well did she know him?

What did she truly know about Ian Patterson?

Everyone else seemed so certain he was guilty.

What if she was wrong about him?

He must have realized she was wavering, because his expression suddenly darkened and his lips curved cruelly. "I want you to leave," he suggested. "I'm not interested in taking on another charity case, and I have no interest in helping you find some kid. Right now, I'm more concerned about keeping my ass out of prison."

Augusta's feet planted firmly. "I don't believe you!"

His eyes narrowed as he took a step toward her. "Why? Because you know me so well?"

And then he was suddenly right in front of her, so close that if she leaned forward, her lips would have touched his chin. Though even in her heels, she would have had to lift herself on tiptoes to feel the stubble against her lips.

"You don't know me at all," he assured her.

Augusta straightened to her full height, though she couldn't find her voice to speak.

He didn't touch her, didn't move his hands from his sides, but the tension in his body was palpable and the look in his eyes was threatening. Suddenly, he looked frighteningly unfamiliar standing in the empty kitchen.

She glanced around. There was nothing anywhere to give her a sense of *who* this man truly was—no pictures. No dirty dishes. No glasses on the counter, save one—hers. No intimate little kitchen table. No lists on the fridge. Her gaze was drawn there, to the solitary item under a Piggly Wiggly magnet—a much-folded computer rendering of a photo of Jennifer Williams standing out at the ruins. Her smile was genuine as she posed for someone unknown. The look in her eyes was full of adoration. Her strawberry-blond hair was something like Augusta's, and something about her was so shockingly familiar that Augusta stood there staring.

She recognized the photo. Caroline had a copy of it, as well, given to her by Jennifer's mother, who had told Caroline that her daughter had e-mailed the photo to Ian. But Ian *could* have taken that picture. She peered up at Ian and blinked.

"Time to go," he announced, clapping his hands together, and moving toward her, forcing her to take a step backward. Getting the hint immediately, she turned and headed toward the living room. He followed closely at her heels and despite the fact that she was leading the way toward the door, she felt like a stray sheep being herded. On the way out, she reached down and seized her purse, feeling as though if she paused for two seconds too long he would run her down.

She reached the door, and he was right there behind her, reaching around her, his arm skimming her waist. She jumped at his touch, but he merely pulled open the door. Clearly, she wasn't welcome. That night on the beach meant nothing to him. She was stupid—stupid to have come here.

"Take care," he said, and then nodded in the direction of the car still parked discreetly on the curb. "Don't forget to smile for the camera."

Augusta shot him a beleaguered glance, but all he said was, "And tell your sister I said hello." Then he slammed the door.

Stunned by the haste and animosity with which he

had disposed of her, Augusta stood outside on his front porch, clutching her purse. She glanced only briefly at the black unmarked car, and knew for certain it was not the press. It looked to her like a police-issue Dodge Charger similar to the one Jack drove. The only thing she knew for certain was that it wasn't Jack or he'd likely have lots to say about her being here. She made a beeline for her car and hoped no one recognized her.

She ran across the yard to the Lincoln and slid inside, closing the door. If she wanted to help Cody, she was going to have to do it herself, but where the hell was she supposed to start?

Maybe Ian was right? Maybe she should stay out of the way? Wanting, or even needing to help, didn't make it the right thing to do. Whatever the truth of that matter, the one thing she knew she for sure was that she couldn't face her sisters yet, so she didn't go home.

6

Thursday, August 19, 12:22 p.m.

While hardly the same obscene spectacle her mother's funeral had been, Magnolia Cemetery was a crush of people. At eighty-seven, Rose Simmons came from an old-school Charleston family. Among those present today were politicians, Daughters of the Confederacy and socialites. But though Rose and Augusta's mother had run in the same circles, most of these folks had red-rimmed eyes and lips that quivered—not like the blank faces and emotionally vacant eyes of the mourners attending Flo's funeral. Rose Simmons was beloved by her neighbors. Flo had been lionized. There was a difference.

Listening only halfheartedly to the pastor, Augusta scanned the faces in the crowd. Grief-stricken expressions, thin lips beneath dark glasses.

Across the grave, Sadie stood quietly next to Josh. Neither of them peered in Augusta's direction and she guessed Josh must still be angry with her, too, although she was pretty certain his reasons weren't the same as his mother's or her sisters'. Behind Sadie stood Daniel Greene, and if Augusta needed proof those two were involved, she had it now. He stood at Sadie's back, with a hand resting solicitously upon her shoulder, reminding her of his presence. On Sadie's right stood Rose's housekeeper, Queenie Pritchett, who had been making the trek in from St. Helena Island once a week for as long as Augusta could recall. Queenie and Sadie were distant cousins, and Queenie made some of the best damned red beans and rice Augusta had ever eaten, although she would never admit as much to Sadie. Queenie at least acknowledged her with a quiet nod of her head and dark, melancholy eyes.

It was pretty certain Rose would have left Queenie very well off, though her life would no doubt change now. None of Rose's three children was the sort to keep servants, and so it was the end of an era for the Pritchetts and the Simmonses. Augusta wondered if Sadie would follow in her cousin's footsteps. She hoped so. One would think she would have severed the ties that bound their families long ago, but until now, she had remained steadfast, ready to give up her life to care for the Aldridge home. That Josh had never resented it was a wonder in itself. But after all these years, Sadie deserved to retire.

The sound of clay and damp earth striking hollow wood breached her reverie. "Help us to find peace in the knowledge of your loving mercy," the pastor intoned. "Give us light to guide us out of our darkness into the assurance of your love, in Jesus Christ our Lord."

"Amen," the crowd responded.

Augusta took that as her cue and didn't wait for her sisters. In her escape to the car, she meandered through the plots to avoid conversation.

"Augusta!" called a familiar voice.

Augusta turned to find Nick Simmons following her.

"Hi," she said, stopping beside a moss-stained stone cross.

"You're not with your sisters?"

"I came late," Augusta confessed, and nodded in Caroline and Savannah's direction. The two of them were heading toward their mother's grave—something Augusta desperately wanted to avoid. She supposed neither of them could justify coming here without at least setting eyeballs on Flo's gravestone, though Augusta had no interest in lingering for five minutes over her mother's memory.

Nick watched them for a moment and then turned to say, "You three never could be together in one room for long." He didn't mean to be offensive, but Augusta frowned. It wasn't precisely true, and the perception disturbed her, but she didn't correct him. It was his mother's funeral after all. She shrugged. "We're good these days," she offered, though he didn't ask and it wasn't entirely true. "Mom's death, you know."

"Guess that's what it takes sometimes." His gaze sought out his own sisters, and found them huddled together, walking toward the limo. It looked a little as though Claire was supporting Janet.

"What about you?" Augusta asked. "How are you holding up?"

"Fine," he said, watching his sisters. "Mom really worshipped Cody, you know? I guess it's better she isn't around for this."

Augusta nodded, but he wasn't looking at her. "No news yet?"

He shook his head, and his gaze returned to her. "Not a thing."

"How's Janet?"

He lifted a shoulder. "On diazepam and you know how she feels about meds." He sighed. "Anyway, we're not having a big to-do at the house. Didn't seem right. Hope everyone understands."

"Screw rules," Augusta said with a tiny smile.

Nick nodded. "Come by later if you feel like it," he offered. "I'll be in town for a little while." And then he gave her an awkward little two-finger wave and left. He was walking in the direction of her car so she stood there awkwardly, not wanting to follow. She let people pass her by, and then she gave up after a few uncomfortable waves and made her way to where her sisters stood by Flo's grave, bracing herself for an argument.

NEAR A CLUSTER of newish gravestones belonging to the final crew of the H.L. Hunley, between two untarnished headstones, a garden spider had spun its web—a masterful double weave with a zigzag center. The female was more than an inch long, her markings yellow, black and white. One would think she might conceal herself with those bright, warning colorings, but no. She sat there, waiting in plain sight.

Today, a baby green anole lizard struggled in vain to remove itself from her sticky web. Every move it made only served to seal its fate. The spider remained some distance away, in the center of her silken bed, where she could control the undulation expertly, each move a manipulation to further entwine her hapless victim. Later, once she was certain the lizard was hers for the taking, she would approach gingerly and then inject him with her venom, and wrap him up neatly to feed upon.

There were lessons to be learned from nature.

Patience now.

He had the boy in a safe place; no one would find him.

But even if they did, the kid wouldn't be able to identify him.

Better to wait, like the spider.

This one excited him—not like the others, who didn't deserve to be buried in sacred ground. No more games now. No more vanity. He was smarter than they were. This one would be worth the wait. There was time; a healthy person could live maybe nine or ten days without water and food. But he wouldn't have to wait that long.

He watched the spider without blinking, thinking of the irony that she had chosen the graves of the Hunley's crew to make her home. At least for him. The crew of the historic sub, only recently raised from its watery grave, had suffocated in their iron prison at the bottom of the Atlantic, less than four miles from Sullivan's Island.

He knew better than anyone what they would have looked like in the moment of death, eyes bulging and bloodied with broken vessels. Those who drowned would have foam in the airways due to the mixing of mucus and water as they struggled to breathe. Their hearts enlarged. Under a microscope could be found the presence of algae and other water-borne substances ... usually in the stomach or airways, and the chemical makeup of the blood would change.

Some of his kills were clean.

Some were not.

His first was not.

The boy was little more than four. His tiny raft had begun to sink, filling with water. Sobbing quietly, he'd called for help, but no one heard ... except him.

At first, the child's eyes had been full of trust, then confusion and finally fear. But there was a moment beyond the fear, when a look of comprehension had entered his eyes— a moment when he'd understood his salvation lay right be-

fore his eyes, and instead of trying to get away in those final seconds, his little fingers had clutched his flesh possessively while he'd held him below the water's surface. Close enough to watch the process with the same sort of morbid curiosity that made a man slow down after an accident, and pass by with eyes downcast to the black tar, only half-horrified at the prospect of spying death. With those little arms held firmly within his grip, the legs flailing—like the lizard was doing right now—he'd felt a sense of power unlike anything else.

Filled with wonder, he watched the spider approach now, fangs bared. They appeared to him like little fists rubbing together in glee.

His gaze lifted to the name upon the headstone: Arnold Becker. Died 1864. Buried 2004.

On that day, he had stood right here, along with other curious onlookers as they had buried eight wooden coffins —all huddled together much as they had died on that ill-fated sub.

That was the beauty of a place like this ... elite though it might be, anyone could come here and tourists often did.

Not far from where he stood admiring the spider, Augusta Aldridge was approaching her sisters after talking to some guy. Her body language had caught his attention. Flirtatious. She'd touched his arm.

Slut.

Instead of stealing her phone, and leading her sister out to the ruins, he should have lured her out there instead. And instead of leaving her to be discovered... he should have killed her and buried her out in the marsh.

Just like her little brother.

"WERE you ever going to tell us, Augie?"

"Eventually," Augusta replied, though she hadn't intended to answer that way. Caroline's attitude simply annoyed her. Flo might have left her at the helm of the *Tribune*, but no one had appointed her head of the household.

Savannah met her gaze, but said nothing, and Caroline apparently wasn't content to leave it at that. "I would have appreciated a heads-up so I didn't have to hear it from Sandra Rivers. You made me look like an idiot, Augie!"

"I wanted to tell you, Caroline. Really." She looked at Savannah. "I wanted to tell both of you."

"Why didn't you?" Savannah asked softly.

Augusta shook her head, meeting Caroline's angry glare. "I don't know ... I just couldn't."

"Damn it, Augie! How could you pay that man's bail?"

Augusta bristled over the question, because she realized *that*, precisely, was why she hadn't been able to tell either of them—because neither of her sisters could possibly understand and she couldn't—didn't want to—explain Ian to them. To sum it up, she said simply, "Because I believe he's innocent."

"He might have killed me that night!" Caroline argued.

"Yeah, he might have saved you, too!" Augusta countered, wanting Caroline to see the situation through different eyes. "What if, in fact, he's telling the truth and if he hadn't found you in time—you'd be as charbroiled as those woods!"

There was nothing Caroline could say to that.

Her sister had spent literally months trying to prove that Ian was a cold-blooded killer. She seemed to *need* to believe that he had lured her out to those ruins with the intent of murdering her, but it didn't add up for Augusta. Okay, so it happened that Ian was caught with Caroline in his arms. But that didn't mean he'd actually intended her harm. He was carrying her *out* of the fire. And with police sirens racing down Fort Lamar Road and only one way out, where did anyone think he planned to take her? More and more Augusta believed he was telling the truth—about everything. She wasn't precisely thrilled with him at the moment, but she didn't believe he was guilty either.

She and Caroline stood glaring at one another, at an impasse. Augusta realized Caroline had taken this personally—as though somehow by paying Ian's bail, she had taken Ian's side. But Augusta only ever wanted to be on one side—the side of truth.

She wasn't going to apologize for that.

Wisely, Savannah stayed out of it. She stood beside them, hands linked in front of her, smiling with chagrin at the people who passed them by. Augusta didn't really care what anybody thought. Caroline had started this.

Sensing that Caroline was wavering, she asked, "Do you *really* believe he's guilty, Caroline?" Caroline set her jaw stubbornly, but didn't answer, and Augusta persisted, "Do you think they would be setting him free on bail if they had any real proof?"

Augusta could see the uncertainty in Caroline's eyes, and knew it was the most she could ask for right now. Caroline had a good heart. If she thought it through, Augusta knew her sister would come to the same conclusions she had.

"I don't know what to think about Ian Patterson," Caroline finally snapped, "but I deserved for *my* sister to be honest with me—especially when it potentially makes me look like an incompetent ass! You knew enough to come to me when you wanted to offer that reward for Amanda Hutto—this is way worse, Augusta! That man is accused of trying to kill me! Despite what you may believe, they haven't dropped the charges against him. You're not thinking clearly where he's concerned!"

"Neither are you!" Augusta countered stubbornly. "I swear to God, you have practically crucified that man!"

"I did what I thought was right," Caroline countered.

"So did I," Augusta told her, standing her ground.

With that, Caroline stalked away, leaving Augusta and Savannah standing alone together. A few people gave them curious stares as they passed by.

"Look at it from Caroline's perspective," Savannah interjected, although without any anger. "You paid bail for a guy accused of—"

"I know what I did, Sav! I don't need you to spell it out for me. I didn't mean for it to happen this way, but I believe in my heart that Ian is innocent and Caroline did him an injustice! He's not a murderer," she insisted.

Savannah peered down at the grass between them for a moment, seeming to weigh her words, and then up again. "For the record ... I think he's innocent, too," she offered. Her gray eyes were so full of compassion that it unsettled Augusta, taking her off guard. Savannah sighed heavily. "But we both know you really aren't thinking clearly where he's concerned. Caroline is right about that much."

Augusta knew the truth when it stared her in the face. The thing was... she *was* thinking with her heart, but her head wasn't arguing at all. A wave of emotion nearly choked her. "Maybe not," she admitted.

"Anyway," Savannah said, "we're heading over to the Simmonses'. You coming?"

Augusta shook her head, knowing that she should, but too confused to be much comfort to anyone.

"Well ... I'd better go before she leaves me," Savannah said, glancing toward the car. Caroline was already seated behind the wheel, checking her makeup in the rearview mirror. "Call me later if you need to talk," she offered.

Augusta nodded, and Savannah hurled herself into Augusta's arms so fast that Augusta had no choice but to hug her as she fought off another wave of emotion almost too unbearable to deny. All the feelings she had kept pent up for months now threatened to erupt right here in front of half the city. Somehow, she sensed Savannah knew more than she was saying, and her sister's compassion was her undoing.

In that moment, she regretted not having kept in closer touch with both her sisters. But it wasn't too late to change that ... and she desperately wanted to. She missed Savannah, missed the easy camaraderie they used to share as children. And she really, really missed Caroline. Somehow, Augusta had built a fortress of ice around her heart and stayed far enough north of the Mason-Dixon Line to keep it frozen and intact.

Maybe it was time to change that?

Maybe it was time to take the restoration of the house a little more seriously?

Maybe it was time for healing?

"Gotta go," Savannah said, and tore herself away.

Augusta felt the separation acutely. She swallowed hard as she watched her younger sister walk toward Caroline's silver Lexus. She stood rooted to the spot for a moment, trying to temper her emotions. At this point, the funeral crowd had already dispersed from the area, and she didn't want to talk to anyone. She lingered a moment, watching her sisters drive away, watching so intently that she was startled by the unexpected voice at her side.

"Hi," the man said. In his late thirties, he looked vaguely familiar though Augusta didn't immediately place him. He extended his hand. "Brad Bessett," he said. And then noting her confusion, he offered, "I work with Caroline at the paper."

Augusta swallowed and nodded. "Oh. Hi," she said, and forced a smile.

"I was watching you with your sisters," he said, his blue eyes canny. "Caroline can be a bit of a firecracker, can't she?"

Augusta decided she didn't like the guy. No matter what she might call her sisters in private, she was fiercely loyal to both of them. Still, she held back, not wanting to light into her sister's employee without cause. "Are you a friend of the Simmonses?" she asked, her tone curt.

He gave her a little smirk, as though he knew exactly what she was implying—that otherwise, he was intruding. For Caroline's sake, she was being uncharacteristically tactful, so she was glad to see that he wasn't obtuse. "Nah. I'm covering the funeral for the paper. Not really my beat, but since this one is connected to the investigations, I figured we'd kill two birds with one stone."

Augusta's back went rigid. "I see." Obviously, another Sandra Rivers, except with a penis dangling between his legs.

Sensing Augusta's withdrawal, he said, "We met when you came in a few weeks ago to inventory the office. Remember?"

"Yeah," Augusta lied. She had been way too distracted that day to remember anything at all. She had gone in to inventory the *Tribune* offices for the fundraiser, to hone in on her mother's extravagances and expunge them, and had walked out with a single item on her list—a gaudy chandelier—and a brand-new crusade in the form of Ian Patterson.

Recalling Ian's expression as he'd kicked her out of his house, she swallowed another wave of emotion.

"So how's the fund-raiser coming along?"

Nosy little shit. "A little off track for obvious reasons." Augusta glanced around to see if there was anyone left who might save her from this conversation. Most of the guests were already gone, and only a handful remained—no one she recognized.

"Understandably," he said and grinned, and Augusta wanted to ask him what the hell he wanted. As cute as he might be, there was something about him that just grated on her nerves—maybe it was the sense that he thought he could pry open doors with his smile. He reminded her of one of those guys in high school who expected girls to trip over themselves whenever he passed by.

His expression changed suddenly, sobering. "Anyway, I'm also covering Pam Baker's funeral... too bad ... she was a nice girl. Reminds me of those murders way back in the nineties, remember? The ones where Realtors were all being picked off while showing houses? Talk about being in the right place at the wrong time, huh?"

A shiver raced down Augusta's spine at his choice of words.

The right place at the wrong time.

Her brain flashed on the ruins. Pamela Baker had gone missing after being there. But how widely known was that? Augusta knew about Pam's photos, placing her at the ruins on the day of her disappearance, but only because of Jack and Caroline. As far as Augusta knew, Caroline had not shared that knowledge with the paper. In fact, Augusta was pretty sure Jack was trying to keep that particular information out of the media entirely. But maybe that wasn't what Brad was implying. She narrowed her eyes at him.

"Look, I've got to be going ... to the Simmonses'," she lied, and felt a tiny stab of guilt for it. "It was nice seeing you again ... Brad?"

He nodded and shoved out his hand, and Augusta shook it, even though she didn't want to. Then she walked away as fast as her legs could carry her.

"Catch you later," he called after her as she hurried toward her car.

Not if she could help it, Augusta thought.

7

For once, reporters weren't camped in his front yard, so Ian decided it might be a good time to get out and take care of business. Unless he wanted to spend the rest of his life behind bars, he needed to find a good attorney to take his case—not one ap-pointed by the state.

On his way out the door, he snagged the list he'd printed from the Internet, determined to continue his search for Jennifer.

Her mother had still heard no word from her or the authorities. In so many ways, it was as though she had walked out of her house and vanished into thin air. She'd texted Ian a few times and sent him that photo of herself at the ruins, but other than that, he hadn't much evidence of her ever having been in this city. He'd checked the shelters, couldn't locate where she might have been staying, nor anything that indi-cated she might have held a job. And yet her cell phone bill was being paid—he knew that because of the texts and photo she had sent him.

He remembered that she'd signed off as Jennifer Leigh—her first and middle name, having adopted the signature after the actress, Jennifer Jason Leigh.

Apparently, she'd been influenced by watching the actress in *The Hudsucker Proxy* where Leigh played a reporter. That's what Jennifer most wanted to do with her life when she grew up—be a reporter.

A thought occurred to him.

Shoving the list of lawyers into his pocket, he wondered if Jennifer had been drawn to the Aldridges because of the *Tribune.* Maybe she'd tried to get a job there? Augusta might be able to help him find out, but the last thing he wanted to do was get her involved. Damn it. She was a distraction he couldn't afford.

He shut the front door and locked it, checking it twice.

She was like a tick in his brain. She had planted herself there, and no matter how hard Ian tried to remove her, she wasn't withdrawing. The hurt look she'd had on her face before he slammed the door gnawed at him now.

He wasn't sure why, but he felt inexorably drawn to her. And it had nothing to do with the semi he'd been carrying in his pants from the instant he'd laid eyes on her. Damn it. He couldn't think straight in her presence—or even out of it, apparently.

Fuck him if he didn't want to see her. But that wasn't all he wanted. He wanted to bury his face between those beautiful breasts—wanted to make love to her properly—not on a beach under a pier with sand creeping between the cheeks of his ass. And when all this was over, if she was still willing, he planned to do exactly that.

If he didn't end up back in jail for the rest of his life.

He got into his car and shut the door, then stared at his cell phone, determined not to punch in numbers that were becoming far too familiar.

———

FEELING A LITTLE FRIENDLESS, Augusta walked into the house, grateful to find Tango waiting by the front door to greet her, his black tail wagging happily. He whined and she laughed, despite her mood, and she patted his head affectionately. "Do you have to pee, boy?"

He whined again, pitifully, and she took that as a yes, and led the way into the kitchen, setting her purse down on the counter as she searched for Tango's leash.

"Where does Sadie keep the leash, Tango?"

Tango whined, slapping his tail on the kitchen floor.

"Of course, it wouldn't be in plain sight," she complained, and then turned to look at Tango. "Why is it you like Caroline so much when Savannah's probably the one who walks you, huh?" He was a male, she decided, and men always liked Caroline. Probably because she was far more amenable than Augusta and didn't have a chip on her shoulder. Augusta accepted that. She realized she wasn't the most approachable person. But Savannah was far more agreeable than Caroline. Augusta gave her youngest sister a hard time but it was probably because Augusta wished she could have even a fraction of Savannah's patience.

Tango didn't answer—not that she expected him to—and she continued searching for the leash, thinking about her elder sister. Even though Augusta couldn't live her life by Caroline's edicts, it was probably true that both her sisters were far less inclined to forgive her these days for marching to her own drum. In many ways, after all these years, they were strangers now. And how much had she actually contributed since her return? She had spent so long being pissed off about her mother's will that she hadn't truly checked out of limbo. Well, it was time she pulled her weight around here, even if it was a temporary stay. And now, with Sadie gone, everyone would need to do their share. Hopefully, Savannah would get her cast off soon.

She'd talked to a builder who'd said he could begin as early as tomorrow, the twenty-first. She felt good about that. And in the meantime, it was probably time she got to know her mother's dog a little better since they had nine more months of incarceration together.

However, the leash seemed to be avoiding her. She rifled through drawers to no avail, trying to think like Sadie. Where would Sadie put the leash?

Despite the fact that the dog seemed to have become Caroline's shadow, she knew Caroline wasn't around the house much to take care of his daily necessities. And Savannah, with her cast, probably needed help walking him.

There was some comfort to be found in everyday drudgery, especially in these dire circumstances. Missing kids. Dead neighbors. Mutilated women. With all that was going on, was it any wonder Augusta couldn't keep her mind on her given task? And then there was the fund-raiser ... she still needed all this junk out of her way before she could really get the restoration underway. Rifling through the crowded drawers only drove that fact home.

According to the terms of her mother's will, she had approximately nine months left, and then the clock stopped ticking and all three of them either walked away with everything or nothing at all. But how the hell was she supposed to work on the house when people were getting murdered left and right?

Literally.

Not only were the ruins smack-dab on their property, but the first body in the Secessionville murders—a college student—had been discovered not more than a stone's throw away, in the backyard of one of the brand-new houses that were still for sale on Backcreek Road. She could literally spit out her back window and it would land on their docks.

Augusta thought about the girl who had been playing onstage the night she'd met Ian. Judging by the way the girl had been staring at them, she was smitten with him.

Would she have lied to give him an alibi?

She couldn't start second-guessing everything she did right now.

Frowning, she took a break from searching for the leash. Thirsty and needing a drink before continuing, she opened the fridge and grabbed a bottled water, then twisted off the cap and guzzled a few swallows before setting it down on the counter. "Sorry, boy," she said, and then resumed her search. Tango followed her around the kitchen, whining at her heels as she opened more drawers.

Finally, she found his leash in a drawer beside the pantry and set it on the counter. It was only then that she noticed the old photograph sitting on the kitchen island. She hadn't seen a Polaroid in years—not since her father left. Picking up the photo from the counter, she furrowed her brow. It was overexposed. She imagined sun glinting into the eyes of the photographer, but she recognized the subject of the photo and the little inflatable canoe. Both had disappeared on the same date.

Sammy.

Tango whined again, but she ignored him, studying the old photograph.

For all she knew, the photo might have been taken on the same day Sam had disappeared; she wasn't sure. But it was the same stretch of beach they always went to—north of Folly. In retrospect, a dumb place to set a kid free in a little inflatable raft when the currents there were infamously treacherous.

Not far from that spot, the Morris Island Lighthouse fought a losing battle with the sea. When it was first constructed the lighthouse had stood in the middle of an island, some 2,700 feet inland. Now it was 1,600 feet offshore and slowly inching into the Atlantic. In fact, the currents around there were so intense that during the 1700s there had actually been three islands stretching four miles between Folly and Sullivan's islands. The lighthouse had been constructed on the middle island, and eventually, because of the currents, and partly because of efforts to deepen the channel, the inlets that separated those islands silted in, resulting in a single strip that later became known as Morris Island. Lives had been lost in those waters. Nowadays only stupid people swam that stretch of ocean ... though sometimes even dumber surfers braved the whitecaps.

But no one in their right mind would let a four-year-old sail around in an inflatable canoe supervised by three flighty little girls, all eight and under. Augusta had been seven at the time, Caroline eight and a half, and Savannah five. What idiocy to leave them all with that burden.

Augusta was still angry with Flo over that one. She hoped her mother had enjoyed every one of her margaritas that day on the beach—and every one thereafter. For her part, Augusta couldn't see a salt-rimmed margarita glass or a froufrou paper umbrella without thinking of that terrible day.

She wondered which of her sisters had unearthed the photo. What was it doing on the counter? Turning it over revealed nothing. Her dad would sometimes write on the backs of his Polaroids but this one had nothing written on it.

Both Savannah and Caroline had been rummaging around the attic lately, trying to help Augusta gather items for the fund-raiser, but neither had mentioned discovering the photo. Nor was it something any of them was inclined to just leave lying around. As much as they all loved their little brother, neither she, nor Caroline, nor Savannah relished the memories his name evoked—and Sammy had long been banned from discussion and reminiscence. For a while, they hadn't even been allowed to speak his name or refer to his death. Flo had been so certain for so long that he had simply gone missing and that he would just turn up one day. She had set her heart on finding him ... and then had become depressed when she couldn't.

Augusta tossed the photo down on the island with a sigh, wondering how Amanda Hutto's mother was faring. She had tried to help Karen find her daughter by offering a reward, but now that so much time had passed without a single lead, the poor woman had stopped calling and Augusta tried not to think about her at all. Cody was different. His disappearance was recent and so close to home.

She remembered when the kid was born. Going to visit him in the hospital was one of the last things she remembered doing in Charleston before she'd left the city. He was so cute, with his tiny red face and little balled fists. Augusta remembered feeling such an incredible stab of envy, thinking that maybe she would never get close enough to anyone to justify having a child of her own. And so far, she had been right. A string of bad relationships had left her happier alone ... until Ian. Although apparently Ian wasn't the answer either. Even if you put all other troubles aside, he didn't seem to want anything to do with her.

Tango whined again and she grabbed the leash off the counter, shaking off her self-reflection. She hooked it on his collar, shifting her focus away from all the drama, away from Ian, and away from the photograph on the counter.

Still, it was strange that it would show up today of all days, when they had just buried Cody's grandmother ... and Cody was still missing.

She glanced at the calendar hanging by the door, and an unexpected realization head-butted her.

It was August nineteenth.

She glanced back at the photograph and a sense of foreboding assailed her. Today was the twenty-fifth anniversary of Sammy's death.

8

Frowning, Augusta went back to snatch the photograph of Sam off the counter. She tucked it into her purse and grabbed her cell phone before leading Tango out the front door, feeling completely unsettled. On the porch, Tango whined when she stopped to untangle his leash from around the cell phone in her hand. "Hold on, boy," she appealed.

She had forgotten how eerie Oyster Point could be when no one was around. Even in broad daylight, there was something about being at the end of a lonely road, with only one way out, surrounded by the croaking marsh, that had always given her a bit of the willies. Add to that her reservations about the property's history and it wasn't exactly a place she had ever longed to be. Flo must be laughing it up in her grave right now to have forced her into sleeping under this wretched roof again.

It didn't help much that Cody's disappearance brought Sammy to mind, and that today of all days she would find Sammy's photo lying on the kitchen counter.

Sweat beaded between her breasts, dampening her bra. August in Charleston had always been a bit of a steam bath and anything but white cotton in this weather was a mistake, but Tango couldn't wait long enough for her to change out of her funeral garb, so she adjusted her bra, then wrapped the leash about her hand, and took the opportunity to look around.

Oyster Point was completely isolated at the end of Fort Lamar Road, but with the nearby woodlands decimated, it seemed vulnerable and open to scrutiny, even with the front gates closed. She had the feeling someone was watching ... probably just paranoia. Lightning never struck twice in the same place, right? Simply because her sister had found herself in the crosshairs of a killer didn't mean Augusta was in danger. In fact, Augusta thought maybe they were safer than most, because they were now living under a magnifying glass. Still, she wasn't stupid enough to wander off alone without her cell and didn't plan to take Tango far from the house.

Her sisters were at the Simmonses by now, and Sadie and Josh were probably there, as well. Augusta wondered if they would find a way to get past the argument, or if they would walk around avoiding each other forever. Knowing Savannah, she wouldn't let Sadie go very long without another attempt at an apology.

Her gaze was drawn to the peeling blue paint on the porch ceiling. The entire house needed to be repainted at some point, and the looming restorations were beginning to weigh heavily upon her. If she didn't begin soon, she would never get them done in time and in accordance with her mother's will. Her sisters would never forgive her if she cheated them all out of twenty-seven million dollars.

Hell, they probably wouldn't forgive her anyway.

Out of the corner of one eye, the old joggling

board caught her attention. The sixteen-foot bench sat exactly where it had always sat, though, unlike the house itself, it sported a newish coat of green paint that hadn't yet been buffed thin in the middle by too many rear ends. Augusta doubted anyone had sat on the bench since they were kids. Obviously, it was simply for show now, a throwback, not only to their youths, but to a bygone era. As children, she and her sisters had used the board to annoy one another. As far as benches went, it wasn't an ideal place to sit, though it sat off to one side of the porch, surrounded by plants that offered a modicum of privacy. But Caroline in particular had used it often and Augusta was pretty sure it was where Caroline had gotten her first kiss from Jack. She smiled at the memory of her and Savannah hiding in the azaleas, spying on the two of them. Poor Savannah had always been dragged into her schemes.

On the other side of the porch, her mother had gathered a collection of rocking chairs, all handmade by a local craftsman. True to the man's word, the chairs had outlasted Flo's lifetime, and probably would outlast theirs, too, although the thought of growing old sitting on this particular porch, staring out at the bowing spartina grass, didn't do much for her peace of mind.

Tango tugged her down the stairs, past the gravel drive and into the grass. She was still clutching the cell phone in her hand when it rang, startling her. And then her heart leapt again at the sight of the number on the caller ID. *Ian.*

She dropped the phone on the edge of the gravel drive—fortunately in the grass. "Shit!" she said and bent to pick it up, fumbling with it. "H-Hi," she stammered, and rolled her eyes at the note of desperation in her voice.

"Hi," he said, and then without preamble, "I owe you an apology, Augusta."

Augusta didn't know what to say. She was just glad to hear his voice.

"Look, I appreciate that you paid my bail. It was ungrateful of me not to say so to begin with. Can you forgive me?"

He sounded sincere, with none of the anger that had seemed directed at her yesterday. Augusta's heart twisted a little. "Of course ... I told you, Ian ... I believe in you."

She heard him blow out a sigh. "Listen," he said, getting to the point. "I wouldn't have called ... except I need your help."

"Of course," she said again and stood there, clutching Tango's leash, trying to sort through the emotions that assaulted her—most notably disappointment. Her sister's words echoed in her head: *You're not thinking clearly where he's concerned.*

"My house has been crawling with reporters," he continued. "Do you think you could meet me at The Shack?"

Her heart lurched. "In Folly?

"Yeah."

"When?"

"Now."

Augusta took a deep breath, her emotions rocketing, feeling giddy in a way she hadn't in far too long. Maybe he was simply using her, maybe not. She heard sincerity in his tone. She wanted to believe that if the circumstances were different, their relationship would be also. "Sure," she said. "Let me finish walking the dog and I'll be on my way."

There was a moment of silence, and then he offered, "Want me to pick you up? I know you hate driving that boat of a car."

"No," she said at once, and smiled because he'd remembered. "I'm getting used to it." Uncertain what else to say, and feeling awkward, she offered, "See you in about twenty minutes?"

"See you then," he said.

Augusta hung up and grinned, realizing belatedly that she had been so excited, she'd hung up without even saying good-bye.

So what if he'd called just because he needed her help? It was a start, she reasoned. Simply hearing his voice made her feel better somehow. She waited for Tango to finish his duty, then led him back toward the house, cutting his walk short.

Her mother's dog stared at her, dark eyes full of censure. If Augusta didn't know better, she might think Flo had taught him that look.

"What?" she asked defensively. "The days of long walks are over," she argued as though he could possibly comprehend what she was saying. "At least for a while," she reasoned.

Tango stared at her.

"Hey, be glad I don't make you pee on newspaper!"

He flipped his black tail back and forth and peered toward the woods, and Augusta gave him a gentle tug, starting him back toward the porch, feeling guilty. Poor dog couldn't possibly understand everything that was going on. Even if Ian hadn't called, she wouldn't have gone traipsing through the woods—not with dusk falling. She gave Tango a pat on the head when he listened, and then made sure he was settled and fed, before checking her makeup in the foyer mirror. At her reflection, she shook her head, thinking Sadie must be right about the mirror being haunted, because right now, she looked a little like the living dead. Hopefully, Ian wouldn't notice. She gave Tango a last pat and rushed out the door.

———

FROM HIS VANTAGE point on the patio, Ian watched as Augusta pulled up in front of The Shack and finagled a parking spot large enough for that rig she drove— her mother's, she had said. The vintage Town Car was difficult to miss, with its mint-condition lemon-yellow paint job—about as hard to miss as that undercover car sitting outside the T-shirt shop. It was the same car that had been positioned outside his house earlier— about as inconspicuous as fireworks with its short radio antennae on the trunk lid, the front bumper lights and remote spotlights.

Ignoring the car, he set his beer down and watched Augusta walk up, starved suddenly, but not for food.

Today she was wearing black—black skirt, black shoes and black button-down shirt. She looked as though she had just come from a funeral—probably had. He'd heard on the news that the old lady whose grandson had gone missing had passed away. He felt bad for the family, and figured Augusta must have known them. From what he knew, their families ran in the same circles—at least her mother had. He still didn't know all that much about the Aldridge girls, and all he knew about Augusta was that her mouth tasted like lime—that, and the girl had serious altruistic tendencies. He had never known anyone so ready to bleed for the world at large. Except for him. The simple fact that he had been so willing to set his life aside—sex, children, love—without any true religious conviction, solely for the purpose of helping others, seemed extreme ... but only now that he had met Augusta.

He watched her walk up to the front door, and stop at the hostess stand. She must have asked where he was seated, because the hostess poked her head into the patio and so did Augusta. She waved, said something to the waitress and walked his way.

Like some kid in high school, his palms began to sweat and the monster in his pants stirred. Damn it to hell. It was almost as though she had her own little relationship with his penis and the little Benedict Arnold didn't give a crap what Ian had to say about any of it.

His heartbeat skipped as she slid into the seat across from him and gave him a tentative smile—one that was so sweet he had to stop himself from reaching out to brush a wisp of hair from her lips.

"Hi," she said, looking a little uncertain.

Ian wanted to kiss her before saying another word, but he held back. "Glad you came," he offered instead.

"So what's the mystery?"

Ian sucked in a fortifying breath and decided to get straight to the point. Neither of them was much for beating around bushes. There was a lot they had in common; he sensed that without needing to be told. "I lied," he admitted. "But I'm sure you already knew that."

Augusta braced herself for the next words to come out of his mouth.

She wasn't really sure she wanted to know what he'd lied about—especially since he'd thrown it out there before she was even settled in her chair. She set her purse on the seat beside her and demanded, "Okay, so spill it."

He stretched back in his chair, crossing his arms. "I'm still looking for Jennifer."

A feeling of relief swept through her, and she sucked in the breath she hadn't realized she was holding. "That's not news to me, Ian. I was pretty sure you wouldn't give up."

He tilted his head, the gesture a little boyish and uncertain, completely at odds with the hard lines of his face and his day's growth of whiskers. "I didn't think you'd buy it. I just didn't want you involved. You understand that, right?"

Augusta lifted a brow. "But you do now?"

His pale blue eyes pierced her. "No."

"So what's changed?"

"Like I said, I need your help."

Augusta tried to look away, but his gaze held her fast. She couldn't even begin to understand what it was about this man that held her so enthralled. "What is it you need from me, exactly?" she asked, resigned to help him however she could. The unfortunate truth was that she was beginning to believe she would give Ian anything he asked for.

Anything.

Including her heart.

But he wasn't asking for that, apparently. "I just need to know if Jennifer Williams ever applied for a job at the paper."

Augusta furrowed her brow, surprised by the request. "The *Tribune*?"

"Would you like a beer?" the waiter interrupted. His tone wasn't particularly friendly, and Augusta peered up at the guy—a surfer-type dude in his early twenties. Her gaze zeroed in on the bottle in front of

Ian. She raised a brow. "No, thank you," she said, and gave a little laugh. The last time she'd had alcohol with Ian, they'd ended up not even in bed, but on the beach, and the smell of wet sand and salt air was far too near. "Tea," she told the waiter, clearing her throat.

"Sweet or unsweetened?"

Augusta smiled, largely for the waiter's sake, because she felt so anxious at the moment that she really thought she might puke. "You mean I have a choice?" she quipped. It used to be that restaurants in the South gave you sweetened tea, nothing else. The waiter gave her a nod, seeming not to understand her question, or maybe not in the mood for jokes. He eyed Ian circumspectly. "Unsweetened," she conceded. "Thank you."

The waiter left, moving to another table at the other side of the patio to take an order. The couple there put their heads together when he left, and looked their way. Augusta turned to Ian, ignoring them. They probably recognized Ian—or her—but she refused to let them bother her, or give them the satisfaction of her annoyance. "I'm confused. Why would Jennifer Williams have applied at the paper?"

Ian took a long pull of his beer and set the bottle down in front of him, eyeing Augusta over the rim as he rocked the bottle on its edges. "She wanted to be a reporter once upon a time."

"Did she actually *study* journalism?"

He shook his head. "She was a runaway," he reminded her. "I doubt it."

"Then she wouldn't have gotten far with an application at the *Tribune*. Mom was a stickler about education. She barely allowed Caroline to intern there."

"Could she have gotten a job as an intern maybe?"

Augusta shrugged. "Maybe, but I think Flo would

probably have hired students. Still, I guess it's possible."

Ian nodded. "I would have asked your sister, but obviously, she doesn't like me much." He grinned, and Augusta laughed nervously, and shook her head.

"Honestly, I can't believe we're even having this conversation," she admitted. "Considering the circumstances ..."

He placed a hand on the neck of his beer, wrapping his long fingers around it. "You either believe I'm innocent, or you don't, Augusta," he said in that slow, sexy drawl of his. "If you do believe me—as you say—I need your help."

Augusta sighed.

Outside the porch, two sparrows chased each other from the rooftop to a perch on the porch screen. Muted late-afternoon sunlight filtered into the patio, turning the room a glowing shade of orange-red. There was nothing nefarious about this moment. Her gut wasn't screaming, and she didn't feel as though she was doing anything wrong. Being with Ian—believing in him—*felt* like the right thing to do.

Still, she was the last person on earth who might be able to help him with this particular issue right now. "My sister isn't exactly speaking to me," she confessed.

He lifted the bottle. "Because of me?"

Augusta gave him a sober nod. There was no use lying or skirting issues. She slid her hand across the table to play with the saltshaker. "Partly ... and partly because I was stupid enough not to tell her about you before she heard it somewhere else."

He eyed her pointedly, lifting a brow. "What about me exactly... that you paid my bail ... or that you happened to be my alibi for the night of Kelly Banks's murder?" Ian set the bottle down and reached out, closing his fingers over hers. The feel of his warm hand sent Augusta's pulse skittering. "Or maybe you're talking about the fact that we've done a little more than trade spit ... you and me?"

"She only knows about the bail part," Augusta replied, staring at his hand, unable to look him in the eyes. "Why haven't you told the police about the night we spent together?"

"My attorney knows, but the police haven't asked," he said. "The case so far has been focused on the abduction and attempted murder of your sister."

"Which you didn't do..."

It wasn't a question, but Augusta peered up to gauge his expression anyway.

He nodded belatedly. "Which I didn't do. But since I have one alibi already—one they don't seem to want to believe—for both the nights of Amy Jones and Kelly Banks's deaths, your sister's case was the strongest and that's been their focus. Until now there hasn't been a body for Pamela Baker, and we both know exactly where I was when she took her last breath."

Sitting in jail.

On the nights of Amy's and Kelly's murders, Ian had claimed to be at the Windjammer, watching his friend perform. On at least one of those nights, Augusta knew beyond a shadow of doubt that he was telling the truth.

He was watching her intently.

"Will you tell them I was with you that night?" she asked.

"More to the point ... will *you* tell them you were with *me*?"

Augusta hesitated, but only an instant, and then nodded with certainty.

It seemed to be what he needed to hear. He rewarded her with a smile. "It probably wasn't the smartest thing not to tell your sister about the bail," he allowed. "But I do appreciate your help, Augusta. I realize it couldn't have been easy for you."

Augusta swallowed the oversized lump that grew in her throat. She averted her gaze, thinking about how Caroline might perceive even this simple dinner invitation. She wondered if she should tell her, and knew the answer, though their relationship would suffer more because of it.

His hand squeezed hers. "I wasn't trying to hurt your sister that night, Augusta. You have to believe me."

It took all of Augusta's willpower to release the breath she was holding and speak. "I do believe you. I said I did, and I do."

He released her hand and slid his own back across the table into his lap. "I'm at a loss," he admitted. "I feel in my gut that Jennifer is part of this whole picture somehow, but I can't figure out how she fits." He scratched absently at his jaw, a gesture she was coming to recognize as one of frustration.

As much as she hated to say it, Augusta had to ask. "Ian ... Jennifer has been missing for months now ... long before Pamela Baker. Have you considered the fact that maybe she's ..."

"Dead?" He gave her a nod and met her gaze. "Of course."

"I would think finding Cody would be a higher priority."

"I don't know Cody," he countered.

"But I do."

He gazed at her, unflinching. "That's a job for the police, Augusta."

"I could say the same to you about Jennifer."

He nodded. "Fair enough."

"Look, the police are doing their best, but they never found Amanda Hutto—or Jennifer either—or my brother for that matter. Do you know how long ago that was? Essentially, my brother is *still* missing." She eyed the purse where the photograph was stashed. "We put *all* our trust in the authorities all those years ago and guess what? To this day, we have absolutely no idea what happened to my baby brother. Do you know how debilitating that is? I *know* how that feels."

"Thousands of people are reported missing every day, Augusta—adults and kids both. Only a fraction of them are actually abductions or kidnappings. Most are just unlucky."

"Like Jennifer?" she pressed.

He narrowed his eyes, but Augusta couldn't quite read his expression. "You think you can do a better job than the police?"

Augusta shrugged. "Maybe—maybe not, but how can we not try, Ian? If they send out an Amber Alert, aren't we supposed to take off our blinders and start looking at the faces we pass on the street?"

She could see that his jaw was working. "Yeah, but noticing a face in passing on the sidewalk is *not* the same thing as going after a killer."

"Really, do you think I don't know that? Jesus, look at what nearly happened to my sister! For all we know my brother drowned—and maybe so did Amanda Hutto. But Cody Simmons is a different story altogether. He disappeared from a known crime scene. I *know* you know something more than you're letting on."

"I know basically what you know," he lied. Augusta could tell by the set of his jaw.

"Whatever. At this point, Cody has a better chance than Jennifer. If you know something, he's the one you should be searching for."

"Stay out of it," he said quietly and they locked gazes, neither of them willing to give an inch.

After what seemed like an eternity, the waiter returned to take their order, but Augusta hadn't bothered to look at the menu. Ian picked up the plastic trifold and handed it to her, then changing the subject, said, "Are you hungry?"

"A little."

"Do you know what you want?"

Augusta shook her head.

"I can come back," the waiter offered, his eyes fixed upon Augusta. Clearly, he wasn't comfortable acknowledging Ian, or lingering by their table.

"Why don't you bring us a bucket of oysters and let us think about the rest," Ian suggested. "And bring the lady a beer," he demanded. His lips curved into a tight smile and he said, looking straight at Augusta, "With a lime."

Augusta licked her lips, remembering the way his mouth had tasted that night. He was staring intently at her lips right now. So intently that she couldn't think straight—and that was probably his intention.

"Cody's just a kid," she persisted when the waiter left again. "Maybe we won't find him, but I don't see why we shouldn't at least try. I think you know something," she tried again. "In fact, I know you do. It's part of the reason I paid your bail."

"I see," he said, his voice changing slightly. "Not

because you believe in my innocence, after all ... or maybe even because of something else?"

"What else?"

His lips thinned.

"I do believe in you," she protested. They were skirting a dangerous subject here. She knew he was aware of what she felt for him. The question was ... did he feel it, too?

Right now, Cody was far more important, she reminded herself.

What if he had been her child? She couldn't simply walk away, knowing he was out there somewhere, alone. She wouldn't want anyone setting him aside—as they seemed to have already done with Amanda Hutto. Poor Amanda had disappeared from her own front yard. No one saw anything and not even the reward that had been offered had netted any leads. Six years old and the child had simply vanished into thin air. The same way Sammy had vanished. If the community had banded together, instead of going on with their lives as though nothing had ever happened, maybe Sammy would have had the chance to grow up to be a man.

Or maybe at least they would have had a body to bury.

So many things might have been different.

Their mother might have been different.

Augusta might have been different.

But she was beginning to realize that her strength was truly a weakness. He was still staring at her, and seemed to be studying her, but his eyes were so full of secrets.

Did he know hers, too?

"Tell you what," he suggested, relenting. "We can

help each other ... if you promise you'll go nowhere and do nothing without me, Augusta."

The waiter dropped off her beer, and she seized it, avoiding Ian's gaze. She took the lime, squeezed it and shoved it down into the neck of the bottle, trying not to think about the way his fingers had pushed their way inside her body that night. She shivered at the memory.

He reached out and seized her bottle, wrapping his hand around hers, and tugged firmly to get her attention. "Do you hear me, Augusta?"

Augusta met his gaze, and nearly gave him a typical Augusta response—one without commitment and with plenty of sarcasm, but he threaded his fingers between hers until they were both holding the cold bottle, their fingers entwined—and dear God, her body convulsed in secret places. They stared at each other, long and hard.

"Okay," she relented, frustrated. "I won't do anything you don't want me to do—but you have to tell me everything you know!"

She tried to extricate her hand, but he held the bottle firmly and his smile turned suddenly wicked. "What about the things I *want* you to do? Do you want me to tell you about those, too?"

Augusta tried for one of her most unaffected looks, though she was certain she failed entirely. "That depends..."

"On what?"

She smiled back at him. "On whether I want it, too ..."

9

———

*L**ulled by the last minutes of sunshine, a swallowtail butterfly landed on the windshield, diverting his attention. Its yellow and black wings fluttered elegantly, slowing as it settled. Behind it, the air bent as the heat from the black hood cooled and dissipated into the dusk. A female. At least in this species, males were far drabber. And she was young, he could tell by the pristine wings and the long projections beneath the wings. She had likely been drawn to the butterfly bushes that were planted along the sidewalk. This one had particularly brilliant blue and orange markings with black tiger striping that bled into a stark blue tail. It went perfectly still, enjoying a moment of serenity. He watched for a long moment, mesmerized by the insect's grace ... and then casually reached out and flipped on his wipers, flicking the butterfly off onto the hood of his black car, onto its back, where its wings began to fry in the heat, leaving a dusting of yellow powder where it struggled to right itself. He watched for an instant as it floundered, and then bored with the display of weakness, returned his gaze to the couple seated on the porch of the Crab Shack.*

What were they talking about?

Was she trying to figure out how to get his cock be-tween her legs?

Or was she talking about the kid now?

It wasn't difficult to figure out what made Augusta Aldridge tick ... especially after she had placed that reward in her sister's paper for information leading to the return of Amanda Hutto. She wasn't a nosy reporter type like her sister, just a do-gooder, who thought she could change the world.

All these years he'd struggled in vain to find peace.

He'd gotten his first true thrill when the breath left the youngest Aldridge's lungs ... maybe he would get his last with the demise of his slutty sister? Maybe then he would find peace from the voices in his head?

Somewhere in the part of him that wasn't dead, he knew he should stop. But like a smoker craved nicotine ... or an alcoholic needed liquor, he was powerless to resist the siren song. Only difference was that his habit needed proper planning... and willpower.

He had to be smarter than your average junkie.

He had to get small fixes where he could.

His gaze returned to the butterfly as he recalled that first day out on the beach...

He'd been watching them. Their mother drunk on sun and margaritas, leaving the girls to look after their little brother ... but no one was actually watching the boy. The same way no one ever noticed him.

Unless he made them notice.

He'd recognized that look in the child's eyes as he'd called out to his sisters, waving his little flag on a stick.

"Yo ho, yo ho—look at me, Cici! I'm a pirate—just like Blackbeard!"

No one paid attention to his shouts for attention, and he soon became sullen and silent as he resigned himself to a solitary voyage. And then he drifted ... far enough away that he was no longer in his family's sight.

Still no one noticed.

That day ... he really hadn't intended for anything to happen.

The kid was sitting there in his little canoe. Alone. Angry at his sisters, and probably his mother, too, and he took the little flag he was holding and started to pound it into his plastic canoe, his little face twisting with frustration. Farther and farther he floated... until he was well beyond the shallows and drifting into deeper water.

The canoe popped with a whoosh of air, penetrated by the end of his wooden flagstick, and the look on his face was one of surprise ... still he didn't realize the danger he was in, too young to understand that his boat would soon be gone from beneath him.

Compelled, he'd waded out toward the kid while the raft slowly deflated. But the boy hadn't been afraid even then. He had seemed more concerned with the fact that his feet were tangled in the plastic and the water was beginning to leak in.

Wading in chest high, he'd stopped there to watch, curious as to what the child might do next. His little brows had furrowed as he peered up, spying him for the first time. For the longest moment they'd simply stared at one another, until the canoe deflated beneath the boy and his little body slid into the water, dumping him with a gasp. It was only then he decided to cry—when the water could enter his mouth as he sank beneath the surface.

He didn't know how to swim.

His little hands flailed desperately. His mouth opened to cry out, gulping in a lungful of water. The water churned at his feet, but he didn't kick fast enough or hard enough to stay afloat.

No one had taught him how to swim.

What kind of mother put a child in a rubber raft and let him float away without teaching him how to swim? The selfish kind. The kind who didn't give a damn about anyone but herself. The kind who put the needs of others ahead of her kids.

The boy was better off dead.

Still, he didn't move, undecided ... simply watching.

Finally compelled by something deeper, he moved forward, a feeling of excitement building inside him. He snatched the boy into his arms. For merely a second. No longer. No time for the boy to scream, or even catch his breath. And then he shoved him beneath the surface and held him there, knowing he could save him if he chose to. If he chose to. Knowing all he had to do was raise the kid's head above water. Instead he stood there, holding him beneath the surface, and he felt in that moment in control for the first time in his life—a heady sense of control that burgeoned in his breast.

The boy was sad, he reassured himself. Killing him was a mercy. Killing him was a kindness. Letting him live, on the other hand ... would simply create another monster ... like him. Because that's how he was born ... out of the fires of anger and resentment... and in that instant, as he watched the boy suck the last of the cold water into his lungs and his eyes bulge, his blood vessels pop ... in that incredible instant, he was transformed.

Augusta Aldridge had that same sad look about her.

She fought it with every crusade she waged against the world. She would be much happier if she could join her brother, he thought idly. He watched her with the ex-priest a few minutes longer ... then started his car.

It wasn't the right time.

Not yet.

But soon...

Because he already knew Cody wasn't the one to quiet the voices in his head.

His gaze returned to the hood of his car.

Cody was like the butterfly.

A fix to tide him over.

Ian was lying to himself, he realized. Of course, he needed Augusta's help, but he wanted to see her, plain and simple.

They picked their way through a mountain of boiled shrimp and oysters, and drank half a dozen beers between them. Augusta inspected the clusters of shells, searching for one that wasn't already pillaged while he watched, contented for the first time in years.

For the moment, faced with her easy smile and assured manner, he could almost forget that their presence here had drawn the curious, disapproving eyes of almost every patron. Thanks to her sister and the rest of the media, the only people in Charleston who didn't recognize him were those who lived under rocks. Luckily, no one made a stink, but Ian half-expected the management to throw him out for disturbing the clientele.

Augusta was easily the most stubborn woman he had ever met. She was also the loveliest, although her beauty wasn't simply skin-deep. If he wanted to keep her safe, he knew now that he had to keep her close. But he wasn't sure how much to tell her. She was equally as smart as she was stubborn.

His eye was drawn to the silver cross that hung on a worn leather band around her neck. He had the distinct impression it wasn't a religious statement. The cross was intricately carved, with depictions of the four elements at each arm and tiny roses threaded through the circle. He wanted to ask her about it, but wasn't sure he was ready to open up that can of worms. Thankfully, aside from that first night, she hadn't even acknowledged his ex-affiliation with the Church. In fact, she seemed to prefer ignoring it.

So did he, frankly.

When it came right down to it, he had always been more drawn to the works of the Church than he had been to the idea of God. His decision to serve the Church was no more mysterious than a plumber's son following his father into business. Still, he had been fully prepared to do whatever he had to do to make a difference, and celibacy had never been much of an issue. Relationships were too complicated to justify the exchange of body fluids...

Until Augusta.

Even now, when he *knew* he should go, he couldn't seem to muster the will to actually do it. Somewhere in the back of his head he realized that nothing good could come of this, but he sat there anyway, enjoying her company ... loving the way her blouse clung jealously to those lovely breasts ...

He'd meant simply to ask for her help—in person—since he also owed her an apology and a thanks for paying his bail, but now that he was with her, he felt a sense of peace that not even the Church had ever been able to instill in him.

But it was an illusion, he realized, because there would be no peace for him until he found Jennifer Williams ... until the man responsible for all these deaths was finally behind bars. ... until the man who had hurt Jennifer was answerable to for his actions.

Despite what the papers claimed, he hadn't been excommunicated from the Church. He'd left of his own volition. But admitting that now would expose the lie that everyone—including Jennifer's mother—was still trying to hide. A lie that had led Jennifer to whatever end she had found. Finding her wasn't simply about putting his guilt to rest. Jennifer was the only one who could set things straight.

"I think you got them all," Ian told her, referring to the oysters she was so diligently inspecting.

"I made sure to leave you enough."

"Enough for what?"

She was flirting with him, clearly. He recognized that look in her eyes, but taking her to bed wasn't the smartest move for either of them—and his reluctance had nothing to do with the vows he had already forsaken.

"Just enough," she said, grinning.

He leaned forward onto his elbows. The lights had dimmed about an hour ago, and he wanted to see her more clearly. "Actually, that's a myth, I think."

She shook her head, her eyes gleaming slightly. "Nope. They're loaded with zinc, which actually raises the libido," she informed him with a wink. "In case you didn't know."

Ian grinned at her. There wasn't a damned thing wrong with his libido—not around her. If she only knew the dance his little monster was enjoying beneath the table, she might actually be frightened by it. He certainly was. He forced himself to withdraw, leaning back in his chair. "Yeah? Well, I guess I always thought it was because of their shape. I figured some dirty old man came up with the idea."

She laughed. "Could be, but it also just so happens that a lack of zinc can make a man impotent, while an abundance ..." She winked again, an exaggerated version of her last wink. "Well, we both know what effect that can have."

He loved that she spoke her mind. And yet, she never crossed the line. She took him to the edge, teasing him ... but never crossed it.

"Want to put it to the test?" he asked. The words came out of his mouth of their own accord, defying his will. Or maybe it was just the beer?

Their gazes locked, neither speaking, uncertain where to go from here.

Her cell phone rang, breaking the spell for the moment.

She shook her head, looking flustered, and tossed down the cluster of oysters she held in her hand. She'd found one after all, but even the steam hadn't coaxed its muscles to part. There were no cracks in its armor, no way in. Somehow, despite all their flirtations, he sensed they were both like that. Words were one thing, but Augusta Aldridge's emotions were locked up tightly on the inside. Only patience and persistence would get her to open up, and neither of them had time for that. As far as Ian was concerned, sex alone wasn't enough. She fished her cell phone out of her purse and glanced at the number. "My sister," she said.

"Which one?"

"Savannah. You'd like her. She's nothing like Caroline. Nothing like me either, really." She laughed at that.

"Let's take a walk on the beach," he suggested. "I have something I want to show you ..."

IT FELT like there was sand in Cody's eyes.

They were gritty and dry and he could barely keep them open. The air felt like it was burning the inside of his nose. His stomach hurt almost as bad as his head and his wrists and ankles were on fire where the skin was chafed and swollen around the cuffs. His heartbeat wouldn't slow down even though he couldn't stay awake, and he was afraid to cry anymore, because snot was caking on the inside of his nose and if it closed up, he wouldn't be able to breathe.

The inside of the building was steamy ... or maybe everything was getting blurry. All he really knew was that he was thirsty and scared. Mosquitoes were biting him all over. Desperately, he pushed his tongue up against the rag in his mouth and then coughed a little and puked in the back of his throat...

With some effort, he worked the pukey rag away from the back of his throat and he thought maybe he looked like a boa with a half-eaten rat down his neck. Except that instead of shimmying the cloth deeper into his mouth, he was slowly working it out by widening his jaw and wiggling his tongue.

He didn't understand what was happening.

Why would someone truss him up like a Thanksgiving turkey and then just leave him here to rot? He expected the man in black to come back and kill him, but so far he hadn't, and he was afraid maybe he was going to die before anyone found him. He felt a little like he was dying already. Maybe. He wasn't sure. His head hurt so bad it was easier to just lie here on the cement floor and wait with his eyes closed.

But he wasn't ready to die.

He didn't hate his little sister, and he didn't want to go away without telling her that he never meant to squish her doll's head. Or set her Barbie's hair on fire. Or put gum in her skate wheels. He was just mad. Because until she was born, his mom had always had way more time to read to him. Now, he always had to read to her, though he didn't really mind. He kind of liked it. And he felt proud when she asked him about the hard words. Lila was only six, but she was smart. Who would help her learn to read if he couldn't go home? Would his mom get another boy to replace him?

Sadness filled him, because he knew in his heart that if he hadn't done all those bad things to Lila, then his mom and dad wouldn't have separated them after school and made him go stay with his grandma Rose.

He had been bad, he knew, and maybe that's why he was being punished now.

If he had been a good boy, he would never have gone to look at stupid blood at some old broke-down church. He would have gone home instead and had a real good supper and then his mom would have picked him up with Lila and brung him home.

Why did he have to go with TC? Why had he listened to TC? Cody wished he could take back every bad thing he had ever done in his life.

Please, God, he thought, *don't let me die.*

10

Ian and Augusta left The Shack and headed east down the beach. When they reached the Washout—literally a washed-out block of beachfront homes where the wind tore across the shore to the Folly River—they cut through someone's yard to East Ashley.

"This is all I need," he said, "to end up back in jail for trespassing."

Augusta laughed. "This is Jack Shaw's house."

"Great!" he said. "Even better." He shook his head.

"Relax," she said. "He's not home." She winked at him. "Probably sitting in his office right now trying to figure out how to get you back behind bars."

"That's not particularly funny," he suggested, but laughed anyway.

They followed the road past Karen Hutto's sun-bleached yellow cottage, where Amanda had vanished from her front yard, and finally onto the beach access road that wound past the old defunct Coast Guard station. The farther they walked east, the darker the sky grew, untouched by artificial lights. "I keep wondering, what is that?" he asked, pointing to a graffiti-covered cement foundation that was surrounded by beach scrub. Whatever it was, covered in psychedelic writing, it appeared man had waged a war against nature, both of them trying to claim the lost building for themselves.

"An old Coast Guard station. Apparently, it played a huge part in protecting the naval base here from German spies during World War II. I think Hugo flattened it."

"As in Hurricane Hugo?"

Augusta nodded. "Yep. Same storm that flattened those beachfront homes at the Washout. It's a surfer's haven now."

"Anything worth taking a look at here?"

"And brave sand spurs?" Augusta shook her head. "Not really. But it might actually draw that cop out of his car if he thinks we're messing with a historic landmark."

Peering over his shoulder at the red parking lights that clicked off at the end of the beach access road, Ian laughed. "I know. Damn. I thought we'd lost them."

"There's only one street that runs this far east," she told him. "Not even a good guess, really. He'd have to be stupid not to figure out where we're going."

"We can still ditch 'em," he boasted, and grinned. He took the sandals from her abruptly, plopping them onto the ground. "Put them on," he directed. "I want to show you something anyway."

Augusta did and Ian led her through the dunes to show her where a loggerhead turtle had recently laid her eggs. Known nests were marked, but apparently, one loggerhead mommy had braved the tourist-infested shoreline to deposit her brood along a secluded spot on the far northeastern beach. Carefully, Ian uncovered the nest so Augusta could look inside, where there were literally hundreds of eggs. "Talk about sibling rivalry!"

He smiled up at her. "Spoken like a true middle child."

Peering into the nest, hands on her knees, Augusta shrugged. "What can I say, I was the one who ended up without Mommy's attention, right?"

He gave her a knowing look. "Something tells me you fared just fine without it."

Augusta smirked. "Depends on who you talk to."

He chuckled low. "From where I'm sitting, Augusta Aldridge, there's not a damned thing wrong with you."

Augusta blinked and met his gaze, a shiver racing down her spine. He was staring up at her, his blue eyes intense. Uncomfortable with his scrutiny and uncertain what to say next, she peered down into the nest at the golf ball–sized eggs.

Her head was clear—as clear as the moonlit sky.

She knew exactly what she was doing.

Didn't she?

Ian covered the eggs back up with sand, gently ... the way he had once handled her body ... as though somehow she might break beneath his touch. "Apparently, it takes about thirty or so years for them to get the maternal itch," he said, "but when they do, they travel back to lay their eggs on the beach where they were born. Pretty incredible stuff."

Except that those loggerhead babies would soon discover there was no mama around to care for them. Something Augusta had firsthand knowledge of. But that was a reality she had come to terms with long ago. She sat on the beach and sighed.

She was thirty two now. Maybe that's all that was wrong with her? Like the loggerhead turtles, maybe she was just getting a maternal itch?

Except that ... when she looked at Ian ... it wasn't

the thought of having babies that sent her heart skidding to a halt ...

Ian sat beside her, scooting near, their legs so close now, their knees were almost touching.

Augusta buried her fingers in the warm sand, lifted up a handful, letting it trickle through her closed fist, like a broken hourglass. "So how did you find the nest?"

He glanced at her, pulling his shoulder-length hair away from his face. "I've done a lot of beachcombing lately."

"Cool," she said. But it wasn't cool, because they both knew exactly why he was searching.

Is that how the killer found his victims? Scavenging along the shore?

Uncomfortable with his scrutiny and the turn of their conversation, along with her thoughts, she peered up at the darkening sky.

From where they sat, they could see the Morris Island Lighthouse in the distance, standing in the middle of moonlit, white-capped waters. Beyond that, the city of Charleston gave off a mellow glow. In between, the water was dark, and the silhouettes of numerous sailboats dappled the harbor. "Did you know there's a light curfew around here?" she asked him.

"Nah, but I figured. The place goes black after ten."

Augusta raised a brow. "I guess they try to keep the beaches as dark as possible at night... for the turtles."

"Mood lighting," he suggested, and winked at her.

"I think it disorients them," she countered. "The lights apparently lure them away from the ocean where they're supposed to go."

In the growing darkness, the breeze whispered through the sea oats. Augusta could see dark spots on the beach moving ... probably hermit crabs or other sea creatures scavenging, too. Opportunistic creatures, operating under cover of night.

But Ian wasn't a killer. Her instincts were good. She wouldn't be here with him if there had been even a single red flag.

She took in a deep breath of salt air, afraid to hope for something more than what they had in the moment. If she let it, her entire life could be defined by a string of bad relationships. It was all she knew, and her parents had been a poor example. Her father had come from a long line of politicians and her mother had been a "daughter of the Confederacy"—Charleston royalty, so to speak. While her dad's political aspirations had no doubt been served by her mother's pristine heritage and unshakeable façade, Flo's idealism was hardly benefited by her father's unprincipled career. On the surface, the marriage might have seemed perfect—like Jackie O. and John Kennedy—but their dysfunction had been preordained. Add to that the fact that Flo had been a strong woman, uncompromising, and it was no surprise their family had unraveled so quickly after Sam's death. Her parents hadn't married for love. She doubted either of them had ever known the meaning of the word. She worried maybe she didn't either.

"So here we are again," he said.

Augusta swallowed, and lay back in the sand, staring up at the sky above, listening to the ocean smash into the rocks below. Here the beach was uncharacteristically rocky—by design, to keep the shore from eroding in the powerful currents.

"Here we are again," she echoed, and gooseflesh rippled over her skin.

No matter that she tried to deny the attraction, it was there, as thick as a Lowcountry mist in the morning. She was barefoot, her sandals lay beside her on the beach, and the ends of her skirt were damp from walking through the surf. The warm, soft breeze tousled the neckline of her cotton blouse and Ian shifted beside her, turning to face her.

Augusta held her breath, not daring to look at him. "What are we doing?"

She watched in her peripheral vision as he leaned on an elbow, staring down at her. "Damned if I know, Augusta. The world is going to hell around us and here I'm sitting on the beach yet again... staring down at your gorgeous lips ... thinking how much I want to kiss you."

His voice sounded raw, as though he meant every word.

Augusta swallowed, and shifted her gaze to peer up at him, gauging his expression, her heart pounding fiercely. Under his scrutiny, her nipples began to ache for his touch, burning despite the cool night air.

He reached out and placed a hand over her cheek, barely touching her, turning her face toward him. "You deserve to be made love to... in a bed," he said.

Augusta tried to find her voice. She met his gaze straight-on. "This is the last thing we should be doing," she agreed.

For the longest moment, neither of them spoke.

His heart beating like a drum, Ian stared down into Augusta's lovely face.

She was the last thing he needed in his life, he told himself—the last person he should be involved with. If he were even half the man he used to be, he would take her by the hand, walk her back to her car and see her safely home.

At the very least, he would take her home and make love to her the way she deserved to be made love to, with cool, clean sheets beneath her soft, sweet body.

But they were alone. Here on the beach. For the first time in so long there weren't a dozen pairs of eyes locked on him, and the night was as beautiful as she was.

Moonlight reflected off the white sand, leaving her aglow in soft light. Behind them, the dune grass shimmied with the breeze.

She lifted her face into his hand, and he couldn't stop himself. He bent to cover her mouth with his, savoring the taste of her mouth. "I want you," he whispered.

In answer, she reached up, sliding her long, graceful fingers around his neck, pulling him closer, and Ian was lost from that moment forward.

He shifted his body so that he lay beside her in the warm sand, hooking his hand around her thigh and drawing her leg over his, reveling in the feel of her lithe body and the soft skin beneath her skirt.

He kissed her deeply, knowing that whatever it was that was happening between them was meant to be. It felt right, even if it was the wrong damned time.

But his conscience warred with him. She deserved better than this. Could he really even be certain their relationship would survive all the drama? It was possible—innocent or not—that he could spend the rest of his life behind bars. The simple fact that police were tailing him told him they weren't going to simply drop the charges. Nor should they—not when there was so much at stake.

They shouldn't be here right now.

Augusta moaned beneath him, but he tore himself away, looking down into her confused eyes. "This isn't the way it should happen again," he said with con-viction.

But he wanted her to know that it wasn't an easy decision. He placed a hand on her bottom and pulled her tight against his erection, pushing it into the hollow of her body.

He was hard as granite and his body ached for release, but he couldn't take it, not here, not now. He slid his hand up to her waist, pulling her close, desperately wanting her to understand it wasn't a rejection.

The confusion in her blue eyes was endearing, and he wanted to hold her all night long. He hugged her then, burying his face into her shoulder, and for the longest moment, simply held her, reining in his desire. "Let's revisit this after it's all over," he whispered into her hair.

Augusta nodded, shivering. The heat of his body was blistering, but she trembled as he held her. It was exactly what needed to be said, but it filled her with regret ... for not having been strong enough to be the one to say it.

Her sister was right; she couldn't think straight where Ian was concerned.

He didn't seem in a hurry to disentangle himself from her arms, so she let him hold her, resting her head against his chest, listening to the steady thumping of his heart. After a long while, he turned so she could lie in the crook of his arms and together they stared up at the sky.

The scent of the sea was strong here. Combined with the familiar scent of his skin, it was as close to feeling at home as Augusta thought she'd ever come—inexplicable as that might be.

The sky was clear, with nearly every star visible in the heavens, and the sound of crickets filled the night air. It seemed they were completely alone, with only the sound of the ocean for music. "I don't think I've ever seen the stars so clearly."

"That's Cassiopeia," he said, pointing up into the north sky. "That cluster that looks a little like a lazy *W*." She listened quietly and he continued, pulling her closer. "As the story goes, Poseidon banished her as a punishment for her arrogance. Supposedly, she's bound to a throne in a position so that as she circles the poles, she's upside down."

Augusta smiled beside him. "Poseidon must have been a pervert," she determined. "Isn't that some kinky sex position—upside-down sex?"

He laughed, then glanced at her, nudging her gently. "Only you would say something like that. Hell, I don't know." He grinned. "Never tried it." But something about the tone of his voice told her it wasn't quite the truth.

"Liar!"

He laughed. "Maybe when I was younger." And then his voice turned sober. "Truth is, you're the only woman in nearly six years, Augusta."

Augusta sucked in a breath and buried her toes in the warm sand. For some reason, knowing that made her feel better, not worse, though she couldn't say the same.

"But damn it ... I'm trying to get our minds *off* that particular subject and you're not helping."

"Sorry," she said, though she really wasn't. It was the right thing to do—to wait—but the simple fact that he had been the one to suggest it only made her want to make love to him all the more. "Do you think they'll drop the charges?" Augusta dared to ask after a moment.

It took him a while to answer. He continued

staring up at the night sky, his jaw tight and his profile hard. "They don't have a case," he suggested. "Or I wouldn't be here with you right now..."

PATTERSON WASN'T GUILTY.

The thought squirmed around in Jack's brain like a maggot.

He sat at his desk, staring at the lab report, uncertain how to process the newest information. The feeling that arrived in his gut as he stared at the blood results was a twisting jumble that manifested itself as pain.

Through this entire investigation, he had been so certain Caroline was wrong. He had been furious with her for interfering when she went after Patterson using the *Tribune*. And then Patterson had been caught red-handed—so it seemed—and his arrest had shaken Jack's morale. Enough that he'd strongly considered retiring from the force. But right now... that sick, niggling feeling was back in force. Despite evidence that seemed to point to the contrary, Patterson didn't *feel* like the perpetrator, and little by little the evidence they had acquired was breaking down.

He had allowed his personal relationship with Caroline to interfere with his instincts. He'd held his ground, right up until the night of Caroline's abduction, but seeing Patterson with her in his arms had shaken him to his core. He'd immediately judged the man guilty from that moment forward, despite Patterson's insistent claim of innocence.

Patterson claimed he'd been sent a text and photo from Augusta's cell phone, luring him to the ruins. Apparently, those two had been in communication, though Patterson completely clammed up after the arrest, keeping the nature of their relationship to himself—and his lawyer. Now Jack was beginning to understand why. Augusta had not only paid his bail, but they were together right now. Patterson's tail had just relayed that news.

He pushed back the screen of his laptop, examining the photos of Amy Jones. He had them up on his screen, comparing them to the photos they had taken of Kelly Banks after her body had been dumped at Brittlebank Park, along with the new photos of Pamela Baker. Except for the laceration from Baker's pelvis to her breastbone, the rest was the same. All three women had been found stripped completely bare, their hands tied and posed prayerfully, their mouths taped and their tongues removed. The inside of their mouths were dyed blue with common-variety food coloring—the type that could be bought at most any grocery store. All three had died of asphyxiation associated with drowning. No hands or bindings had been used around the vic's throat. During the autopsy they had discovered evidence of cyanosis and petechial hemorrhaging in the eyes, and blood staining around the mouth and nose. They also found water in the lungs, which suggested all three girls probably died sometime after entering the water.

Maybe some sort of baptism?

In his notes for ViCAP he had already entered asphyxiation, strangulation, manual, non-manual, blue dye, nudity and now baptism and sacrificial wounds. Although not all law enforcement agencies contributed to the FBI's violent crimes database, most did, and he wanted to be sure the killer was on everyone's radar.

It was beginning to feel a bit religious in nature—

especially in connection with the notes the perp had left on each of the women's windshields: *Death and life are in the power of the tongue, those who love it will eat its fruit. Proverbs 18:21*

What did that mean? Had the victims been targeted because of something they'd said? Something that was said about them? Something they didn't say? Was the perp eating their tongues because he believed they held some sort of divine power? Was he removing them symbolically to keep them from talking?

In Greek mythology Tereus raped his wife's sister and cut out her tongue to keep her from telling anyone of his crime. Andrei Chikatilo, a Ukrainian serial killer, bit off the tongues of his lovers as a way to get off. Natives in the southernmost part of New Guinea supposedly ate the tongues of slain enemies to steal their power. Serial killer and cannibal Joachim Kroll killed and ate his victims simply to save on his grocery bill. And Dennis Rader considered his victims projects. He compared killing them to putting down animals. He strangled them multiple times, reviving them, getting off on their struggles, until he finally killed them and ejaculated into one of their personal items. So the gist of it was that their guy could be removing the tongues for any number of crazy reasons, though it was definitely part of his MO. In every case, he had cut out the tongue and painted the mouth blue. But if it was about keeping trophies, nothing had ever been discovered in Patterson's possessions.

As for the blue dye ... Jack couldn't even begin to decipher that one. Ancient Picts painted themselves blue as a form of war paint, though some claimed it was a form of antiseptic. Blue was the color of water. It was also the color of the sky. And it was the color of flame at its hottest point. Blue was associated with peace, serenity and spirituality. It was associated with the blood of aristocracy and little boys. The god Krishna had blue skin. The associations were endless. But if Ian had been messing with blue dye, you'd think that at some point, he would have spilled it on himself or somewhere in his house. His house had been clean. So was his car. So was he. They'd inspected him from head to toe after his arrest.

On the scene they had discovered a wet suit in Patterson's trunk, along with a "hit bag" containing a roll of the same tape used to cover the victims' mouths, rope, a half-used vial of blue food coloring, as well as a bloody knife and a rag that had both blood and blue dye stains—which proved the killer wasn't spill-proof. But the only piece of evidence Patterson had actually claimed was the suit—purchased, he'd said, to make his search of the river easier. But he also claimed he hadn't used it as yet, and sure enough, an examination of the suit showed it had never been worn.

Patterson claimed he'd arrived only minutes before the first squad car, saw the rising flames after spotting Caroline's car and ran toward the ruins to find her lying unconscious with flames licking all about her. He saw no one—conveniently—but said he didn't waste time looking either. He lifted her up and ran toward the road, where he heard sirens.

The rest was history.

The squad cars arrived, they held him at gunpoint, he dropped Caroline, put his hands up and stopped cooperating from that moment forward.

In retrospect, it was entirely possible Patterson was telling the truth and that he had actually been trying to *save* Caroline, not harm her.

According to Caroline's testimony, she arrived first and didn't recall another car being there, which meant

Patterson must have arrived after her. His car doors had been left wide open with the trunk easily accessible. Anyone could have popped the trunk and tossed evidence inside. In fact, when the squad cars arrived, Patterson's trunk had been left wide open, which made absolutely no sense for someone who planned his kills so meticulously. Everything about that night seemed rushed. Cars left in plain sight, doors ajar, trunks wide open.

And then, with sirens racing toward them, and no way off that peninsula but the one road—except over salt marsh—where did he intend to go? If he'd planned to escape into the marsh, he had been walking in the wrong direction. Nor had they found any evidence of stray boats in the surrounding creeks.

All Jack's deliberations brought him to the same place.

Ian Patterson wasn't guilty.

Jack picked up the lab report—the final nail in the coffin of their case against him as far as Jack was concerned. The blood from the knife and rag in Patterson's car had been sent to a private lab. Normally, the state would have processed the work and the turnaround would have been six months to a year, but this was the case of the decade. No expense had been spared. Even before Patterson's arrest, they had gathered the DNA of all known missing persons and entered them into CODIS, the national DNA indexing system.

According to the lab report in his hand, there was more than a 99 percent probability that the blood found on the rag and the knife in Patterson's car belonged to Pamela Baker, but her time of death posed a serious logistics problem since Patterson couldn't have killed her while sitting behind bars.

The rest of the evidence was compromised, as well —a notebook belonging to Amanda Hutto, a camera belonging to Amy Jones, complete with photos cataloguing her grisly death. Those had been seized from Patterson's house, though he claimed the evidence had been planted. His prints weren't found anywhere on the items. Not even the surfaces that would have retained latent prints had produced anything of value. The truth was that it felt to Jack as though it had been planted—all of it—just like Patterson said.

And then there was the tongue ring: Discovered in the ashtray of Patterson's car, they had pinned so much hope on it, because they'd learned belatedly that Amy Jones had had a tongue piercing—something they'd missed during the investigation—something Amy's roommate couldn't have known to tell them because they'd never fully disclosed the details of her friend's mutilation and death. But the organic matter didn't match Jones's DNA. Nine to one it belonged to the girl who gave Patterson his alibi, just as he had claimed during both polygraph tests he'd passed—and that was easy enough to find out.

Although Patterson could be working with an accomplice, Jack didn't think so. Why the hell would he agree to be the fall guy? It didn't make sense.

No, the killer was still out there, somewhere, and now he had Cody Simmons. It didn't matter that Cody didn't fit the profile of his past victims. Neither did Amanda Hutto, but he was starting to believe they were all connected. Jack just had to find the kid before he turned up dead, as well.

He got up and lifted his jacket from the back of his chair, leaning over to turn off his computer before shrugging into it. Then he picked up his cell phone and called his partner. Don Garrison answered on the first ring—probably bored as hell. "Where is he?"

"He left The Shack and headed down East Ashley with Augusta."

"Just the two of them?"

"Yep."

"Do you know where they went?"

"There's only one way to go from here, boss, and they had that look, if you know what I mean. I didn't follow into the dunes. I figure she's safe enough since they both made me."

Jack sighed. "Alright, let them go. Moving forward, we'll just check in on him. Go on home, Garrison."

"Will do, Jack. Thanks."

Jack hung up and shoved the phone in his pocket, then grabbed his keys off the desk and sighed. Augusta's involvement with Patterson was something else for Caroline to be upset about, but he sure as hell wasn't going to keep it from her and jeopardize his relationship. As far as he was concerned, she might as well hear it from him since Augusta didn't seem the least inclined to share that information. As far as he was concerned, Augusta was on her own.

11

On the street in front of The Shack, the lights were on, but dimly lit, obscured by bell-shaped black shades to keep the glare down. Only Augusta and Ian's cars were left on the road. His sat conspicuously beneath the streetlight in front of The Shack, while hers was guarded by the half torso of a plastic shark that protruded from the building above a law office sign. At this hour of the night, the flickering streetlights lent the shark movement, giving her a creepy feeling.

Ian walked her to the Town Car, and they stood in front of it for a moment before Augusta unlocked the door and slid behind it, using it as a shield.

Ian was right. There was enough going on in their lives that they didn't need to add relationship drama to the mix. Besides, for the first time in her life, she was determined to do this differently. Sex wasn't the smartest reason for any relationship and somehow, she felt closer to Ian now. Sex alone couldn't have accomplished that. They'd talked all night, baring secrets, wishes and fears ...

Ian had been a troubled kid, whose life before the Church had been filled with difficulty—one of those for whom the Scared Straight program had actually worked. In his case, probably because the man who had put the fear into him was his own dad. He got involved with his local church because of an uncle, and from there ended up in the seminary, intending to spend his life in service to the community. They were more alike than she might have realized. No wonder she was drawn to him.

"I'll be right behind you," he reassured. "I'm not letting you out of my sight."

Augusta smiled and leaned on the door. "Despite everything that's going on, I had a really nice time, Ian."

He smiled back at her, shoving his hands into his pockets—Augusta sensed it was his way of controlling himself. The impulse to kiss him was strong, and the tension between them was palpable. "Me, too."

"What's that?" he asked suddenly, withdrawing his hand from his pocket and reaching toward her.

Augusta assumed he'd failed his own test of willpower, but he reached past her to the windshield to pluck up a little yellow paper umbrella that was stuck into the black plastic of the wiper.

She grimaced as it flashed past her eyes. "Some drunk's idea of a parting gift, I suppose. I hate those things!" she told him. "They remind me of my mother."

He lifted a brow. "I take it that's a bad thing."

Augusta eyed the little umbrella with no small measure of disgust. "You might say that." But she volunteered no more than that. Another day, another time, and she would tell him anything he wanted to know, but at one-thirty in the morning, this wasn't the time or place.

He lifted a brow and twirled the little umbrella daintily between his fingers, lifting it mockingly over his head. "It matches your car," he remarked.

Augusta laughed. "Keep it," she directed him. "Call it a memento." And then she slid into the car before she could do or say something she might regret—before he might begin to feel obligated to give her a kiss good night. One rejection for the night—even if it didn't really feel like one—was quite enough.

He started to toss the umbrella away, and then at the last minute shoved it into his pocket. Augusta raised both brows, and said, "I was kidding. You don't have to keep that junk."

He shrugged. "With my luck, a cop will jump out from behind a bush and charge me with littering. I'll use it to pick my teeth clean on the way home."

Augusta laughed and started the car, fighting the urge to say three ridiculous little words. At this point, it was hardly appropriate, no matter what her heart was telling her.

"I'll call you tomorrow," he promised, then turned and made a dash for his car. Augusta waited for him to start his car before pulling out into the road and heading home, giving him time to get behind her. As he said he would, he followed all the way, stopping just outside the gate when she went through. He made a three-point and turned around, but sat there, waiting. Staying within his sights, she parked the Town Car in the circular driveway and lingered only long enough to wave good-bye. Then she unlocked the door and hurried inside.

Caroline's car was outside, but the house was dark. It was two in the morning. Everyone was probably in bed, and not even Caroline's righteous anger would have kept her from the opportunity of being bright-eyed and bushy-tailed in the morning. God forbid she might be off her game. The thought made Augusta smirk a little.

With just the briefest glance in the hall mirror, she made her way up the stairs toward her room. The stairs creaked on the way up, and in the dark, she passed over the loose board at the top of the steps, tripping.

"Damn!" she said, and remembered her appointment with the contractor tomorrow. Hopefully that would make Caroline happy.

Tango barked in Caroline's room, and Augusta dove for her bedroom door, unwilling to brave even a brief discussion before bedtime. Thankfully, the dog settled down after another halfhearted *woof*, and she closed her bedroom door, dropped her purse. She kicked off her shoes, and shrugged out of her skirt before making a beeline toward the bed, intending to sleep in her tank top and underwear. It was too late to brush her teeth. The idea of sand in her mouth was far more inviting than an encounter with her wrathful sister.

Once in bed, she stretched out, feeling the tiny grains of sand that had followed her home. But all in all, sleeping in a grainy bed was a small price to pay for the evening, and a tiny smile curved her lips as she thought of Ian, holding up that silly paper umbrella.

IGNORING HER LUNCH, Caroline shook her head over the wedding announcement in the newspaper. "The woman apparently wanted a full-blown plantation wedding, with servants dressed in period costume and everything."

"Jesus!" Jack said, and laughed. "I wouldn't say I had a clue what's appropriate, but even I know that doesn't come close." He took a halfhearted bite of his gyro.

They were still in the planning stages of their own wedding, though Caroline would be happy if they simply eloped. They had yet to set a date and a big wedding didn't feel right—not with everything that was going on. Jack had surprised her by insisting on a big to-do. He said he wanted the entire world to know she was his wife. It was a sweet gesture, but she knew it had roots in a previous life, when weddings had been among her mother's most coveted affairs. That Flo hadn't lived long enough to see a single one of her daughters stand before the altar made Caroline feel strangely obligated to carry it through, despite her reservations.

She set the paper aside with the realization that her mother was still her greatest weakness. The need to prove herself persisted, like a gnat floating before her face. While some people tapped away on their phones over lunch, tethered to Facebook, she couldn't seem to stop reading the newspaper—not simply the *Tribune*, but every newspaper within reach. She read voraciously, trying to gauge the competition to make certain the *Tribune* hadn't missed any opportunities or leads. Jack was extremely patient with her, and for that she was grateful, but she also knew that his pensive mood probably had just as much to do with the ongoing investigation. For Caroline's part, it was never far from the edge of her mind, but she had promised Jack not to get involved beyond her personal relationship with the Simmonses. That wasn't easy to do, especially now that it seemed she had some sort of influence. The key was in learning when to flex her media muscle.

"Okay, so what was so important that you had to see me *right now*—not that I'm complaining, mind you. I'm counting the days until we can be together every second."

Jack lifted a brow, obviously mistaking her tone for sarcasm, since Caroline wasn't the most forthcoming with her feelings. She'd caught him with a bite of his lamb in his mouth, and he continued to chew. She smiled to reassure him.

"How can you count days when you're avoiding setting a date?" he challenged her.

"It just doesn't seem right yet," Caroline defended. "And now with Rose and Cody ..."

He'd been tense from the instant they'd sat down, avoiding the reason he'd asked her to lunch in the first place. As pleasant as the morning was, and as happy as she was to see him after spending the night away from him last night, they had been seated now for more than thirty minutes since opening the place up.

"Augusta was with Ian Patterson last night," he blurted.

Caroline's stomach sank somewhere beneath her chair.

"If it's any comfort, Caroline, I don't believe the man's guilty."

For a moment, Caroline stared at her own plate, trying to determine what to say. She couldn't control Augusta, but she couldn't handle Jack defending the man, too. Somewhere in the back of her mind, she was struggling with the burgeoning possibility that Patterson could be innocent, but if she accepted that fact, it meant she had gone after an innocent man with the tenacity and grace of a pit bull, thinking of nothing else but the story. Right now she couldn't figure out which was worse—the idea that she had been so terribly wrong, that she was becoming exactly like her mother or that her sister had taken a total stranger's side over hers—because that's what it felt like, even though her rational side told her it wasn't true.

"He didn't kill Pam," Jack said more certainly. "We know that."

She knew better than to ask him *how* he knew. They had made a pact to stay away from potentially explosive subjects. "Okay," she said, taking a moment to process the information he had given her. "So what about Cody?" she asked, steering the conversation to safer ground. "Any word there?"

He shook his head. "No."

He peered down at his plate, suddenly shoving it away, with half a gyro still on it. She realized he was taking Cody's disappearance hard. Did he feel they had wasted time with Ian Patterson and that it was Caroline's fault they didn't have the right man behind bars?

She couldn't blame him for those thoughts, because they were exactly the same thoughts she had been struggling with herself.

Her desire to help—in some way—was overwhelming, but this time she had handed the story over to her editor-in-chief, Frank Bonneau, and walked away, putting her energy into comforting Cody's family. It made it easier that she trusted Bonneau implicitly—nearly as much as she trusted Jack, so she let the subject of Augusta and Ian Patterson go entirely ... for the moment. Still, she had to ask. "It's been days, Jack. Do you think he's still alive?"

Jack nodded, but then shook his head. "I don't

know. It's impossible to say. I don't think this guy's killing them right away. The official stance from the public information officer is that we're hopeful he's still alive."

So that was what she was bound to report.

Caroline hoped it was true.

THE PHONE RANG, waking Augusta out of a dopey sleep. She fumbled for the receiver, wondering who would be calling on her mother's landline. It wasn't a private number, but neither was it a number she gave out.

"Hello?"

A dial tone was her answer, but not right away. For a few brief seconds, she heard the sound of music playing on the other end of the line ... or maybe the music was playing here in the house? She couldn't tell. She hung up and heard the music like an echo in her brain.

Admittedly, morning wasn't her best time of the day.

Within seconds, as soon as she set the receiver down, the phone rang again, and she stifled a curse as she lifted the receiver to her ear. "Yes?" she said, irritated.

"Lucas Skywalker, Skywalker Construction," the voice offered.

Augusta lay there, disoriented and confused for a moment. It might have been a prank, except that she had actually gone to Skywalker Construction yesterday afternoon to meet with a contractor. She simply hadn't realized that was the guy's full name.

Correctly interpreting the silence, he offered, "I

know, sorry. It always takes people by surprise at first. That's why I rarely use my real name. I'm part Cherokee," he explained. "At least that's the explanation I prefer over admitting my parents were stoned when they signed the birth certificate."

Augusta laughed. "Hi," she said.

"You can call me Luke."

"Hi, Luke," she said, and spoke to him briefly about his schedule, relieved to hear that he could start first thing this morning. Luckily, her mother's reputation in the community still loomed large, even from the grave. Plus, Augusta had hinted at their first meeting that money wasn't an object. She supposed she wasn't above throwing her name around after all —not when it meant saving her and her sisters from having to forfeit twenty-seven million bucks.

He reassured her that he was gathering his crew as they spoke, although they wouldn't be available until after lunch. "That's fine," she said. "I'll be here. Thanks so much," she said, and hung up.

Still groggy, she sat up in bed, cocking her head toward the persistent sound of music coming through her closed bedroom door. A small headache lurked in the back of her brain, but not enough to make the idea of rising all that daunting. The clock by her bedside read 11:38 A.M. and she grimaced. She had never been an early riser, but the last time she had gotten up near noon, she had had a roommate and test scores to worry about. Since then, she'd been running on a gerbil wheel. Without a doubt, life was slower paced here than in New York, but waking up at noon was just unacceptable.

Stumbling out of the bed, she opened the bedroom door, and the sound of music spilled into the room. She could make out the disoriented melody of

Harry Nilsson's "Blanket for a Sail" playing downstairs as she went back to fish a pair of shorts out the dirty pile of clothes in her closet. As a child, Savannah had loved that song, but it was a weird choice to be listening to now—not that she had anything against Harry Nilsson. The man was a genius. But it was a song she recalled from a children's collection—one that included songs like "This Old Man" and "Itsy Bitsy Spider."

"Savannah?" she called, as she made her way back into the upstairs hall.

Savannah didn't respond, but Augusta knew she must be around because she didn't have anywhere else to go—nor would she have simply taken the car without waking Augusta to ask for the keys. They were sharing it right now, but it was understood that Augusta needed to be mobile if she was going to get the house restored, while it was Savannah's job to plant her ass in the office chair and write. Although neither of them had done much to those ends, Augusta had been busy with plans for the fund-raiser—something she still wanted to get done, though it didn't seem appropriate now to have some huge community gathering when women were being murdered and kids were disappearing.

The thought gave her a shiver as she walked down the corridor, stopping at Caroline's room on the way to Savannah's. She found the door shut. She opened it, throwing it wide. Empty, of course. Caroline would be at work right now.

Augusta's room was the farthest down the hall, away from the stairs. Caroline's was closest, with Savannah's on the other end of the corridor past the stairs. The closer she got to the stairs, the louder the music played.

"Savannah!"

With the music blaring downstairs, shouting was pointless, she realized. Clearly, Savannah was not in her room, unless she had cranked the stereo so she could hear it upstairs. But that wasn't like her at all. A peek into her bedroom revealed that it, too, was empty. The door was open. Unlike Augusta's room, it was neat and orderly, not a shred of clothing out of place. That was probably the only character trait Savannah had inherited from their mother, though physically Savannah was the spitting image of Flo, with her willowy frame and deep gray eyes.

Expecting to find Savannah downstairs, Augusta made her way down the stairs, belatedly wondering where Tango was. He wasn't at the bottom of the stairs where he seemed to plant himself all day long, waiting for Caroline to come home, so she called his name, too.

Neither Tango nor Savannah answered, and Augusta wandered toward the sound of music, her nerves a little on edge. The music was coming from the den, the string accompaniment sounding a little like the *Psycho* danger music in its percussive intensity. "Blanket for a Sail." Nilsson was talking about a tiny little skipper keeping the boat afloat. The song immediately reminded her of Sammy. He'd loved that little inflatable raft of his, and would run around with his little pirate flag, waving it like a banner, yelling, "Yo, ho, yo ho, it's a pirate's life for me!" The memory would have made her smile, except that she began to feel a little creeped out when the song came to its orchestral conclusion, paused, then started over again.

In the den, she found her mother's vintage turntable on, the receiver blaring. Savannah was nowhere in sight. Harry Nilsson's voice was crooning the refrain, "Way out on the ocean..."

Augusta yanked up the arm, dropping the needle on the vinyl. It scratched briefly before she caught it and placed it back on its perch, shutting off the turntable. "Jesus," she said, and called out again, "Savannah!" She turned to assess the room and cursed softly to herself.

Where the hell was Savannah?

The house appeared empty. At the moment, it felt a little like one of those eerie mansions in a horror flick, where ghosts were tormenting the home owners, but Augusta didn't believe in ghosts. As unlikely as it seemed, her sister must have left the stereo on. Maybe she'd taken Tango for a walk?

Augusta poked her head into the kitchen and called for Tango again. She heard a whine coming from the pantry and went straight to it, opening the door. Tango stood there, panting heavily, looking at her with gratitude. The pantry was hot.

"How the hell did you get in there?" she asked him.

He came out, wagging his tail sheepishly, drooling on the kitchen floor, as though he thought he'd done something wrong, and Augusta decided someone must have accidentally locked him in the pantry and left the house in a hurry. But if Tango was in the pantry, obviously Savannah wasn't walking him, so she continued looking for her sister, walking through the house, not once, but three times, before wandering outside and heading out toward the dock. The car was in the driveway, exactly where Augusta had left it, so Savannah must be somewhere on the premises.

Tango followed her around, and she was grateful

for the company as she made her way toward the dock, half-expecting Savannah to be out in the boathouse for some reason. She wasn't there. Back inside the house, the attic stairs were up, not down, so there was no way she was up in the attic again, rummaging through boxes for the fund-raiser.

Tango followed at her heels, panting heavily as she made her way back to her room. She glanced at the clock and, seeing that it was nearly twelve-thirty, snagged her cell phone out of her purse. In the process, she spotted the photograph of Sammy in the side pocket.

A tiny chill ran down her spine.

It was eerily coincidental that she would find that photograph last night and then wake up this morning to that music, but it was entirely possible Savannah had found the picture, and then feeling sentimental, had woken up with a desire to hear that song.

Either that, or they had a ghost in their house. Maybe Flo was around here somewhere wandering around, trying to explain why that stupid shoe of hers was out in the woods. Or maybe she was simply pestering Augusta to begin the renovations, she thought wryly.

Feeling a little anxious, she punched in Caroline's number.

12

"It's about time!" Caroline said, answering her phone on the first ring.

She mouthed the word "Augusta" and got up from the table to walk outside, hoping to spare Jack the sight of her foaming at the mouth. "Where the hell have you been, Augusta?"

"Sleeping. I just woke up."

Caroline slid outside the door of the tiny Greek restaurant, narrowly avoiding a shoulder bump with a businessman. "Last night?"

"What do you mean, *last night*? Since when did you become my mother, Caroline?"

"Never mind! I already know where you were, no thanks to you!" Caroline countered. "Don't even throw out that mother bit!"

"If you knew, why bother to ask?"

Caroline clutched the phone tighter. "Maybe because I wanted to hear it from your own two lips, for once."

"You wouldn't understand."

"How would you know? You haven't tried me, Augusta! You don't talk to anyone anymore. You keep to yourself and assume nobody gives a crap—well, some people do, and you had me worried out of my mind last night!"

Augusta's tone was full of her usual sarcasm. "Right, so you're okay with Ian and all you care about is my well-being?"

"Of course! There's a murderer out there, in case you haven't heard?"

"Jesus, how could I miss that, Caroline? You shouted it from the rooftops, even before you had a clue what the truth was." Her words were defiant and angry, though she sounded deflated. Caroline's anger wavered as she realized there was truth in Augusta's accusation. "Are we really going to fight over this, Caroline? I'm thirty-two years old. I have a right to see whomever I want. And I don't believe Ian is guilty. It's that simple. It's my money, not yours."

"Believe it or not, I wasn't going to bring up the bail money. There's not a lot more I have to say about that. What's done is done."

"Good," Augusta said. "Anyway, I only called to ask you where Savannah is and why she left the stereo blaring."

"If you had gotten up this morning, instead of sleeping off a party night with Ian, or if you'd bothered to talk to anyone but Ian, you'd know I took Savannah to the airport this morning. If she left the stereo on it was an accident."

That disclosure seemed to deflate Augusta's anger completely. She paused for a moment, and then asked in a subdued tone, "Savannah's gone?"

Caroline took the opportunity to encourage a cease-fire. "Yeah."

"But she's coming back, right?"

"Yeah, she's just finally doing what you and I did

when we first resigned ourselves to mother's will. She's gone back to D.C. to put her affairs in order. Though I'm pretty sure she's getting rid of her apartment and moving back to Charleston permanently. She's done in D.C. Besides, I think she needed time to think about this whole ordeal with Sadie. She's pretty upset over it all."

"How did yesterday go at the Simmonses?"

"Not great," Caroline admitted. "Sadie pretty much had nothing to say to either of us. She's clearly not in a forgiving mood. Josh wasn't there."

"Well, that sucks. But on a brighter note, I have a contractor arriving in a few minutes—oh wait," she said suddenly. "That could be him now. I gotta go. I'll go by and talk to Sadie after he leaves."

Caroline didn't even have a chance to say good-bye. Augusta simply hung up on her, and Caroline found herself shell-shocked by the fact that Augusta had actually taken steps to complete the task their mother had bequeathed to her. "Wow," she said to herself, and made her way back into the restaurant to give Jack the details.

SKYWALKER CONSTRUCTION CAME PREPARED to work, Augusta noticed.

Luke—she had a hard time taking his name seriously—arrived at the house about thirty minutes ahead of his crew, and took some time to look over the problem areas Augusta had identified—most notably the peeling exterior and deteriorating siding and the loose boards at the top of the stairs. The boards themselves weren't such a concern, but Augusta worried that somehow Flo had painted over water stains on the ceiling and that there was, in fact, damage from a past leak in the roof.

That was his first order of business once she was done showing him around; she wanted to be certain there wasn't anything of structural importance to be corrected. The siding itself wasn't a structural issue. But in the muggy Charleston climate, it wasn't unusual to hang a wooden garage door and find it completely rotted away the following year. Wood had to be treated before being painted, and if it wasn't, it was common to find moisture damage, particularly around the marshes. Replacing the siding with vinyl or composite was not an option, because Augusta thought the house should remain true to its original construction. How she'd come to that conclusion when she hated the original house, she didn't know, but somehow it didn't seem appropriate to alter its construction with plastics or metals. The closest she could come to comprehending her own decision was that she was a bit of a purist. In this, she knew her mother would approve.

Luke was clearly the right man for the job because he knew exactly what needed to be done. Augusta thought he was kind of cute, in a rugged, alpha sort of way, and wished Savannah was around to meet him. Her sister could do worse, she decided. The man owned his own construction company but sounded like a professor. But since Savannah wasn't around, and she had a renewed sense of purpose, she set him loose on the house on his own. Feeling a sense of accomplishment, she decided she had earned enough goodwill to go ask Caroline about Jennifer Williams.

Leaving Luke with instructions and a key, along with her cell phone number, she headed out the door.

THE MAN WAS HERE.

Staring down at him.

Cody heard him come into the building from somewhere near the lockers. He slithered in through a hole in the floor, dripping wet, his footsteps slapping like fins against the floor. He could hear banging and the hollow *ting* of metal being abused. And then the rotting floor creaked as he neared.

It was the heat of the day, as his grandma Rose would say. Cody's hair was plastered to his face and the inside of his face felt like it did when he stood on his head and all the blood rushed into it.

He kept his eyes closed, afraid to open them, afraid to see the man, though he could sense the light from the window being blocked by his body. Possums played dead and sometimes it worked. He waited a long time, slowing his breathing, hoping the man would leave, but he stood there so long the water he'd brought in on his shoes puddled beneath his feet and trickled down the slanted floorboards toward Cody's face, tickling his chin.

Cody resisted the urge to open his eyes.

He was so thirsty ... the rag in his mouth felt like a ball of fire. The water against his face felt good. The man nudged his chest with his boot and he stifled a whimper, his chest heaving. He kept his eyes closed, praying harder.

Please, please, God... I'll be good!

The man said nothing, and Cody hoped that if he didn't look, the man wouldn't kill him. In the movies, the minute you saw the killer, you were a dead man. Cody didn't want to be a dead man. He wanted to live.

Desperately.

He heard the sound of knuckles cracking as the wet puddle gathered around his face, cooling the fever in his cheek. Resisting the urge to sob, he lay thinking about his mama and his grandma and the pool in their backyard.

Don't worry, Mama. I'm real smart. Like Daddy.

Cody had learned to swim in that pool. He could float on his back like an otter, his mom said.

Against his will, Cody shivered as the man toed his chest again, nudging gently, as though he were inspecting him. Still he resisted the urge to open his eyes, focusing on his sister, Lila. He thought about her Barbie doll, the one he'd burned the hair off, and tried to recall how much money he had in his little piggy bank at home. His grandmother had given him the freckled pig with the sunglasses, and he'd thought it was a real dumb gift, until he'd begun to stick in the spare change he'd found lying around the house. He always made sure to ask first, and now maybe he had enough to buy Lila a new doll. She would like that, he thought. Maybe he had enough to get her two ...

"Thank you, Cody," he heard her sweet voice say in his head. *"Do you want to play dolls with me?"*

Next time, Cody would say yes.

He would sit with her and enjoy it and he would talk his dad into showing him how to build a dollhouse for her—like the ones some people built with wooden furniture and shingles on the roof. Lila loved her dolls, and Cody wondered if that was because he wouldn't play with her. He would from now on, he promised himself. He would even let her come and play with him and his friends if she wanted to and he wouldn't complain when his mom asked him to watch over her. Now he understood ... she needed watching over and he would never, ever let anyone steal her ... like they had stolen him.

He would keep her safe.

Always.

As soon as he got home.

He saw himself removing his handcuff and ropes, tearing the tape from his mouth and getting up and walking home. It was probably a long ways through the pluff mud with the smell of the marsh caked up in his nose.

A little delirious from lack of food and water, he disappeared into his head for a while. When he came back out, he found his cheek swimming in stinky water. The puddle had worked its way down to the lower spot in the warped floor and the tape was getting wet on one side of his face. Slowly, he cracked his lid and found himself alone again, but he was uncertain how much time had passed.

The sun was softer in the sky now, like it was late afternoon, and he wriggled into a more comfortable position, scraping a piece of the tape away from his cheek into the water.

His heart kicked against his ribs in surprise.

He wriggled his cheek a little harder and the tape loosened a little more.

His heart beat even faster.

Suddenly, he was like a mindless animal, working furiously to scrape the tape away from his blistering skin. Scraping his face into the puddle he rubbed until his skin was raw and finally the tape popped away and Cody spat the cloth out of his mouth, turning his lips into the puddle and lapping it up like a dog.

Water, water, water!

Yes! He was going to go home!

13

It was more than a simple attraction. Ian realized that now. Despite everything going on, the taste of her lingered on his tongue. Every so often his memory zeroed in on the two of them lying in the sand, her legs wrapped around him. It had been all he could do to turn her away when he wanted more than anything to make love to her right there on the beach.

Again.

Despite the fact that he'd had sand chafing his ass for hours after the first time. She was one hell of a little seductress and it was a good thing she hadn't come into his life while he wore the white collar. Or maybe it would have been exactly the thing to show him how unsuited he was to the life of a priest. But he knew that now. That was all that mattered.

He'd gotten a call from Jack Shaw. He was on his way into the Lockwood station to pick up the paperwork to retrieve his car—a good sign, he thought. Maybe, finally, they had decided to spend their energy looking for the real killer.

Inside the station, he asked after Shaw and was instructed to wait for the detective to come out and fetch him, which he did in his own sweet time, Ian noticed.

When Shaw finally appeared, he looked haggard and far less presumptuous than he had during their last meeting.

"Have a moment?"

"Sure." Ian stood, ready to follow. "As long as you aren't still looking for ways to dress me in green. It's not really my color."

Smiling without mirth, Shaw waved him down the hall, reassuring him, "In fact, you won't be wearing any jumpsuits at this point," he said, leading him down the hall.

Ian followed. "Does that disappoint you?"

Shaw didn't bother to look at him, but said, "For what it's worth, I don't believe in the death penalty."

"Your employer does," Ian suggested, referring to the state.

"Let's get to the point," Shaw said, leading him into a tiny, airless office that Ian assumed belong to him.

"Nice. You must be important," Ian baited.

Shaw eyed him pointedly. "Cut the crap before I decide to take my time about dropping these charges."

Ian sucked in a breath and sank down into one of the two chairs facing Shaw's desk. "You're dropping charges? No shit?" he asked. It wasn't meant as a question. The fact nearly bowled him over. Shaw was watching him intently. "Wow," Ian said, sobering, and scratched the back of his neck to hide the burn of tears in his eyes. He felt suddenly like a little girl, emotional as hell and ready to cry. He swallowed, crossing his hands, and peering down at his fingers, trying to regain control. He sat there like that for a good minute, and to his credit, Shaw allowed it, sharing the space with him but saying nothing.

"I didn't think you were guilty to begin with,"

Shaw offered finally, when it was clear Ian wasn't going to break down like a baby and bawl.

Anything Ian might have said in response just didn't seem appropriate. But he still couldn't talk over the lump in his throat.

"I need you to square up with me," Shaw said, settling behind his desk. "I need you to tell me everything you know, Patterson—*everything*."

Ian nodded, regaining his composure.

"Help me catch this guy," he pleaded. "Before an innocent kid is killed."

Ian met his gaze straight-on. "Just tell me what you need me to do."

So much for working up the nerve to talk to Caroline—her sister wasn't in her office. Apparently, she had met Jack for lunch and had yet to return to work.

This was the first time Augusta had returned to the *Tribune's* offices since the day she'd come in to do her inventory for the fund-raiser—the same day she'd found Ian's name and information among her sister's notes—notes that all pointed to his guilt. It was strange to walk in and see someone new at the reception desk that Pamela Baker had once manned.

The gaudy chandelier was still hanging in the reception area, its massive bulk dangling from thick black iron chains. As beautiful as the ironwork appeared, the antebellum-era contraption gave her a sick feeling in her gut, because it reminded her of galley chains and irons clapped around the ankles of slaves. But it was simply a light fixture—a stupid, expensive one, but hardly worth getting upset over. When the time came, she'd have them haul it down and sell it to some wealthy banker with questionable political motives who might hang it above his private collection of fake Fabergé eggs.

She was still standing there, peering up at the monstrosity, when Brad Bessett came up and stood beside her.

"I heard the thing cost twenty-two thousand just to have it restored."

Augusta peered at him over her shoulder and sighed. "I wouldn't doubt it." But that was all she said. The fact that their mother hadn't blinked an eye over such an extravagance, while asking her for fifty dollars was an ordeal, wasn't any of his business. It wasn't Augusta's style to share her family's dirty laundry. Ignoring it—as she did her own—was more her style. Proof of that fact was sitting in a heap in her closet. It was crazy that she was an heir to this legacy, yet she couldn't bring herself to wear clean clothes.

Realizing suddenly that as annoying as the guy was, he might be able to help her find out what she needed to know, she turned to face him. Maybe she wouldn't have to deal with Caroline?

"Hey, it's Brad, right?"

A smile spread across his face, and he nodded, his hand immediately going into his pockets.

"You're exactly the person who can help me. How long have you been here?"

His brows drew together. "Working?"

Augusta resisted the urge to ask him if that was what he was doing. "Yeah. How long have you worked for the paper?"

"Going on five years now," he said, peering over at the receptionist, who got up suddenly.

Augusta waited for the girl to leave before asking.

"Yeah... so, maybe you can tell me if Jennifer Williams ever applied for a job here?"

His face suddenly tightened. "Jennifer Williams? As in the missing girl?"

Augusta nodded. "Yeah," she said, watching his body language. His hands came out of his pockets, and he crossed his arms. "I got a tip that maybe she did."

He shook his head, but his lips thinned, as though the question perturbed him.

Either he didn't know. Or he did. Either way, Augusta knew how to handle him. She was a gifted middle child, after all, and knew how to play both sides. "You realize, if somehow the *Tribune* missed that bit of information, Caroline will see red," she suggested. "You're the investigating reporter, right?"

"Yeah," he said, clearly irritated now.

"Then you would probably know, right?"

He tipped his head back and cracked his knuckles. Augusta couldn't tell if it was a nervous gesture or if he simply felt uncomfortable over having been caught with his pants down, so to speak. "I can look into it," he offered.

"Alright. Well, if you find out, let me know, please. I'll let you be the one to share that bit of info with Caroline. I know what a pill my sister can be. Let me give you my number," she offered, and dove into her purse for a pen and piece of paper. She walked over to the receptionist's desk and scribbled her name and number on an old business card, then handed it to him as the receptionist returned.

"Frank wants to see you in his office," she said.

"Me?" Brad asked.

The girl nodded.

"Thanks," Augusta offered, and winked at him. "Just give me a ring when you figure it all out."

"I will," he said, and left without another word.

"Do you want to wait in Caroline's office?" the receptionist asked.

"Nah. I'll catch up with her at home. Thanks," she said, and turned away, indulging in a private smile. She had a feeling Brad would look into it at once. So now, with a second task accomplished, she set her sights on Sadie. Two down, one to go.

Maybe she would have better luck this time.

SOME SAID the dead could not cross over water. So that's where he put them, his flock of wayward souls, who in life had been nothing more than vessels filled with the putrid stench of hate and fear.

He'd once read that all actions could be reduced to one of two motivations: fear or love. Killing might be construed as an act of fear or hate, but it wasn't true, because he loved every member of his growing congregation. With their deaths, they had given him their greatest gift.

And he returned it tenfold.

They lay beneath the muck, earthly beauty preserved for the rest of eternity.

The smell of decay hung in the air. Most would blame it on the pluff mud—a ripe Lowcountry stew made of bacteria, water and organic matter decomposing in the muggy Southern climate.

From experience he knew that if a body was submerged soon after death, the soft tissues—skin, hair and organs— were preserved. Here, the soil was so dense, and the thick mud held so little oxygen, it literally suffocated the life from the microorganisms that caused decay ... in a way, that was what he was doing, too ... smothering disease ... the same way Mother Nature did. But he was still perfecting his craft.

He cast his fishing line out into the water and watched as the weighted bob landed nearly seventy-five feet out, radiating ripples that reflected the late-afternoon sun. Standing nearly knee-deep in the pluff mud that caked his beige waders to his thighs, he lifted his boot as a matter of habit. It made a sucking sound as he shifted to a new spot, and he watched idly as the tide pooled into the cast of his leg, washing sediment into his prints until they began again to fill. He'd watched novice fishermen wait too long, and then struggle with the mud, sinking hip-deep before extricating themselves at last. But he knew exactly how far out to go. Knew precisely where not to step. He was so familiar with these salt marshes that he knew the tidal flats like the back of his hand.

From here he could see for miles.

He wondered what it must have been like in the old days, when you could see clear to downtown Charleston from the middle of the island, over miles and miles of white cotton fields that looked like snowy tundra in the middle of summer.

Beyond that blanket of cotton lay black water.

Not blue. But black.

Certainly not that washed-out shade of blue that superstitious Southerners splashed on their shutters and porches to keep out the souls of the dead—souls tethered to the material world by forces of revenge.

The mouth of the righteous brings forth wisdom, but the perverse tongue will be cut out.

That's what Proverbs ordained.

The knife in his leg sheath itched to be used on something bigger than fish.

There was still time.

Maybe a good four or five more days.

At the end of his line, he felt a tug and jerked the line to set the hook, then he reeled in his catch, the blood singing in his veins.

Patience is a virtue.

14

———

Spotting Sadie's silver BMW in the driveway, Augusta veered toward her cottage instead of continuing on to the main house. The black iron gates closed automatically behind her as she turned down the drive and came to a crunchy halt in front of Sadie's house. Luckily, Josh's car was nowhere in sight. She wasn't in the mood to deal with him today. They had grown apart. They were nothing alike anymore. He cherished his shiny Italian shoes far too much.

Sadie's home badly needed a coat of paint, and Augusta decided she would send the painters over when they were through with the main house—a gift from all three of them for everything Sadie had done since their mother's death. It would be impossible to pay her back for everything she'd done for them throughout their lives. She was certain neither Caroline nor Savannah would protest the added cost to the project.

On the other hand ... Sadie was very particular about the shade of blue she used on her porch, shutters and door, so maybe she should send them over here first, and then use the same color on their own porch?

In Hoodoo folk magic, water and sky were cross-roads between heaven and earth, and therefore bar-riers between the living and the dead. Sadie strongly believed in the power of the dead. It was why she hated that old mirror in their house. She said it had seen far too many deaths.

Outside her own home, she had constructed a bottle tree made of dead red cedar. It was the real deal, with antique cobalt blue bottles of all types—old can-ning and medicine jars—nothing like the sculpted creations you might order from a Web site. Sadie's Geechee roots were stronger than her accent. She used to say that when the wind blew past in the evenings, you could hear the moans of trapped spirits whistling on the breeze. Come morning the rising sun would burn them up, preventing them from coming in to steal the souls of the living.

Not that Augusta believed in old haint supersti-tions, but the sight of the bottle tree comforted her somehow.

On the porch, she recognized the cracked terra-cotta pot she'd painted for Sadie when she was nine. It was still intact after all these years—same crack, same place. How it had remained in one piece after all this time was a mystery. The only explanation Augusta had was that Sadie had cared for it lovingly. She and Josh had dropped it soon after painting it and they had reinforced the cracks with glue and then re-painted it, but it could only have made it all these years if it had been cared for by a loving hand. She stood a long moment, lost in reverie, and Sadie an-swered the door before Augusta got the chance to knock, opening it wide.

"Hey!" Augusta said, feeling suddenly awkward, despite their history together.

Sadie lifted a brow and Augusta peered down at the purse in her hand. It could hardly have gone unnoticed that she hadn't knocked on this door since she was seventeen. "You gonna stand there all day? Come on in, eah!" Turning her back to the door, Sadie wiped her hands on the dishcloth in her hands.

Augusta followed her inside and back toward the kitchen, where they had an unimpeded view of the spartina flats from the kitchen window. The house sat far enough back from the water that Sadie didn't have to worry about high tide, but she was still close enough that she could see the end of their dock. Seagulls and terns dotted the skyline. One year, there had been an osprey nest right outside the window.

"I'm pretty sure you didn't come by lookin' for coffee, but I've got some made fresh if you want."

"Sure," Augusta said, and set her purse down on the counter.

"Half-caf okay?"

"Yeah, fine."

For a moment, Sadie busied herself with preparing the coffee, and Augusta watched, feeling uncomfortable. This wasn't her home and she was Sadie's guest, so she couldn't really insist on getting her own. Instead, she sat down on a stool at the kitchen counter, inspecting the newly renovated kitchen.

Dressed in shades of indigo and white, the cupboards looked old but new—not quite as cutesy as gingham, but just as down-home. The Sub-Zero fridge was hidden behind dark blue wooden doors and the rest of the appliances were all obscured from view, as though Sadie didn't want to be reminded of housekeeping duties while in her own home. After working her fingers to the bone for nearly sixty years, Augusta was pretty sure she might develop a similar aversion to kitchen chores. Who could blame her?

She was simply making conversation when she said, "Looks like you're putting your money to good use, Sadie. Good for you. I'm sure Mother would approve."

Sadie set a mug of coffee down in front of Augusta —one that read CITADEL MOM—and put her hands on her hips. "I redid this kitchen ten years ago, child. If it looks new, it's 'cause I just started using it and you ain't been around. Now what are you doing here? Like I said, I know you didn't come for coffee."

Augusta raised both brows, feeling sheepish. "Is it that obvious?"

Sadie's chin tipped downward. Her black eyes narrowed. "What do you think, eah?"

Augusta sighed and told her about Savannah's sudden departure. "She's upset because she knows she hurt your feelings."

Sadie sat down on the stool beside her with her own mug of coffee, listening quietly. When Augusta was finished, she said, "I'm already over it, Augusta. Truth is, I don't blame Savannah one bit. We're all a little emotional these days."

"How is Queenie holding up?" Augusta asked. "I know she loved Rose."

"Heartsick over Cody. You know she helped raise that little boy." She gave Augusta a meaningful look. "I hope they find him ..."

Alive.

The word hung in the air between them, unspoken. But they both felt it.

Augusta took a sip of her coffee. "Yeah, I know."

Sadie reached out and touched her hand unexpectedly, her expression sincere. "It's really good to see you, Augusta. I thought I'd never see the day you'd walk back through my door. I know you don't like this place. And I'm so sorry for anything Joshua may have said to upset you the other day. You know, he just feels a little rejected by you, but it's for the best he stays away right now." That revelation seemed to make her uncomfortable and she withdrew her hand and peered inside her coffee cup, then shook her head, setting it down.

Augusta set her cup down, too. "I don't think he ever forgave me for moving away," she acknowledged.

Sadie nodded. "Maybe so, but that boy has plenty of other things to worry about."

"Like what?"

"A job, for one. He quit—did you know that? He's no longer with the DA's office."

"Why not?"

"Well, you know, originally he resigned because of the upcoming mayoral election on James Island, but I don't think he's put his name on the ballot and I don't think he intends to. He's been so preoccupied with that house on Tradd Street—holed up in it all day long!"

Augusta's face screwed up. "Dad's house?" But it was no longer her dad's house; it was Josh's now.

Sadie nodded and reached out to pat her hand again, as though working up her nerve to say something. "Yeah, but that brings me to another point ... something I've been meaning to talk to you girls about. I suppose I've been avoiding talking altogether, not so much because I've been angry with Savannah, but because it's time to clear the air and I don't know where to begin."

"Oh-oh," Augusta said, and gave Sadie a lopsided grin. "You stole the silver?"

Sadie didn't crack a smile. "Child ... your mama never wanted me to tell you this, but Florence is gone now and I gotta do what's right, eah? Didn't you ever wonder why your mama willed the Tradd Street house to Joshua?"

Augusta thought about it a moment, and then shrugged, picking up the coffee cup again. "Not really. You're family. I thought it was the least you two deserved. In fact, I was pissed that her will doles out your inheritance like a monthly salary. You deserve better than business as usual."

"Never mind about all that!" Sadie burst out. She patted Augusta's hand again, looking nervous. "You see ... it ain't so simple as that, so I might as well spit it out and get it over with. Robert and I had an affair," she said quietly. "Joshua is his son."

Augusta nearly dropped the coffee cup in her hand. "Daddy?"

Sadie nodded.

"Josh is my brother?"

Sadie nodded again, her black eyes looking melancholy. "So many lies!" she exclaimed, and started to weep. She placed her hands to her face while Augusta simply stared, feeling numb. "God forgive me, I wish I could undo it all!"

Sadie continued to sob, uncontrollably, and Augusta couldn't move, unable to comfort her. Inside, she could feel her façade cracking, the fissures widening by the second. It was all she could do to keep from flipping out. How she maintained her calm, she didn't know. "I don't know what to say."

It was more than simply not knowing what to say.

This was the woman who had raised her, loved her. Based on this new revelation, everything Augusta knew was a lie. Her life sped by all at once, all of it foreign now, with actions and reactions that made no sense. Everything she'd believed she understood about her life, she no longer did.

Josh was her brother.

She'd kissed him once.

Out behind the boathouse.

What if she hadn't said no?

After another moment, Sadie composed herself. "You don't have to say anything, Augusta." Her eyes were red-rimmed now, and Augusta realized they were already swollen, as though she had been crying about this for days. "I'm glad I'm telling you first. That's why we never wanted you ... and Josh ... well, you know." She dabbed at her eyes and picked up the dish towel, blowing her nose into it.

Something volatile was stirring deep down. Something Augusta was afraid she might not be able to control. But her tone betrayed nothing. "Does Josh know? Did Dad know?"

Sadie blew her nose again. "Yes and yes. I'm pretty sure that's why Josh isn't in so much of a hurry to run for mayor anymore. I think he's furious with me and he's mad at Robert, and has no desire to follow in his shoes. At least that's how I think he sees it."

"Wow," Augusta said . Her skin prickled all over. "He hasn't said a word. How long has he known?"

"I told him the day he ran you off. But it's something I've been struggling with now for a long time. After that fight with Savannah ... I did a lot of thinking, and I just can't keep any more secrets. It's too hard." She set the dishcloth down.

Probably still numb, Augusta sat and listened to Sadie's entire confession, somehow holding everything inside. Apparently, her father had been a bigger whoredog than any of them had realized. But even

Sadie's part in the affair wasn't what was most shocking. They had long ago decided Josh's father must have been a mistake, someone Sadie didn't care to talk about, but that Robert Samuel Aldridge II was that man, and that he had actually known about his son, and that her own mother had known about the affair —and Josh—and covered it up, was shocking. What was more, that Sadie would continue to work for Flo —and that Flo would allow it—seemed somehow to raise their family's dysfunction to biblical proportions.

Augusta guarded her expression, uncertain how to process any of it. The amount of information she was downloading made her head spin and her stomach ache. Her hands shook. She brought a trembling hand to her forehead, her thoughts racing, suddenly unstoppable.

Evidently, Sadie had loved Robert, had believed him when he said he loved her, too. But in retrospect, Augusta doubted her dad had even loved himself. He certainly hadn't loved his children. Or her mother, for that matter!

As she sat there, staring into the now empty coffee cup, she felt, for the first time in her life, a sense of sorrow for her mother.

How truly awful it must have been to walk in her shoes, to have everyone expect you to be bigger than life ... when in fact, you were feeling small and vulnerable, and everyone in your closest circle was betraying you. Then your son died. And your daughters hated you ...

"Oh God," she said, unable to hold it back any longer.

She experienced the greatest desire she'd ever felt to hug her mom in that instant, but Flo was gone. She was buried in a grave in a teak coffin beneath an old oak, in a place where none of her children would ever venture, including her beloved son.

Augusta sat there, focusing on the coffee cup, feeling wired, but not from caffeine.

She had thought to ask Sadie about the photograph of Sam, but she couldn't bear the thought of fishing it out of her purse now. At the moment, it didn't seem important. Neither did 99 percent of the fights she'd had with her sisters lately. All of it was pointless. All that really mattered was family, and you couldn't really know how much they mattered until they were pulled out from under you like a rug. Her ears were ringing and she realized she was holding her breath, about to pass out.

She felt sick.

"I wanted to tell you first," Sadie offered, her expression mirroring the ache that was growing in Augusta's breast. "It seemed important."

Augusta suddenly longed for her mother. It was a keen, aching feeling that took her completely by surprise. She blinked away tears, clutching the empty coffee cup in her hand. Not since before her mother's death had she shed a single tear. Now they threatened to flow without stop.

Sadie stood up and clutched her shoulder, gripping it hard, as though to keep Augusta grounded in reality. "Oh Augusta!" she said and threw herself into Augusta's arms, and though the child in her wanted to push her away and run, she held on to Sadie for dear life, sliding her arms around her back and burying her face in her bosom.

The two of them remained that way for what seemed an eternity.

Augusta could hardly find her voice to speak.

"Can you ever forgive me?" Sadie asked.

Augusta nodded but held her tighter when she tried to withdraw, unable to look her in the eyes yet.

Sadie patted her hair lovingly. "We should have told you girls a long time ago," she lamented. "I wanted to so much, but your mama said no, Augusta. She said she didn't want to drag you girls through any more drama ... so we took care of each other and our kids together. Do you understand now why I could never leave?"

Augusta didn't, but there was no point in saying so. Everyone had to handle their lives their own way, but she wanted to believe that, in their shoes, she would have told everyone to go to hell.

"You okay, child?"

Augusta pulled away suddenly, swallowing hard. "I gotta go," she said, and grabbed her purse.

"Augusta!" Sadie called after her.

But Augusta was gone.

IAN NEVER INTENDED to set about becoming a one-man army for justice. When he'd first arrived in Charleston, he'd attempted to ask the police for help but ended up with doors shut in his face, both literally and figuratively. And then Caroline Aldridge came into the picture and suddenly he'd found himself dodging accusations like bullets.

So his decision had been easy.

He'd told Jack everything he knew. He'd explained how Jennifer Williams's initial charges had come to be, his history with her family, and why he felt so driven to find her—especially now that it seemed she might have fallen prey to a killer. The girl's father was dead, her mother dependent upon an uncle, who happened to be a deacon in the Church. The uncle had molested Jennifer, using her father's death as a way to get close to her. Her mother knew and pressed her to keep it quiet so Jennifer had turned to the Church. Unfortunately, under penalty of *latae sententiae*—automatic excommunication—a priest could not reveal anything learned during confession, even under the threat of his own death or that of others. Later, when Jennifer came to him outside of confession and came on to him, asking for help the only way she knew how, he turned her away, gently, encouraging her to seek counseling with a professional. Angry and confused, she'd accused him of molesting her—all the while the true perpetrator ran around without repercussions. Because Jennifer's mother had known the entire story from the start, she'd talked sense into Jennifer and the charges were dropped immediately, but Jennifer had run away.

Ian had agreed to go looking for her because, well, he'd felt responsible for not having handled the situation better in the first place. But that wasn't his only reason. Without Jennifer, it was his word against her mother and her uncle, and he fully intended to bring her uncle to justice if possible. Now that he was no longer affiliated with the Church, there was nothing holding him back—certainly not the Seal of Confession.

But he was at a dead end. Maybe Jack would have better luck. He handed over every last piece of information he had.

Unfortunately, Jennifer's telephone was a prepaid, and Shaw had already followed that lead, having seized the number from Ian's phone after the arrest. Although Ian hadn't heard from her in months, her picture—the one she'd sent him—was still on his phone. But her phone records had revealed little else except that she had not used the cell since April sixth —less than half her credits used with more than six months left to go on her three-hundred-sixty-five-day recharge. It was as though on April sixth, Jennifer had simply disappeared.

They were searching for her car, which was missing, as well. Not much to go on, but far more than Ian had uncovered in all the time he'd spent searching for her.

In return, Jack gave him his first helpful piece of information about Jennifer since arriving in Charleston. Jennifer had, in fact, legally changed her name to Jennifer Leigh. The records, held at the local level, were public record if you knew exactly where to look and whom to ask. She had, in fact, gotten into a bit of trouble under that name, but because she was now eighteen, her mother was never notified of her arrest. The terms of her release were negotiated by pro bono attorney Daniel Greene—the same Daniel Greene who was also the estate attorney for the Aldridges.

On the downside, although he had a more complete picture now, Jack warned him against interfering with the investigation and had prohibited him from speaking with Greene. As a man who only twenty-four hours before had been at risk of losing his freedom and his neck to the state, he sure as hell wasn't about to place himself in jeopardy, but at least he knew something more than he had before.

He wasn't sure he should tell Augusta about any of it. Jack hadn't given him any classified information per se, but somehow he knew that telling Augusta about Greene could be detrimental to Jack's investigation, or he would have already told her himself. Augusta would tell Caroline and Caroline had already proven once that her relationship with Jack wasn't enough to keep critical information out of the papers. Then again, Greene was their family attorney. Maybe they would feel obligated to protect him—or alert him that his name was being bandied about the investigation—particularly since apparently the longtime housekeeper was romantically involved with the guy. That was something Ian knew simply from poking around. Daniel Greene spent a great deal of time at Sadie Childres's home.

Pitching old and new facts around in his brain, he made his way home, enjoying the sound of his own car engine. "Yeah, baby," he said, patting the dash, grateful the Acura was still in one piece. All in all, they had taken pretty good care of the car, and he was suddenly feeling a lot better.

As he headed over the expressway, the phone rang on the seat beside him. Without looking at the number, he picked it up and answered. "Ian."

"Hi, it's Augusta."

She'd been crying.

"Where are you?"

"On the way to your house."

"Are you alright?"

"No."

"I'll be right there."

Shocked at how much her revelation affected him, Ian hung up and punched the gas.

15

Like Charleston's estuaries, the meandering back roads in James Island's Secessionville Creek area wound in and out of neighborhoods, seemingly devoid of any organizing principle. There were only two outlets spilling directly onto Folly Beach Road.

As upset as Augusta was, she made a few wrong turns. It was only after making the second that she realized she was being followed, though she didn't recognize the car. As far as she was concerned, a good description of a car was black or red, new or old. Give her a bicycle and she could probably tell you the model and approximate year, but cars were not her forte.

After Sadie's bombshell revelations, instinct drove her straight to Ian's house instead of home. The construction crew was working outside today and Luke had a key besides, so she didn't have to worry about locking up, and the last thing she wanted to do was to walk into a worksite full of strange men, sobbing like a child—particularly since Savannah wasn't even home and Caroline would be there any minute. Until she gathered her thoughts, her sister Caroline was the last person she wished to see. She had no clue how to feel about anything right now, but she couldn't deal with more drama. The only thing that seemed certain was that Ian always managed to make her feel better. He had an easy way about him that helped her forget everything except the moment they were occupying. Somehow, despite his own tribulations, he seemed able to put aside anxiety and anger—like The Dude, she thought. In fact, he looked a little like a young Jeff Bridges, she mused, as she pulled up in front of his house.

The car following her pulled over to the side of the road and parked three doors down, in the tall grass, but the car door never opened. Parked in Ian's yard, Augusta sat, waiting and watching.

Probably a reporter, she decided. Poor Ian. She didn't know how he managed. This was the first time she'd come by his house when he didn't have half a dozen strange cars parked in his yard.

However, this one was clearly tailing her—probably trying to figure out what her connection was to Ian. Nosy hounds. Let them say whatever they wished to say. Unlike other people in her life, Augusta had nothing to hide.

Curious, she sat and watched in her rearview mirror, trying to make out the driver, but it was dusk now and she couldn't see much inside the car with the last bright streams of sunlight beaming down on the windshield. As Ian's black Acura came racing around the corner, the car's headlights flicked on; then it pulled out into the street behind him. She watched as the car drove slowly by, but the windows were all tinted too dark a shade to see inside. She was pretty sure that wasn't legal anymore. She caught the first three letters on the license plate before the car turned the corner: NZ3. It was an older black Dodge that looked as though it had seen way too many miles on the road—maybe even a rehabilitated police car.

NZ3, she repeated to herself.

Ian was out of his car before she managed to open her door, and she walked toward him, tears suddenly stinging her eyes. He held out his arms, and without warning they began to flow, breaking through her carefully laid barriers.

"Hey, hey," he said, lifting her face. "What's wrong?"

"I don't know where to start," she said in a voice that didn't sound like her own.

He wiped away her tears, and with his arms around her, turned her toward his house. "Let's get you inside. I've got beer, and pretty much nothing else, but you can tell me everything when you're good and ready."

Augusta nodded, allowing someone else to direct for once.

"I've got good news," he offered, squeezing her gently. "Maybe it'll help to hear that first?"

With watery eyes, Augusta peered up at him, and she knew before he said it. "Oh Ian! They dropped the charges?"

His grin widened, and he nodded, and she felt suddenly more lighthearted—even more so once the door closed behind them, shutting out the rest of the world.

ACCORDING *to experts there were three types of anger: the first, a low-grade temper that manifested itself in a person's character, like grumpy old men; the second, a slow, simmering reaction to perceived wrongs; and the third, a fight-*

or-flight mechanism. When it came to punishment, it could mean the difference between manslaughter and premeditated murder.

Anger was not his friend, so he stilled his heartbeat, cleared his mind.

She was a bitch and a whore, but that wasn't why he wanted her out of the way. He wanted her out of the way because he thought it was smart.

AUGUSTA RAN her fingers along the fireplace mantle.

It appeared not to have been dusted in a decade. Clean spots, where knickknacks had once resided, stood out against the ivory paint, conspicuous without the usual baubles to hide them. Behind the grate, though the bricks were stained with soot, there wasn't an ember to be found. It was as clean as a dog's bone. "So you must be renting?"

Ian returned to the living room with a glass of water, no beer. "What makes you say that?"

Augusta gave him a lopsided grin. "Oh, I don't know ... maybe the simple fact that your rooms are all empty and it seems they've been that way for quite a while."

He winked at her. "Not *all* my rooms are empty. In fact ..." He wiggled a brow at her as he set the water glass down on the mantle beside her and pulled her into his arms. "Maybe later I'll give you a tour of my postmodern-style boudoir, as well as a demonstration of how the single-purpose minimalistic bed works. You'll be so impressed," he assured.

Augusta laughed, but a thrill raced down her spine at the thought of being naked with him again. Her body responded to his touch. "Single purpose?"

He nodded slowly, grinning. "Sleep is overrated," he said, his lips curving a little mischievously. "Of course, all this happens only after we've had a chance to talk."

Augusta's heart beat faster. "Taking is overrated," she said, and her nipples pebbled against her blouse, drawing his gaze.

"Damn," he whispered, and she knew the instant he put the joking aside. His gaze became hooded, moving from her breasts to her mouth.

The mood shifted suddenly and his voice grew sober now. "This time I don't want alcohol on my breath or sand up my ass. I just want you in my nice, clean, soft bed and I want to show you exactly how I feel about you, Augusta."

Augusta slid her arms around his waist, leaning back to gauge his expression. "Yeah? How is that?" He had never really seemed like the priestly type, but gone was the ex-priest entirely and in his place stood a bad boy she had never met before this moment. His eyes glittered with the intensity of blue flames.

He reached between them, lifting her chin, and seemed to need to ask. "Why don't you tell me what upset you first?"

Suddenly, nothing seemed as important as hearing how he felt about her. She slid her arms up along his back, reveling in the sinewy strength along his lats. "Later," she promised. "Right now we're celebrating."

He lifted a brow. "Are you celebrating with me?"

Augusta nodded slowly and held her breath. There was no music to move their hips to, no smoky lights to hide behind, no champagne in her veins ... but the moment was as sexy as any Augusta had ever experienced. She moved against him, shifting her weight with a lover's instinct, melting into his embrace, daring to tease him.

"Augusta," he said, his voice gruff. It sounded every bit like a warning.

He caught her hand about his neck, but instead of pulling it away he leaned to kiss her gently on the lips. Augusta responded by deepening the kiss, offering her tongue. He kissed her deeply, his body tense and trembling and after a moment, he tore himself away, leaning his forehead against hers, staring down into her face.

"Turns out I'm not enough of a gentleman to resist a beautiful woman alone in my bed." He moved to kiss her neck.

"I'm not in your bed yet," she pointed out.

"*Yet* being the operative word." His fingers curved around her throat, holding her still for his exploration.

His body hardened against her and he pressed his arousal into her, letting her feel him through his jeans. She held her breath, her skin tingling with anticipation.

His fingers moved to her blouse, popping the top button, looking her in the eye. Augusta's breath left her in a rush at the gentleness with which he unbuttoned her buttons, one by one, exposing her, the look on his face hungry and purposeful as he worked his way down her blouse.

Unblinking, Ian watched her expression, afraid to miss a flicker of emotion.

This wasn't how it was supposed to go.

He was only halfway joking about the bed, though he'd be lying if he told himself he hadn't purposely set the beers back in the fridge, not wanting anything to numb his senses ... or hers. Just in case. But he'd meant to give her a chance to breathe ... to lean on him if she needed to, and even then, if she hadn't wished to make love tonight, he would have simply held her and told her he loved her.

Because he did.

He knew that now.

The feel of her in his arms was like manna for his soul. He wasn't sure how she'd gotten through his armored shell, but she had. Slowly, reveling in the satiny feel of her skin, he turned her so that the lamplight illuminated her fully for his eyes. The last time he'd held her in his arms, and the time before that, it had been on a dark beach. He wanted to make love to her in the light, so he could see every lovely inch of her body ... every goose bump ... every blush.

He pressed his erection more firmly against her, wanting her to feel it, wanting her to know the dangers of tempting the lusty beast inside him.

She was the first woman he'd wanted this badly in more than six years... the first woman who'd made him forget his past ... the first who made him yearn to spend every day for the rest of his life lolling in a bed.

Desire thrummed through his veins.

"Say the word and we'll stop," he suggested, and sent a little prayer heavenward that she wouldn't ask him to. Prayers generally failed him, but today he hoped the man upstairs was firmly on his side. He didn't want to have to relieve himself in the shower, with just the memory of her taste lingering in his mouth. His body ached for release. But he wanted her willing and on the same page.

"Don't stop," she whispered, and Ian groaned deep in the back of his throat, taking her by the hand. He led her into his room, flipping on the light, and pulling her gently toward the bed.

Augusta swallowed, unable to speak a word. She

let him guide her into the room and resisted the urge to ask him to turn off the light.

She knew why he'd turned it on ... could see it in his eyes—that barely restrained hunger that made her panties wet with just a glance. And deep in her heart she knew she wasn't going to stop him. What she wanted most in this instant was to have him inside her. Something about him emboldened her; that was the only explanation for this fevered desire she felt every time she was in his presence. Her mouth suddenly felt like cotton. Her tears were completely forgotten. Her palms grew damp and her skin prickled with anticipation—all with merely a look.

Without a word, she backed up toward the bed, and he followed, his blue eyes brilliant and full of purpose. Swallowing the knot that rose in her throat, Augusta sat on the bed and he knelt in front her, pushing her legs apart without a word, sliding her skirt up.

A whimper caught in her throat as she fell back against the bed, clutching the hem of her skirt and pulling it the rest of the way up. "Yes," she said with a sigh, even before his lips touched her.

He settled his nose against her panties, breathing deeply and then pressing his tongue against the soft cotton before taking the damp material into his mouth and pulling the panties off with his teeth. Augusta swallowed convulsively.

After being so long without a woman in his life, Ian might have thought that all he'd want to do was to bury himself inside her sweet body, but he longed for more than that. He wanted to savor each and every moment. He wanted to taste every inch of her body. He lingered on the tiny bud that tempted him beyond reason, teasing her with a finger, and he didn't stop until her body shuddered beneath his lips and she moaned with unrestrained pleasure.

He wanted her to feel appreciated and adored. He made love to her first with his mouth, drinking up the nectar of her body with complete abandon. And then when he was done, he kissed her thoroughly, wanting her to know that there was no part of her that wasn't divine.

"I play for keeps," he whispered against her temple, and then pressed his weight down upon her, pulling her blouse off a little feverishly.

Augusta welcomed his weight, drawing him down atop her, but words failed her.

Eagerly, she unbuttoned his white shirt, and tugged it off, throwing it behind her on the floor. He unzipped his jeans, and stood a moment to shrug out of them. "I want to see all of you," he said, his eyes never leaving her.

Augusta shimmied out of her skirt, and before it hit the floor, he was kneeling over her once more, his body hard and ready.

There was no shame in his actions. He peered down at her, looking primal and ready to take what he wanted. His hand moved to his shaft and he stroked himself while she watched, completely uninhibited. The sight of him touching himself, pulling his thumb over the bead of moisture at the tip, turned her on like nothing else ever had. God help her, she thought she would have another orgasm simply watching, and then he brought his hand to her lips, painting her mouth with the silky moisture, giving her the tiniest hint of the taste of him. His fingers shook with barely restrained passion, and he looked at her pointedly.

"I want you in my life until we both take our last breaths, Augusta. You're the last thing I want to see at night before I go to bed. If you don't want that, too, say no and I'll get up right now, put my pants on and see you to the door."

Wide-eyed, Augusta stared at him. Naked and unashamed, he rested his hand once again on his erection, stroking it seductively, waiting for her answer. His hair fell back behind his shoulders, and the earring in his ear gleamed wickedly. A day's worth of golden whiskers glittered on his face. He was easily the most beautiful man she had ever known.

Augusta couldn't have walked away from this moment if her life had depended upon it.

She was lost—body and soul.

With Ian she felt no inhibition, or shyness. She felt only a primal desire to claim him for her own. She threw her head back in blatant invitation, smiling slightly as she demanded, "Make love to me, Ian."

16

─────────

12:02 a.m.

It took every ounce of willpower Augusta had to get up and go home.

Ian begged her to stay, but she knew she couldn't —not with the realization that Caroline was likely to be home alone. Until the wedding, she and Jack had agreed it was entirely too weird to have him stay at the house, and she rarely spent the night with him at his beach house—never without telling her and Savannah. Augusta couldn't take Ian home either—not until she had a long talk with her sisters.

"Stay," he begged, and despite her halfhearted protests, he coaxed her back into bed. They made love once more before she managed to get up and get her blouse and skirt back on.

"You're such a bad boy for an ex-priest!" Augusta told him, loving that it was true. There was a fine line between sexy and dirty. For her, crossing it wasn't an option, but pushing the boundary was a turn-on. She and Ian had the same sensibilities, she realized. She trusted him implicitly.

He threw his hands up into the air and grinned

unrepentantly. "I wasn't always a priest," he reminded with a wink. "In fact, if you come back to bed I'll show you how *unpriestly* I can be." Snagging her hand, he dragged her down atop him, but Augusta resisted, kissing him firmly upon the lips and tearing herself away.

"I really, really have to go," she insisted.

"Then I'll see you home," he said, and his tone brooked no argument. He got up and dressed without complaint and Augusta watched, for the first time in her life truly appreciating a man's solicitous nature. Usually, it made her feel like running as fast as she could in the opposite direction. But somehow Ian made her feel at ease, despite the fact that he had clearly stated his intentions—maybe even because of it.

But there was something that was hovering at the back of her head—a feeling that she couldn't quite shake, though she was pretty sure it had nothing to do with Ian.

With everything going on, Sadie's confession, knowing she still had to talk to Caroline, there was a heaviness in the air—a grim feeling she couldn't escape. It elbowed its way into her joy, but she pasted a smile on her face as Ian saw her to her car door.

"Want me to drive you home? I can pick you up in the morning."

"Nah ... I'd better take the car."

Accepting her answer, he let her lead the way, following behind her down the isolated road.

The night was clear but balmy. Augusta drove home with her windows only partway down, rolling slowly through stop signs rather than coming to a complete halt. Her doors were locked, but the silence was unnerving. As beautiful as the overlying oaks were, with their mossy curtains spilling down over the blacktop, she couldn't shake the overall feeling of gloom. It was like a black cloud pressing down over her.

Apparently, she wasn't the only who felt that sense of gloom. After Amy Jones's murder on Backcreek Road, a few more houses had popped up for sale. Realtor signs loomed out at her through the darkness.

It was strange how the murders were so concentrated in this area.

She had once read that serial killers lived and worked in areas they were stalking—they got jobs in positions where vulnerable people sought help. It was sinister, but not surprising. The simple fact that people lived and worked around such monsters and couldn't recognize them for who they were was a little frightening.

Augusta liked to think her instincts were better than that.

She had never once gotten a bad feeling about Ian, even though her sister had pegged him as a murderer from the moment she set eyes on him. But his character had never raised a single red flag, as far as Augusta was concerned.

Maybe serial killers had multiple personalities? It seemed the only plausible explanation for how folks could miss what seemed to be right there in front of their faces.

Back in the early nineties, when the state executed Donald Pee Wee Gaskins, reviving the horrors he had committed upon the Lowcountry, she remembered reading that the guy claimed to have bought a hearse to haul his victims to his "own private cemetery." Still no one believed his boasts. All his drinking buddies thought he was joking. But he wasn't. By his own admission, Gaskins had murdered more than one hundred men and women, including the daughter of a state senator. Whether that was true or not, no one knew. He never shared the locations of their bodies and there were millions of acres of wetlands—impossible to search every inch.

After Gaskins, it literally took decades for Charleston to shrug off the cloak of fear thrown over the city—especially considering the public's reawakening to his crimes after his execution. And now, like then, there was an aura of fear surrounding the community ... except these killings were concentrated right here around Oyster Point Plantation ... around the places Augusta had played as a child. That cemetery Cody had disappeared from was a frequent stop on their hikes.

She watched Ian in the rearview mirror with a smile.

Even the spooky evening couldn't diminish the way he made her feel. He made her feel loved, even if he hadn't said those three little words. After so many failed relationships, this time *felt* different. There was little point in denying it: Augusta was in love with him. She had turned to him after Sadie's confession instead of reaching out to Caroline. Because she trusted him even more than she trusted her own family.

Once they reached the gates, as he had before, he refrained from entering behind her and simply waited for Augusta to get inside.

Spotlighted by his headlights, her sister Caroline sat on the top porch step with Tango lying quietly at her side. Her eyes mirrored Augusta's pain, and Augusta saw ... she knew about Josh.

Tango's head came up as Augusta slid out of the car and his tail thumped once against the porch, though he didn't get up. "Sadie just left," Caroline told her as she shut the car door. But that was all; she said nothing about Ian or his presence at Oyster Point—though Augusta knew she had spied his car. It was impossible not to notice because she was sitting directly in his high beams. Nor did she make any accusatory remarks about the two of them having been together.

Out by the gate, Ian's headlights turned away, casting her sister back into shadow, and then his glowing taillights disappeared slowly down the road as she sat down on the porch steps next to Caroline. "Did she tell you everything?"

Caroline looked at her, and inhaled deeply. "I sure as hell hope so. We've had more than enough drama, don't you think?" She reached behind her to stroke Tango, adding, "She was worried about you."

Augusta sat quietly, uncertain what to say. She felt only a tiny bit of guilt for having taken comfort in Ian's arms and leaving Caroline to face Sadie alone.

Tango whined and nuzzled his head across her back.

Tonight, there was a hint of a fog descending out on the water. The tin steeple of the boathouse was shrouded, but the water itself beyond the spartina grass was as lustrous as a sheet of black glass. Crickets chirped. Frogs croaked mournfully. Thankfully, they had missed the mating season this year, but if they were still here in March, she was going to have to buy a good set of headphones. The sound of mating frogs was deafening.

"Is she okay?" Augusta asked finally.

Caroline turned to look at her again. Augusta could tell she'd been crying. "Sad. I guess ... this is hard for everyone."

Augusta nodded, and the sting of tears suddenly

reappeared in her eyes. The gloom suddenly descended a little lower. "Poor Mom," she found herself saying.

Caroline simply stared at her, blinking, probably as stunned by the words that had come out of Augusta's mouth as she was. Caroline's eyes grew glassy as she stared at her sister. A trickle of moisture appeared at the corner of one eye, but was stillborn there.

Augusta took the opportunity to speak her mind—to put into words the things that had been plaguing her from the instant Sadie had revealed her secrets. "I judged Mom based on what I knew—which was absolutely nothing," she confessed. Taking her by surprise, a tear slipped down her cheek.

Hearing the grief in her tone, Caroline threw an arm around Augusta's shoulders. "We all did, Augie—Mom included—she judged herself. I'm pretty sure that's why she continued punishing herself until the day she died."

"Do you think she was *ever* happy, Caroline?"

"I don't know. I think she was sad most of our lives —even before Sam—but she's just as responsible as anyone for that," Caroline offered. But her lips quivered a little, belying the calm, rational façade she was trying so hard to present. "If she wasn't happy with Dad—with her life—she shouldn't have stayed with him ... but that's easy for us to say now."

"She did leave," Augusta reminded her.

"Yeah, after everyone's lives were practically ruined, hers included. Let's face it, Dad was a bit of a sociopath."

Augusta sat there, considering their entire family, leaning into Caroline's embrace. "At one time I would have said Mom was, too."

Caroline shook her head. "No way ... there's a difference between being incapable of feeling and choosing not to feel. Mom medicated herself so she wouldn't feel. It's not the same."

It had been easier to think of Flo as heartless. Thinking of her in so much pain made Augusta feel infinitely worse. But tonight it was impossible not to see her mother as a human being—flawed, but trying to do her very best with what she had. There was a reason her mother had brought them all together here under one roof, and as she sat next to Caroline, listening to the hitch in her sister's breath, she realized they needed each other far more than either of them had known. Flo had cared enough to force them together.

Maybe it was time to stop running? Maybe whether she liked this place or not—with all its sordid history and her mother's ghost stumbling around, margarita in hand—it was time to face the past?

Maybe it was time to let herself feel?

"I worry sometimes I take after Dad," Augusta confessed. "I can't seem to feel what you and Savannah feel."

Caroline lifted both her brows and gave her an adamant shake of her head. "Augusta, there are a lot of things you are, sister dear, but unfeeling isn't one of them. In fact, if you look up *firecracker* in the dictionary, your photo is next to the definition!"

Augusta laughed, despite the morose mood—despite the probable insult.

Caroline peered out into the marsh. "Anyway, it's not really a matter of not feeling. Apparently, sociopaths do feel—they feel pain, anger—they just don't have a conscience. They lack those sirens in their head when it comes to ethics and morality."

"Yeah? When did you become Dr. Caroline?"

Caroline gave her a little smirk. "Probably about the same time I morphed into Mom."

Augusta laughed again. "You know ... I really didn't mean that."

"Oh yes, you did, but it's okay."

"Did you call Savannah?"

"Not yet."

"What about Jack?"

"No. I was waiting for you."

Augusta's eyes watered at that revelation. At one point, long ago, they had been each other's greatest support. "You could have called."

Caroline shrugged. "Sadie was here all night. Besides, I was going to if you didn't show up soon, but I was bracing myself for another lecture about how unsuited I was to be wearing Mom's shoes."

Augusta laughed. And still Caroline avoided bringing up Ian. She was thankful for the reprieve.

"No wonder Josh hasn't been around," Caroline said, after a moment. "Poor guy."

"I guess," Augusta said. "He was spoiled rotten and both Sadie and Mom doted on him. Mom was certainly way more forgiving of Josh than she ever was of us."

"Yeah," Caroline agreed. "He had it best for sure. He was the only man in a houseful of females and got away with murder."

The two of them fell into silence, staring out at the black water. A warm breeze swept in from the marsh, tousling Augusta's hair.

The scent of the mud was strong tonight—a sweet, sulphurous odor that permeated the air, especially now that the azaleas were done blooming. The faded blossoms were hanging on, but a little the worse for wear. Their mother used to tend the gardens herself, deadheading to encourage new growth. Now the bushes were full of petal blight, looking neglected and distressed. Augusta decided she'd do some reading and figure out how to care for them.

"I ran into the work crew today," Caroline said after a long interval. "Thank you for getting that started, Augusta."

She sounded as though she truly meant it.

"You're welcome," Augusta said and smiled. And together they sat, arm in arm, listening to Tango's easy breathing beside them.

SADIE HAD FORGOTTEN to lock her door. She realized that fact only as she shoved her key into the lock. Shaking her head, she turned the handle and pushed the door open, revealing an immaculate living room, everything precisely as she had left it. She had too much time on her hands these days, and didn't know what to do with herself, so she cleaned incessantly and put things away with OCD compulsion.

Good thing she had Gracie to clean up after and feed, or else she might be feeling worthless. Now she understood all the talk about empty nest syndrome. God only knew, she didn't know what she was going to do with herself when the cat up and died.

She was a mess, she realized, as she locked the door behind her and walked straight back to the kitchen to pour a glass of tap water. Some folks didn't like the island water, but Sadie did. She drank it standing at the sink as she stood peering out onto the marsh.

Lovely night—too bad she had spoiled the mood for everyone ...

But whatever might come, she couldn't regret it. It was time to get rid of all the bad juju around here ... never mind that some things were never meant to see the light of day.

Those things she would take to her grave.

She wondered if Daniel had come by. Normally, if she wasn't home, he would have tried her at the main house, but with all that was going on, he'd probably figured that was the last place she would go. He knew she was thinking about telling the girls the truth and didn't think it was a good idea, but Sadie didn't much care. It felt like the right thing to do—no matter what Flo or Daniel thought, and if Daniel truly loved her, he was gonna have to let her be who she had to be.

It was too late to call him now, so she resolved to call him in the morning, and with that decided, she didn't bother searching for her cell phone. She'd had enough talk today anyway. Tomorrow she would call Savannah, as well, because Savannah deserved to hear the truth from her. With a weary sigh, she set the cup down on the counter and made her way back to the bedroom.

Gracie's black form jumped down out of the bathroom sink as she passed, mewing a complaint over her absence. As expected, the cat followed her down the hall, ready to take up her spot at the foot of the bed.

The old cottage was small—a bread box of a house, really, but it was hers. The back bedroom faced the marsh, as well, and she loved that most—looking out her picture window at the spartina grass, dancing in the breeze, while she read.

Making her way to the nightstand, she turned on the lamp and sat on the bed to remove her shoes, glancing at the current book sitting there—*The Road to Forgiveness.* Would she make it through a single page?

Probably not, but it was her habit to read a little every night.

She tossed one shoe on the floor. "Flo," she said. "You got a lotta nerve dying on me like this, eah! Leavin' me all alone with this mess!"

The house remained silent, no response. Not that Sadie expected one. Though she was about as superstitious as they came, she knew the only kinds of spirits that lingered here on this earth were the mean ones—those who couldn't, or wouldn't move on. Flo didn't have a mean bone in her body.

"Then again, maybe you can't go yet," she said to a make-believe Flo. "You certainly made yourself a big enough mess."

Sadie realized she'd had a part in it, and she considered the possibility that maybe she and Flo might haunt what was left of this old plantation together. The thought of that was fitting somehow. It made her smile a bit and she tossed the other shoe on the floor, thinking that the only one mean enough to actually come back from the dead would be Robert.

Selfish. Mean-spirited. Conniving.

Wasn't much positive to say about that man, and although it wasn't Christian, she was glad he was dead. She hated that Josh had inherited the house on Tradd Street—there could be nothing but bad karma in that old place. Maybe Flo had thought she was doing him a favor, but that wasn't the way Sadie saw it. She'd rather her son had stayed in the house Queenie had sold him on John's Island. He'd had plenty of privacy there, and lots of room to grow—even if it was a little too far out for anyone to go visit him. She supposed at least now he was closer.

"They're gonna make a movie about us," she said to Gracie, and reached over to stroke the cat.

Gracie gave her a solemn "mech" and stretched out a paw, seemingly to push her away.

"What do you know anyway?" she said to Gracie. But the truth was, Gracie probably knew far more than most folks did. Cats could see things people couldn't see. With a sigh, she got up from the bed, found her nightgown, changed into it and then got into bed, pulling the covers up. Gracie watched her all the while, her blinky eyes fixed upon Sadie's every movement, assuring her that there was nobody here tonight but the two of them.

For a long moment, Sadie stared at the cat, thinking about that bottle tree outside. If anyone had ever bothered to empty out her notes from inside, they would have discovered all her secrets long ago. It was her way of giving her cares to God and lettin' him deal with them. Once all those bad feelings and stories were in the bottles, all the bad medicine surrounding them was trapped inside. Although some folks believed that to truly be rid of them, you had to cap the bottle and cast it into water. Maybe she would try that someday.

Her grandma used to have a bottle spell for every dang thing, but the only one Sadie had ever tried was the breakup spell. Maybe it was taking things a little too far, but just in case it was all true, she'd placed the hair of a black dog—courtesy of Tango—and the hair of a black cat—she eyed Gracie—into a bottle with both Augusta's and Josh's names. She didn't want them to hate each other, but it was better than the idea of brother and sister getting up and married without even knowing they were related, and Flo had made her promise never to tell.

"Sorry, Flo," she said, and picked up the book lying on the nightstand. Beneath it was a folded sheet of paper. Setting the book aside, she picked up the sheet, unfolded it and read:

> I, Florence W. Aldridge, of James
> Island, declare this to be a first
> codicil to my Last Will and
> Testament dated May first two-
> thousand-fourteen.

Sadie blinked, her heart jolting. It was the missing codicil to Florence's will—the one Savannah had accused her of hiding. She held her breath as she continued to read:

> Item I: I will and direct that item V of
> my said Last Will and Testament be
> cancelled in its entirety. Item II: I
> will and direct that the following
> shall be item V of my Last Will and
> Testament.

Sadie clutched her breast as she read the next words:

> I will and direct that the property
> bordered by Secessionville Creek
> from the byroad to Fort Lamar
> Road, and consisting of the original
> living quarters of Oyster Point
> Plantation, as well as the bordering
> marshlands, shall hereby be
> donated to the County of
> Charleston.

Her gaze fell to the bottom of the page where Flo's

name was placed in a clear, bold signature she recognized at once. Flo had given Sadie's house to the city. She really had done it. But why? Even more important than why ... what was the codicil doing under a book on Sadie's nightstand? She had never seen this piece of paper in all her life. Even after Savannah had told her about it, she'd doubted its existence.

Who the hell had put the codicil there?

At the end of the bed, Gracie blinked at her serenely, her black eyes knowing. With trembling hands Sadie folded the codicil carefully, and placed it back inside the book, slamming it shut. She set the book down on the nightstand, her heart beating painfully, and then turned off the lights and stared into the darkness.

THE NOISE in his skull was rising.

Like the screeching of frogs during mating season, the sound was maddening and incessant, drowning out rational thought.

With fifty-two windows in the sixty-five-hundred-square-foot house, the odds had been in his favor that one would be left open. Finding her bedroom had been easy. Despite the size of the house, there were only four rooms upstairs. Her door was left ajar.

The floor creaked softly as he entered the room.

Killing the dog would leave an unnecessary warning. Luckily, the animal was locked up within her sister's room, sleeping against the door. He could hear its coarse hair brushing the painted wood as he passed. But here ... in this room ... she slept soundly ... the sleep of the innocent ... unaware she had an audience.

But she wasn't innocent, he decided.

Nor was she very intuitive.

He wanted her to be afraid ... wanted her to understand she wasn't in control. He wanted her to know that even when she believed she was alone, the hand of fate was poised above her, ready to strike.

He stood in the shadows at the foot of her bed, watching her sleep ... for a time ... her face illuminated by the silvery hue of the moon. At his side, he flicked the sharp tip of his knife beneath his fingernails, unwittingly pressed the blade into the tender skin beneath his nail. He felt an immediate stirring in his groin, but didn't move.

The clock on her bedside table read: 3:07 A.M.

Some folks claimed the veil between the spiritual and physical world was thinnest at this hour ... so that's when he liked to work. But he wasn't ready yet. First she had to understand ...

He waited until he was certain she wouldn't waken, then he made his way to her bedside and set down his gift, then walked away.

17

———

9:20 a.m.

"Hey, sleepyhead..."

Augusta awoke to the sound of Caroline's voice and a tiny bounce on the bed. One open eye revealed that Caroline was dressed for work, and a glance at the clock told her it was late.

"I slept in, too. Yesterday took it out of me," Caroline said and Augusta shook the sleep from her brain. "I didn't want to leave you sleeping alone with the work crew banging away downstairs."

Augusta sat up in the bed. "Oh God! I completely forgot! Are they here already?"

Caroline nodded. "Yep. Though they seem to know exactly what to do without my having to get involved, I thought I'd stay until you woke up. But I have a meeting in forty minutes."

Augusta stumbled out of the bed and found her clothes, vowing to do laundry today. She glanced at Caroline. They wore approximately the same size and height. Maybe Caroline wouldn't mind if she borrowed an outfit for the day. "Thanks," she said. "I appreciate it. That makes two days in a row I've slept like the dead. I don't know what's wrong with me!"

"Drama," Caroline said, mouthing the word with great emphasis. Augusta smiled and Caroline stood to go. "Need anything while I'm out?"

"Nah, I'm good. I plan to run out for lunch anyway." Lunch, meaning time with Ian.

"Alright, then I'm off," Caroline said and left the room. Her heels clicked against the wooden floor as she passed the rug in the hall.

Augusta pulled her hair into a ponytail and then reached for the band she'd left on the bedside table last night, freezing at the sight of the small yellow paper umbrella.

Abandoning the ponytail, she reached over to pick up the umbrella, inspecting it. It looked *exactly* like the one Ian had put into his pocket last night. *Exactly.* But she didn't remember him giving it back to her. Nor did she recall bringing it home. She most assuredly didn't remember setting it on her nightstand.

Where the hell had it come from?

Combined with the photograph of Sam and the Nilsson song, it was downright spooky. Outside, she heard Caroline's Lexus start up and drive away and she glanced at the indentation Caroline's rear had made on the bed. She'd sat too far away from the nightstand to place it there, and why would she anyway?

She stared at the frilly little decoration, unnerved by the sight of it. But it was simply a paper umbrella, she told herself. Nothing special about it, except for the rotten memories it evoked—memories and bad feelings she could do without, especially this morning when she wanted to feel something different for Flo and for this house.

It was time to put the past behind her.

Her mother was a human being. Everyone made mistakes. Augusta had certainly made enough of her own. For everyone's sake, she needed to put an end to all the disappointments that could no longer be atoned for. If she could forgive complete strangers for perceived wrongs, then why couldn't she forgive her mother?

With that thought, she tossed the umbrella into the trash by her dresser.

———

IT WAS MORNING.

Again.

He thought.

But maybe he was dreaming.

Cody's arms were beyond hurting. Numbness had set into them, making him feel like they weren't part of his body anymore—like his tongue. So far, the man hadn't come back, but now Cody was pretty sure he was going to die before anyone came, so he wasn't afraid anymore.

His eyes were on fire. His lips were cracked and broken. He was so weak he didn't even move when he saw the snake slither in from the locker room. He lay still, watching the reptile slip its way across the cavernous room, too feeble even to pull air into his burning nostrils. But his heart sped up painfully, beating erratically as he watched the reptile come closer. It wasn't the first time since he'd been here that his heart seemed like it wanted to bust through his chest so he lay there quietly, willing it to settle down.

Mind over matter, his dad would say, though he couldn't remember exactly why he'd said it.

Eyes half-closed, he watched as the snake paused to inspect him ... almost as though it sensed Cody lying in the shadows.

Don't breathe, he told himself. *Stay still.*

But he knew snakes could sense heat, so playing dead wasn't exactly the right thing to do. Still, he lay as still as he knew how to do, not daring even to blink.

His chest rose and fell in a quick rhythm.

After a moment, the snake slithered away, into the corner behind Cody's head and curled its long, thick black body around a pile of wood in the middle, where a shaft of sunlight poured in through the broken window.

Cody could see the snake, lying there in the sunlight.

It was large, with a big, wedge-shaped black head. From Cody's viewpoint on the floor, he could see that the underbelly still had some cross bands, but not too many and they faded to brownish black toward the top of the snake's body. That meant it was probably old, Cody realized. It had outgrown its yellow-tipped tail, but Cody recognized it as a cottonmouth the moment it settled into the woodpile and cocked its head back to show Cody the white interior of its mouth. It stayed there, with its mouth gaped, not more than three feet away—close enough that Cody could see the two large fangs, warning Cody to stay away.

Cody tried not to breathe.

He didn't talk to the snake except inside his head.

"I won't hurt you," he said. *"Don't worry."*

The cottonmouth responded by wiggling its tail, hitching its head farther back and turning its white mouth toward Cody so Cody could see its fangs more clearly.

His dad had always told him that if you were near

enough to see a snake's fangs, you were too close, but Cody didn't have much choice.

For the longest time, the snake stayed in that threatening position, watching Cody from the corner of one elliptical eye.

Outside, he heard the sound of thunder approaching, and the sky rapidly darkened, casting the snake's body into shadow along with Cody.

Cody blinked, closing his eyes, remembering the cottonmouth that had come straight up to their fishing boat. They swam with their heads above the water, their fat bodies nearly invisible in the black river. His dad said they were only curious, but the man at the wildlife habitat said they were aggressive and that his buddy narrowly survived multiple bites from one mean old moccasin.

Forcing his eyes open, he watched the dark form in the corner through slitted lids, his brain weary as he fought the need to close his eyes.

After a while, the snake shut its mouth and Cody relaxed, letting his eyes rest.

Somewhere in his dream head, he thought he heard the snake say, *"Don't worry, Cody. I won't hurt you."*

Storm clouds were rolling in.

The work crew had barely begun before they had to pack it up again, promising to return again in the morning. Augusta stood on the front porch, watching the last of Luke's crew head out the gate.

The weather forecast called for light showers, but these particular clouds had an angry, bruised underbelly that promised more than sprinkles. The wind kicked up and even the tidal flats had a few visible whitecaps.

Augusta might have been disappointed, but what she really wanted to do was to see Ian, and this would afford her the perfect opportunity to slip out if he was available.

She knew that despite Jack's warnings, he probably wouldn't completely give up his search for Jennifer, but neither was he going full speed ahead with it either. He had promised to cooperate with the police and Augusta was sure he wouldn't risk ending up behind bars again, especially now that all charges were being dropped. But she also knew he felt responsible for Jennifer.

She stood on the porch, looking out over the marsh. It appeared as though the boathouse door had been left ajar and seemed to be hanging precariously. If she didn't go out and batten it down, it was going to end up being just another repair they would have to make. In fact, judging by the way it was seesawing, it was already too late. But before she could head in that direction, her cell phone rang and she fished it out of her back pocket—Caroline's back pocket, to be more specific, and the pants were a little tight. She'd stolen a pair of jeans from her sister's drawer along with a cottony blouse. Disappointment filtered through her when she saw it was an unknown number. Wavering between letting it go and answering, she tapped the green answer button and said hello.

"Hi," responded the voice. "It's Brad Bessett."

"Oh hey!"

"Hey, so I looked into that tip you gave me— thanks, by the way." He sounded genuine.

A little distracted by the boathouse door, Augusta

said, "Great, you're welcome. What did you find out? Anything?"

"Not what you were looking for. As far as we can tell Jennifer never applied here at the *Tribune*, though I did check with my source at CPD and they gave me a new lead. Seems Jennifer legally changed her name, and apparently, they've got a BOLA out for her missing vehicle right now."

Ian would be happy to know the police were actually following up on the information he'd given them. "That's good news, right? So they've got a lead?"

"Not sure, but I thought you'd be interested to know the vehicle is registered under a name you might be familiar with ..."

"Oh really?"

"Yeah ..." He paused for an instant, as though building suspense, and Augusta found herself instantly annoyed. "Daniel Greene," he revealed before she could speak up.

The disclosure bowled Augusta over for a second; she didn't know what to say.

"The car is an old decommissioned police-issue Dodge," he added, when she remained silent. "With a license plate registered as NZ3 H43."

A chill ran down Augusta's spine. "Repeat that license again, please."

"NZ3 H43."

The car following her last night had been a black Dodge with a license plate beginning with NZ3. Augusta was pretty sure Jennifer Williams wasn't behind the wheel.

Daniel Greene?

But it couldn't be.

"Apparently, the car was auctioned a little over a

year ago. Greene apparently buys and donates vehicles on a regular basis."

"What do you mean?"

"Well, that's about all I know. He was Jennifer's pro bono attorney and he does this sort of thing a lot—donates beaters to organizations like Wheels for Women, which in turn gives them to single moms and such. Except it looks as though he handed Jennifer the keys to this one directly because most charities will assume the title and act as dealer, selling the title to the recipient. This one's still in Greene's name."

"Is this public knowledge?"

"Not yet. So please keep it under your hat. I'd like to cover this properly when I can."

Augusta was too stunned to know what to say.

"I'm sure your sister would appreciate it, as well."

"Caroline?"

"Yeah," he said, and added, in case she didn't understand what he was telling her. "She would probably appreciate your keeping quiet about it."

"Sure," Augusta agreed.

"Oh, and there's one more thing... Greene was also Karen Hutto's pro bono attorney."

Another prickle ran down Augusta's spine.

"Like I said, he's pretty involved with a lot of these charities for abused women. Apparently, her husband was an abuser, and she was attempting to get full custody of her daughter Amanda before she disappeared."

The hairs on the back of Augusta's neck prickled. "Thanks," she said, and then said good-bye and hung up, too dazed to carry on any further conversation.

Daniel Greene knew every single victim, except possibly Amy Jones.

She stared out at the boathouse, at the door slamming violently in the wind, her brain racing over possibilities. Her mother probably would have shown Daniel the codicil, though she might not have given it to him yet, because otherwise he wouldn't have broken into their house to try to find it—assuming that's how it went. The morning after they'd discovered the body on Backcreek Road, someone had broken into their mother's office through the back doors. Nothing had been stolen as far as they could tell, and aside from the broken window in the expensive French doors, nothing was out of place. They'd found no fingerprints—none that didn't belong in the room—and nothing to indicate there had actually been a successful robbery. All her mother's documents and books were undisturbed.

That break-in had happened *after* the break-in at Daniel's law office on the morning of the reading of the will. But it didn't make any sense that Daniel would break into his own office and beat himself up. Supposedly, he had responded to a silent alarm, surprising an intruder who then beat him nearly to death with a bat and put him in the hospital.

Something didn't add up.

Besides, if Daniel had known about the codicil, he couldn't have told Sadie about it because Sadie was one of the most honest people Augusta had ever known. Sadie could never have kept a secret like that to save her life—or so Augusta had believed until yesterday. And yet, her feeling was that Sadie had longed to tell the truth. If she had kept the secret of Josh's paternity from them, it was because Flo had demanded it. That's what Sadie had said, and despite the pain she felt over the disclosure, Augusta believed it.

In the distance, the boathouse door swung to and

fro, but Augusta stood rooted to the spot, too stunned to move, her brain filling up with new scenarios.

Even through all the media hype, Daniel Greene had never uttered a single word about Jennifer Williams. He'd kept that information completely to himself—despite the fact that Caroline had dragged Ian's name through the muck over his relationship with the missing girl. Not only that, Daniel had never once disclosed his relationship with Karen Hutto.

On the other hand, Jennifer had never officially been a focus of this police investigation as far as Augusta was aware. Nor was Amanda Hutto. The only known murder victims at this point were college student Amy Jones and Kelly Preston—Jack's ex-girlfriend cop, who was discovered at Brittlebank Park on July Fourth—potentially her sister Caroline—and now Pamela Baker.

Had Daniel known Amy, too?

She didn't know the answer to that, but she needed to tell Jack about the car last night. And right now, the boathouse door was swinging wildly in the wind, so she made her way toward the dock, hoping to secure it before the weather worsened.

18

12:47 p.m.

Murrells Inlet was about an hour and a half's drive from Charleston, but Ian still couldn't officially leave town, so he did the next best thing. He picked up the phone, walked out onto his back deck and called Jennifer's mother to give her an update.

The conversation was terse and brief, because he still had a difficult time with the fact that she refused to come forward to hold her brother accountable. He gave it to her straight, telling her everything Jack Shaw had shared with him, with the confidence that Shaw wouldn't have given him information that wasn't already known or soon to be made public knowledge. At this point, Jennifer had been missing so long, he knew her mother would be grateful for closure, in whatever manner she could get it. He owed her that much at least. But he hung up feeling a sense of futility where Jennifer and her family were concerned.

He'd spent a long time looking for the girl and it seemed there was a good chance no one would ever know what had happened to Jennifer. She was simply another missing person. There was no evidence to connect her to the recent murders. No physical proof, aside from the photo that she had sent Ian, which just happened to place her at the ruins. But that was hardly enough for the police to declare her dead and the victim of a serial killer. The fact that both Pamela Baker and Caroline Aldridge had come to harm after being at those ruins didn't prove a thing. However, Shaw seemed to believe him—finally—and after their recent discussion, he knew the intrepid detective would pursue every available lead. The police were now working closely with SLED and had called in the FBI to assist. They were working with a bigger picture than the one Ian had. Sure, he wanted to find Jennifer, but he wasn't in the mood to burn bridges with Shaw or with the Charleston police department. A few weeks in lockup was more than enough to keep him at arm's length—his sense of duty be damned. For the second time in his life, you could say he was scared straight.

As for the missing kid ... Cody was the main focus of their investigation right now, and rightly so. The boy had been missing for six days, with no clue as to where he might be. His chances weren't looking great at the moment, and Ian felt awful for Augusta because she was so closely connected with the boy's family.

Not for the first time, it seemed everything came back to the Aldridges ... they were the central connection here ... even if they didn't know it. That was a fact he'd shared with Jack, despite Jack's connection with Caroline and despite Ian's with Augusta.

Come what may ... the guilty should pay for their sins.

Out on the marsh, dark clouds were sweeping in, turning the water a mercurial gray. The spartina grass was being battered by a rising wind, but the cool front was a welcome respite from the brutal August heat.

He wondered what Augusta was doing right now, and resisted the urge to dial her number. He sensed she needed space after last night, so he gave it to her. But there was no reason not to send her a text, he decided. Unlocking his phone, he punched in her number ...

GRAY WITH AGE, but built to withstand weather, the Aldridge dock extended more than fifteen hundred feet out over the salt marsh, with access to deep water. A little more elaborate than most, it had room for three large seaworthy boats. Only one of the ports was empty. Their father had built it in a style to match the Georgian house, and the tin-steepled roof was the same steeple that adorned the widow's walk.

At the far end of the dock, the boathouse door slammed repeatedly, swinging a little drunkenly from one hinge.

Augusta made her way down the long boardwalk, intending to secure the door quickly, then take the car downtown to see Jack. Obviously Daniel Greene's connection to Jennifer wasn't news to the police, because they were already pursuing that lead, according to Brad, but she felt the license plate was somehow a key piece of information. Although she hadn't seen the entire plate, the description of the car seemed similar.

She thought about Sadie and all that Sadie had already been through, and the prospect of telling her about Daniel made her ill.

The wind whipped her hair into her face and into her mouth as she made her way down the long dock.

Water sprayed up from the marsh, sprinkling her arms, and she inhaled the familiar scent of pluff mud into her lungs, walking faster. Overhead, the sky darkened, casting a purple-gray shadow over the water. Out in the distance, she could see other boats heading in for cover.

Finally reaching the boathouse, she peered inside. The place had the scent of a well-loved workspace. Josh had always taken great care of the boats, and Augusta had already brought up the possibility of giving them all to him. They were his anyway, and the simple fact that their mother had overlooked bequeathing them in the will was a moot point as far as she was concerned—especially in light of recent developments. They were as much his legacy as they were anyone's. In fact, one of the boats, a twenty-five-foot Chris-Craft, had belonged to their father's father. Augusta couldn't remember the last time it had even been out on the water. Left to her and her sisters, it would likely rot here. It seemed only fitting that Josh should have his grandfather's boat.

She thought about the house on Tradd Street and couldn't recall the last time any of them had gone by there. That wasn't a conscious decision, but none of them had really acknowledged that part of their family since their early youth. And now that the truth was known, it was entirely understandable why her mother would give Josh their father's house. Despite the growing rift between them, Augusta thought he should have gotten more.

Inside the boathouse, everything seemed in order, except that the smallest of their boats, a dory, was missing from its rack. She went back to inspect the door, checking the lock. It was broken, but still hanging from the latch pin.

"Shit," she said, and rolled her eyes. Something else to add to the growing list of trials. She sighed, uncertain she wanted to bother with a police report, when there was so much else they should be focusing their attention on—like poor Cody.

The door wasn't completely busted yet. She walked through the boathouse, closing all the windows to keep the wind from blowing through, and then somehow, despite the rising wind, she managed to stabilize the boathouse door and shut it. She took the ponytail holder out of her hair and secured the lock as best she could, binding it all together with the ponytail holder. It certainly wasn't thief-proof, but all she really cared about right now was that the door wouldn't go flying off and injure someone. Tomorrow, she'd have Luke come over and take a look to see what repairs were necessary.

She heard the text come through on her phone as she was finishing up securing the makeshift lock, but she waited until it was done to check the message. The text was from Ian; it read: *I love the taste of you.*

She smiled and dialed his number immediately, anxious to talk to him. It went straight through to his voice mail, and she would have texted him back right then, but she shoved the phone into her pocket as the first drops of rain came pattering down on her head.

THE HEADSTONE HADN'T BEEN THERE on Tuesday when Sadie last went by to chat.

One trip to the cemetery per week was normally enough, but today she needed advice, so she took her troubles to Florence, as she always did, except that today she stood before a brand-new six-foot headstone.

It had been placed here without any commemoration, or acknowledgment by the family. Someone from the company where Florence had purchased it had simply delivered it and walked away. Not even Sadie had realized it was being set.

Of all the cemeteries here in Charleston, Magnolia was the most celebrated. Resting near the Cooper River, Charleston's elite lay buried here amidst ancient cedars, magnolias and humpbacked oaks. A few dogwoods and crêpe myrtles were interspersed among the evergreens, and thorny yucca and cactus plants were planted to keep spirits in their place. Not everyone realized that fact, but Sadie did. It was a tradition that came straight from her Geechee roots. In fact, she'd planted one herself at the head of Robert's grave—because he was a mean ole son of a bitch.

Sadie straightened, wishing she'd brought a sweater. There was a rare cool front coming through, and the rising wind held an unexpected bite.

She'd promised Queenie she would go help move her things out of the Simmonses' house, but she wasn't quite ready to leave yet ... she still had some things to say. Staring at the pillar, she considered how to say what was on her mind.

Florence's gravestone was a throwback to the past. She knew Flo had had to get special permission to erect the six-foot pillar. Many of the oldest graves were marked by simple field stone markers, or tablets of slate, sandstone or soapstone, and carved with simply the name, birth and death dates of the deceased, but the carvings in those soft stones were barely legible anymore. It was easy to tell which graves came later ... those were marked with rich marble with grander designs. Before the War, many of the more intricate stones had been imported from New England. And later stones were made of industrial granite and carved by machines instead of chisels and hammers. Florence's was made of granite, so that it would last the years, but it was larger than most of the newer stones. It stood as the centerpiece to the family's plot. In contrast, Robert's stone was barely a pillow upon the ground, and Sammy's was a lovely, but small cross. Florence's stood like a matriarch, presiding over her kin, past and present.

Even in death, she was larger than life.

Sadie stood, looking down at the grave, holding her red purse in her hand. "Florence ... you know I found that codicil to your will—did you put it there, dear friend?"

There was no answer from the grave. But the wind moaned through the tops of the trees.

"Tell me ... what is it I'm supposed to do, eah? You really want me to give up my house after all this time?"

The sky darkened as she stood there, and Sadie frowned and shook her head.

"I wish you were here," she complained. "I got an awful feeling about things, Florence."

The yucca plant Sadie had planted after Sammy's death shivered violently with the wind, and a prickle of foreboding traveled down her spine. In all the years she'd been coming here, talking over these graves, she had never once felt like anyone was listening. Suddenly, she had the feeling she wasn't alone.

For another instant, she stared at the quivering yucca plant, and then her nerve failed her entirely and she walked away, hurrying to her car.

19

They were in the middle of hurricane weather, but this storm didn't officially have a name. It whipped itself up suddenly, sweeping over the Lowlands like an angry spirit. If it weren't for the simple fact that, once again, after last month's record-breaking storms, it threatened to dump a belly full of precipitation at high tide, it would have been a welcome respite from the heat and humidity.

But no one was in the mood for more flooding or cleanup—especially since they were once again dealing with an overall gloom that had absolutely nothing to do with the weather and everything to do with the recent unsolved murders.

Caroline sat at her desk, listening to Brad Bessett talk about information he'd uncovered—tips he'd apparently gotten from her sister, of all people.

Just when Caroline thought they were making progress, Augusta seemed determined to undermine their relationship.

And Jack ... apparently he was sitting on the information, as well, and hadn't even bothered to tell her any of it. While they had certainly agreed not to encroach on each other's work, this was information that brought everything closer to home.

Still, she felt compelled to protect Jack.

"Have you checked with the CPD's public information officer to see what the official story is?"

"Absolutely," Brad affirmed.

Frank Bonneau, her editor-in-chief, stepped forward, arms crossed. He had been listening quietly to the entire conversation, but interrupted now. "Caroline ... I've vetted everything he's bringing to you. It's all accurate."

"Then *why* are you bringing it to me? You have my full support, Frank. If you think we should run with the story, then go with it. If Daniel Greene is a person of interest, and it's okay with the CPD that we print that information, I can't let my personal feelings interfere."

His expression was one of satisfaction. He gave her a nod. "Just making sure."

Brad swept forward to gather his papers and Caroline hesitated, lifting a finger, asking him to wait as she stared at the notes in front of her.

Daniel Greene was the title holder of the car registered to Jennifer Leigh—at least according to her insurance company, which had already terminated her coverage for lack of payment. No one had seen the girl since early April. Her cell phone was prepaid and still had more than half its credits remaining. Not a single call had been made from it since April, but the number was still active. They had called it repeatedly, unable to leave voice messages because the mailbox was full. She wondered if Jack had the authority to listen to those messages but she knew better than to ask him. Even if he knew something, he wouldn't tell her—not if it might jeopardize his investigation, which was taking an enormous toll on their relationship.

She hadn't seen him but for a few minutes here and there since they'd discovered Pamela's body. She knew he was driven to find this killer—and she wanted him to find the guy. To that end, there was no way she was going to risk his investigation—but she had a responsibility to report the news.

"Does anyone else have this information yet?"

By anyone else, she was clearly referring to local or national media. A knot formed in the pit of Caroline's stomach. She had known Daniel Greene all her life. He'd spent many a Saturday at their home, ensconced in her mother's office. Sometimes he would stay for pancakes and now, apparently, he and Sadie were heavily involved. Her heart hurt for Sadie, who was the one person in all this who was completely innocent.

"No."

"What about arrests? Is there one planned?"

"So far, they've only brought him in for questioning."

The *Tribune* couldn't afford to lose the edge on yet another story. Her mother wouldn't have hesitated, she knew. Flo would have handed over her own daughters on a platter if any one of them had crossed the line between right and wrong. Her mother had been a champion of the city and its people first and foremost.

This wasn't Caroline's first test—simply the most difficult so far. Even throwing Jack under the bus—printing something he'd told her in confidence—had been easy compared to this, because she had made that decision, she thought, for all the right reasons.

But if Daniel was innocent, this could ruin his life ... and Sadie's, as well.

She sighed, shoving the papers away as though they offended her. "Run with it. Put it on the front page."

That decision brought an instant headache and she sat down, rubbing her temples. The minute Frank and Brad walked out the door, her new administrative assistant entered the room. "Line two," she said. "It's your sister."

"Great," Caroline muttered and picked up the phone on her desk, feeling tense. "What do you want, Augusta?"

"It's Savannah. Caroline, what's wrong?"

Caroline let out a breath she hadn't realized she was holding. "Savannah," she said with a sigh of relief.

Caroline got up and walked around her desk to close her door, and then sat down to tell Savannah everything.

3:47 p.m.

Augusta hated driving over bridges in this kind of weather. The wind was blowing so hard it actually shook her car and her windshield wipers barely worked. She left her phone in her purse, knowing she needed all her attention for the road. She was soaking wet, but this was important enough that taking the time to look for an umbrella seemed inappropriate.

She drove straight to the Lockwood police station, hoping Jack would be there. If he wasn't there, she would talk to anyone who would listen.

Luckily Jack was in his office. He wore dark circles

beneath his eyes, and looked as though he hadn't slept in a week, and although he greeted Augusta warmly, he seemed preoccupied. He lifted a brow. "Should I be happy or concerned to see you?"

Augusta crossed her arms, feeling a little uncomfortable. She was cold and wet and confused. "I don't know, maybe a little of both."

"Come on back," he directed, leading her to his office. Augusta didn't miss the looks she got as she followed him down the hall. She had purposely kept the TV off, but she was pretty sure the media was having a field day with her relationship with Ian. To his credit, Jack didn't bring it up. In his office, he pulled a jacket off the rack on his wall and handed it to her, then sat down and waited for her to speak.

"I might have a tip," she offered after a moment.

"About?"

"The car you guys are searching for—Daniel's— the one he gave to Jennifer." He narrowed his eyes at her, probably wondering how she had gotten that bit of information in the first place. "I think I saw it last night," Augusta told him, and she described the vehicle. "I'm not sure about the make," she said, and apologized. "But it was black."

"There are a lot of black cars out there, Augusta. Are you sure about the plates?"

Augusta nodded, hugging herself. "That's the one thing I am sure about."

"Shit," Jack said, and then, "Was Ian with you?"

Augusta tilted him a testy look, annoyed that he would once again turn this back to Ian.

"I have to ask."

"Yes," she said with certainty. "And while we're on the subject of Ian. You're doing the right thing, Jack.

The night of Kelly Preston's murder, he was also with me then."

He lifted a brow. "And you're only now coming forward?"

Augusta wrapped his jacket more firmly around herself, embarrassed, but prepared to make amends. "You didn't ask before, and anyway, he already had one alibi you didn't believe." Her gaze challenged him.

"Touché," he said, and got up. "I need you to file an official report. It's going to be a few minutes. Wait here."

Her gaze fell on the ashtray on his desk, where a lit cigarette had burnt down to the butt.

"Don't tell your sister," he said, noticing the direction of her gaze. "I'm trying to quit." And then he walked out the door.

To his credit, Augusta didn't see him pick it up even once, and it didn't appear to have been touched. At least she wasn't the only one who felt intimidated by Caroline, and the thought somehow made her feel a little better, because clearly it didn't stop Jack from loving her.

CODY AWOKE with the first *crack* of thunder.

He blinked to clear the fog from his head, but didn't bother looking around. He didn't want to see this place anymore.

Outside, he could hear the sound of rain pelting the trestle. It plopped against the wooden roof in fat droplets. The air was full of moisture, but it was not enough to wet his throat. It teased his nostrils like the odor of bread baking in another room.

Without much energy, he stared at the gag that

had come out of his mouth. Filthy and a little blood-ied, it lay in front of his face, like a giant goober. He had been terrified the man would return and shove it back down his throat, but the man was gone now and it was dark again, and Cody was no longer afraid of the dark.

All the real horrors were visible in the daylight.

At least this way he could pretend he was sleeping in his bed at home.

He lay on the floor, awake, watching the rainwater pouring in through the window. It formed a shiny puddle on the floor and grew in circumference like one of those time-lapse videos on *National Geographic*. It grew and grew, until at last it began to spill down the slanted floorboards toward Cody.

Hope flared in Cody's breast.

He felt it like a tiny bird wing flapping against his ribs.

Just a little hope that maybe the water would trickle down his way and he could drink a sip. He was so thirsty.

Peering back at the snake that sat regarding him from the corner with slitted eyes, he was almost grateful for its presence. No longer was its head cocked back in warning. It was simply waiting there patiently for something to eat.

Cody's gaze returned to the trickle of water, learning from the snake, waiting for the stream to come to him ... conserving his energy.

6:47 p.m.

By the time Augusta left the police station, the news about Daniel Greene had already broken on the radio. She considered stopping by the *Tribune's* office, but decided she had better go check on Sadie instead. If, in fact, they were going to arrest Daniel, she didn't want Sadie to be alone. No matter what else they were going through right now, Sadie was still family.

She drove straight to Oyster Point and parked in front of Sadie's cottage, then ran up on the porch. The rain was unrelenting. The sprint to the porch alone had soaked Augusta again. Sadie's SUV was in the driveway, so she knocked on the door, and out of habit, tried the knob. For so long Sadie's house had simply been an extension of their home, and finding the door unlocked, she pushed it open.

"Sadie?" she called out.

Even Jack's jacket was soaked now—but then again, it wasn't really a raincoat. It was a lightweight RiverDogs baseball jacket he obviously didn't wear much. Cursing softly, she removed it and took it to Sadie's back porch, setting it on a chair to dry.

"Sadie!" she called out again, and peered down the short corridor to her bedroom. The lights were out, and she didn't appear to be home. Considering the rain a moment, she walked to the front window, then went back to the bathroom to grab a towel to attempt to dry herself off. She didn't want to sit on Sadie's furniture wet so she made her way into the kitchen, drying off there, hoping that Sadie wouldn't be too upset that she had simply walked in. After all, they weren't children anymore, and Sadie had a right to her privacy.

Gracie the cat sauntered into the kitchen, peering

up at her and giving a long mewl, as though telling Augusta in no uncertain terms that she didn't belong there.

"Yeah, I know, girl. Do you remember me?"

She stooped to pet the animal, and the cat stretched before her, clearly unwilling to stick to her principles at the prospect of a little pleasure. Augusta smiled, picking the cat up to reward her with a few more strokes, but the cat decided she suddenly didn't want Augusta's attention. She leapt down and sauntered out of the kitchen, her black tail swishing anxiously.

Could it be that Sadie was up at the main house?

She wouldn't think so—her car was outside—and the door was left unlocked—but maybe she'd walked up to the house for some reason and got caught in the rain. She still had keys.

She fished her phone out of her purse and rang Sadie's cell phone. No answer, but it didn't ring in the house, so wherever Sadie was, the phone was with her.

Trying to be as unobtrusive as possible, she set the cell phone down on the counter and grabbed a dirty cup from the sink, rinsed it out and poured herself a glass of water.

Maybe Sadie was with Daniel? In which case, there wasn't much Augusta could do to spare her anything. Feeling anxious now, she tried Sadie's phone again, but there was still no answer.

Peering outside at the relentless rain, she decided to wait a little longer and set the phone down again on the counter.

20

He wanted her to understand they weren't her friends.

That was why he'd left the codicil by her bedside—so she could open her eyes and see. But now it was gone. He needed it back. What if he'd misjudged her and she took it to the police?

But no, he didn't believe she would do that.

A few minutes ago he'd heard the door open and hid in the bedroom. The sound of Augusta Aldridge's voice simultaneously gave him a hard-on and angered him to his core. He was convinced now that she would be the one to finally give him peace.

Outside, the rain came gushing down now. Wind battered the house. It was growing darker by the instant. She was right out in the kitchen... it could be so simple...

But it wasn't time, he reminded himself, as the voices grew louder in his head.

Soon, Sadie would be home. He didn't want her to know he had been there. He'd traded cars with her, insisting she drive his to visit her cousin, because he knew she kept an extra key to her house in her glove box. He needed the will back, without raising any brows, without broken windows or jimmied doors. There had been more than enough unexpected surprises, beginning with Florence catching him here alone the day she'd come to tell Sadie about the codicil to her new will.

That was her first mistake.

Her second had been to tell him about her plans for the house and the property.

Her third had been to run from him. He'd chased her through the woods, where she'd lost her stupid shoe and then he'd carried her back to her house and tossed her down the stairs.

Now she was dead.

As her daughter was soon to be.

But he couldn't afford mistakes—couldn't act rashly now.

Plans could change, but it necessitated thought. He had to think—but he couldn't concentrate. There were too many bothersome voices talking all at once.

He concentrated on the image of the kid sitting in his little canoe, sliding into the water, hands flailing desperately, water churning at his feet, but not fast enough or hard enough to keep him afloat.

What kind of people let a little boy float out alone in an inflatable raft?

The kind who didn't know how to love.

And unloved children were the most dangerous of all ...

WHERE THE HELL WAS SADIE?

Augusta sat on the couch, with a towel under her rear end, resisting the urge to turn on the TV. She really wanted to know if there were any new developments, but didn't relish the thought of Sadie walking in with her sitting on the couch watching television. It was enough that she was in her house uninvited.

She got up, feeling a little on edge, and walked back to the bathroom. There, she turned on the sink and waited for it to flow clear, then splashed water onto her face. There was only one bathroom in this tiny cottage and the pipes were all rusty. Augusta honestly didn't understand why Sadie was so attached to the place. She had more than enough money to buy a nice house somewhere that didn't come with so much bad juju—Sadie's word, though it fit.

Augusta was getting hungry. She hadn't heard from Ian since the text he'd sent her earlier so she walked into the kitchen to grab her phone and sat on the couch again to text him back. She didn't want to talk to him yet, because if she did, she was going to walk out of this house and go straight to see him. It was too easy to let him take her away from all these problems, but she owed it to Sadie to stay and face this with her.

Maybe Sadie was with Josh?

She sent Josh a quick text first: *Do you know where your mom is?*

Then, feeling brave, she texted Ian: *I think I love you.*

She set the phone down at her side on the couch but it vibrated at once.

She picked it up and read the text from Ian: *Then marry me.*

Augusta's heart leapt clear from her stomach into her throat. She wrote back: *Are you serious?*

Serious as can be.

A smiley face blinked next to those words, making her doubt.

She sank into the couch, and texted back: *Why?*

Because you give the best head ever?

Augusta laughed and raised a brow. "Bastard," she

said, and started to text him back to say something smart-assed for getting her hopes up, but then he texted again: *Because I love you, Augusta. Why else?*

Augusta found herself grinning from ear to ear, despite what she was writing. *You're really asking me to marry you in a text? How lame!*

It seemed she waited forever for him to text back: *Have you ever seen a grown man cry?*

Only once.

What if you said no? And then, immediately after, he wrote: *Did you steal his heart, too?*

Augusta thought about the day she went off to college—the day she'd told Josh she was never coming home if she could help it. Although he didn't cry, that was as close to seeing a grown man weep as she had ever come. He stood there staring at her with those glassy blue eyes, but regained his composure, blinking the tears away without saying a word.

Their relationship was never the same after that.

She sat there, staring at her screen, uncertain how to answer, because she was pretty sure Josh had never really loved her. She was just familiar to him. And now that she knew the whole truth, the entire situation was a little gross.

Still, he claimed to have loved her, and she took it at face value, knowing that at least he thought he did.

Yes, she wrote back.

SPRAWLED ACROSS THE BED—THE bed he had shared with Augusta—completely naked from the shower, Ian was in no hurry to get dressed—unless it was to go to her. He craved her body. Like a teen, he lay staring up at the phone in his hand, hanging on her every word, aroused by mere words typed across a screen.

The sex was good, but it was more than that. He wasn't a grateful virgin—far from that, in fact. He'd had a string of lovers, beginning from the age of eleven. Women had always thrown themselves at him, and he had very shortly learned how that game worked. He was the bad boy women wanted a roll in the hay with. The guys they actually married had an account with Morgan Stanley Smith Barney. They wore expensive watches and wanted the house and wife with two-point-five kids because it looked good on their résumé.

Ian had never been that guy. He'd come from a broken home. His father was a druggie and a low-rent criminal. He sold meth and stole packs of cigarettes rather than pay for them, even when he had the money. The best thing he had ever done for Ian was hook him up with his brother, who was the reverse image of his dad. His mother had been lost from the get-go. He wanted better than all that, but he didn't need to be *that guy*, because that guy's wife was exactly the type who would hit on him while her husband was busy drinking single-malt scotch and smoking Cuban cigars with clients. He'd had a very rude wake-up call as a young man, and extreme situations called for extreme changes. So he took the hard right turn. Giving up sex had never really seemed like a huge sac-rifice when he had a hand that worked as well as any vagina. Doing something better with his life was what mattered to him. Money didn't make much difference, except that having none sucked. So he'd put nearly every last dime of his earnings into a tidy little bank account that now almost rivaled *that dude's*—espe-cially considering that Ian came debt-free.

But his entire life had changed in the space of a day, and he wanted Augusta at his side for the rest of his life.

Suddenly, making love—to her—occupied at least half his waking thoughts. He was hard again just reading her words, but he didn't even consider taking care of it, because sex meant nothing without her.

He thought about dialing her and listening to her voice instead of texting, but right now, this was enough. He had seen the news, and knew that the instant they spoke, reality would come crashing back into the picture. Of course, it must. Soon enough. But for the instant, he wanted to say what was in his heart, without interruption and without reality to shut him down. He savored the moment.

His heart thumped against his ribs as he tapped away his question. *Yes, what?*

It took her a long time to answer this time. *Yes, I guess I so.*

Grinning, and enjoying the flirtation, he tapped out his question: *Is that yes, you guess you broke his heart? Or yes, you guess you'll marry me?*

Tease. She lingered over the question for an interminable moment. *Depends,* she wrote.

On what?

"Augusta Aldridge is typing" continued for far too long. *On whether you plan to ask me in person.*

Tomorrow, he wrote back at once. And he meant it. Later he planned to go look at rings—something simple to match her frugal sensibilities and his budget. That was the one thing he hadn't come to terms with—the money she seemed to have at her disposal. Luckily, she would be getting her bail money back soon.

What's wrong with today? she fired back.

Ian stared at the text and grinned from ear to ear. Indeed, what was wrong with today? Except that he wasn't about to ask her over the phone. He was going to pick his ass up, get dressed, go get her and when he had her face-to-face, he was going to ask her again.

21

What's wrong with today?

While she waited for his response, she inspected the book on the coffee table. There was barely any light in the house now—just a faint blue glow from the front and back windows—but she was feeling too lazy to get up and go turn one on. Outside, a sliver of moon was barely visible through a steady sheet of rain. Using her phone as a flashlight, she shone it on the book. *The Road to Forgiveness.* It was a big, fat self-help book by an author she didn't recognize. She picked it up, bringing it close and holding the light up to it, curious about the message it imparted. Some of these books were gems. Others were a bunch of drivel. Hopefully Sadie was reading one of the former. For a time, Augusta had devoured these types of books and found solace in a few, inspiration in others. In the end, she realized what she'd needed all along was to come home and face her demons.

She was finally making peace with Flo.

Too bad her mother wasn't around to know it.

Or maybe she was.

Sadie believed in the afterlife.

And sometimes, lately, Augusta felt her mother out there ... so maybe it was true.

Feeling completely contented, if only for a moment, she flipped open the book to a page that was marked with a folded piece of paper. The document had bold handwriting on the inside. You could see it clearly from the other side, bleeding through. Feeling nosy, she set the book down in her lap and picked up the piece of paper with her left hand, unfolding it, using the phone in her right hand to read by. She heard the text come in as she was reading, but continued to stare at the words, too stunned to comprehend what she was looking at, though her brain recognized it at once.

> I, Florence W. Aldridge, of James
> Island, declare this to be a first
> codicil to my Last Will and
> Testament dated May first two-
> thousand-fourteen.

"Mom's will," she said aloud, and held her breath as her eyes scanned the page. She heard a sudden noise in the bedroom, and her stupefied brain attributed it to the cat and kept reading.

> I will and direct that the property
> bordered by Secessionville Creek
> from the byroad to Fort Lamar
> Road, and consisting of the original
> living quarters of Oyster Point
> Plantation, as well as the bordering
> marshlands, shall hereby be
> donated to the County of
> Charleston.

Dumbfounded, Augusta stood, dropping the book on the couch, clutching the piece of paper in her hand, along with her phone. She went straight to the kitchen to retrieve her purse, intending to leave with the will, but stopped at the sight of a man standing at the end of the hall. His face was hooded. He wore black from head to toe. All that distinguished him from the dark were his pale eyes. For an instant, he simply stared at her, looking as surprised as she was.

Augusta screamed and bolted for the front door, abandoning her purse.

Right-handed, and knowing she couldn't manage the door with the phone in her hand, she dropped the phone to snatch open the door and ran out into the rain, slamming the door hard behind her. She heard curses in her wake.

She didn't go for the car, because even if she could get in and lock both doors in time, she didn't have the keys and she didn't want to be trapped inside.

She ran toward the dock, slipping into the brush as the man emerged on Sadie's front porch, a dark shadow against the faded blue porch. She shoved the will down the front of her shirt as she ran to protect it from the rain. Thank God she wasn't one to wear heels! Wet and sloppy, the ground sank beneath her feet, but she ran as fast as she could.

She didn't have the keys to the house. It would be locked. The keys were in her purse. It was late, but Caroline wouldn't be home yet. And the construction crew was long gone. The only phone in the house was upstairs in her bedroom. But if she had to break in to get to it, she wouldn't be able to keep the man out— even if she could get into the house in time. But she knew she couldn't. They had reinforced the locks after the last break-in. But what did that matter? Windows could be broken. There was nobody around for miles to hear her scream.

The docks seemed her best choice. The lock on the boathouse door was already broken. She could get in there fast and maybe there were keys in one of the boats.

She knew the man was somewhere behind her, but didn't dare turn to look. She knew this property better than anyone except her sisters. He didn't. Augusta ran hard, her brain searching for options.

The dock was still a few hundred yards away through thickening mud, but she was camouflaged by brush. Her feet sank into the muck, and the suction threatened to pull off her shoes. She couldn't hear him behind her anymore. He would expect her to run toward the house, toward safety. The porch lights were a beacon in the growing darkness. She knew he couldn't see her in the pouring rain and would have to guess at her direction.

The closer she got to the dock, the softer the pluff mud became, until it began to bog her down. She lost one shoe as the mud sucked it straight off her foot, but she kept running, leaping up onto the dock when she sensed it was there in front of her. She could barely see where she was going now, but despite the fact that she hadn't lived here in ten years, she knew every inch of this property.

On the dock, she made better time, racing toward the boathouse, her footfalls echoing along the wooden pier. She prayed he wouldn't hear. She knew he couldn't see her. The boathouse at the long end of the dock was no more than a black hole in the darkness. She ran toward it, praying for keys.

In the distance, a crack of lightning lit the horizon.

Behind her, the glow of the house porch lights

through sheets of rain looked like fireflies in the distance.

Reaching the boathouse at last, she ripped off the tangled makeshift lock, and the door collapsed with a hollow thud. She knew the instant he realized she wasn't going toward the house because she heard him cursing across the distance. Her time was limited.

Inside the boathouse, she could see that one bay door had been left open. The dory was there and in the water so she made a last-minute decision and skipped looking for keys. She dove into the dory, hoping against hope she wouldn't miss. She landed in the bottom of the small boat with a thud, banging her head on one of the seats and her ribs on another, but the dory slid out of the bay into the black night.

It was only when she was inside the dory that she wondered why the boat was back in the bay and why the door was open. There were no paddles left in the boat, but she had enough thrust to carry her out toward open water.

Her left thigh hurt. So did her chest and head, and she thought she tasted blood in the rainwater that seeped between her lips.

Behind her, she could hear footsteps racing down the dock, but judging by the distance, he was a good ways behind her. She lay dead still, hoping to let her momentum carry her as far as possible. The rain beat down on her back and the back of her head. The tinny taste of her own blood lingered in her mouth. In the distance, another razor-thin bolt of lightning flashed, followed by a *crack* of thunder. Augusta lay quietly, trying to remember what she was wearing. Dark. Thank God. She was wearing denims and a dark plum shirt, nothing bright to reflect light.

The front of her shirt was soaked now and she

could feel the paper of the will plastered to her skin—probably ruined. In the end, she had given up her means of calling for help to salvage a piece of paper that was going to be completely worthless.

The boat suddenly shuddered to a halt as the bow nosed into the muck.

Another bolt of lightning lit the sky enough for Augusta to see that she was stuck in the tidal flats. Yet another flash illuminated the dock behind her. She could see someone standing on the edge of it, but he wasn't coming after her yet. A dark form stood at the end of the dock, silhouetted with each flash of lightning. Thunder cracked between every bolt, closer and closer together.

The inlet creeks were like spidery veins. Even at low tide, the middle of the creek was deep enough to accommodate a good-sized boat that could easily handle Clark Sound and the winding rivers and estuaries around Morris Island. But you needed paddles and you needed light to navigate. Augusta had neither.

If he took one of the boats, he could easily overtake her.

The instant he disappeared from the dock, her decision was made. She slipped out of the boat and crawled into the spartina flats.

IAN PULLED on his left boot, glancing at the phone lying on his rumpled sheets.

Answer your phone, he'd texted, but she'd yet to answer him, and he felt a little silly for feeling so disappointed by that fact. He had no idea where she might be, or what she might be doing. It could be that she'd gotten distracted by something important. There was nothing abnormal about a text gone unanswered. How many times had he done that sort of thing himself?

Mostly on purpose.

The problem was that he was in the middle of asking the girl to marry him, and it didn't seem like Augusta to set the phone down and walk away from a conversation like that. She might tell him to go to hell, but she wouldn't ignore him.

Picking up the phone, he scrolled through their messages for some clue as to her whereabouts, but their conversation had never gone there.

He called her again, for the third time, but the phone rang and rang and then went straight to voice mail.

"Damn it, Augusta."

Pride be damned—this didn't feel right.

He glanced at the clock. It was nearly eight o'clock. The rains had yet to let up and he had to believe she was home. Who would be out in this kind of weather? He didn't have her sister's phone number, or he would have called Caroline, despite how she felt about him. Impatient to hear from Augusta, he tapped out a message completely devoid of humor.

Where the hell did you go?

Setting the phone down on the bed, screen facing up, he pulled on his other boot, and then sat there, staring at the phone, waiting. When the screen faded to black, he rose from the bed.

"Shit," he said and grabbed his phone, sticking it in his back pocket. He went straight for the kitchen to snag his car keys.

He didn't believe Augusta would simply stop talking.

Grabbing his raincoat, he walked out the front door, with the intention of heading toward Oyster Point. He realized her sister probably didn't want him on the property, but he didn't give a damn right now.

He had a bad feeling.

STAYING LOW, Augusta made her way through the spartina flats, panting, trying not to panic. Her ribs hurt from the impact to her chest, but she focused her attention on the tidal flats, trying to pick her way through the muck in the darkness.

With one shoe on and one shoe off, she put the greater weight on the foot with the shoe. There was literally no telling what was in these marshes. Folks claimed they were littered with the bones of the Confederate and Union dead. There were old boats, fishing tackle, glass, broken and otherwise—from stupid drunk boaters who didn't respect the place and tossed out their beer bottles when they were done with them. She'd heard of people unearthing wooden carriage wheels, hundreds of years old, perfectly preserved because of the nature of the pluff mud. Wading in water that was ankle-deep in places, along uneven terrain, she scrambled through the spartina grass, using it for cover.

She had never really come out this far—not even as a child. She had often seen fishermen standing out in the tidal flats wearing their bright yellow waders, but the prospect had never appealed to her. This land was theirs, but while it might seem cool to explore the first few feet of tidal flats, the mystery soon gave way to annoyance over the struggle of walking through what amounted to little more than whipped mud.

If you weren't careful, it was easy to end up in mud to your chin. Nor was it pleasant to pick it out of every crevice of your body because the stinky muck literally oozed into every available crack. Though some people claimed to love the smell, it was not a scent Augusta relished.

She had no idea how far she'd gone through the spartina flats, but she kept going until she heard nothing behind her. When she stumbled across the carcass of a small rotting boat, she dashed beneath it to hide, tripping over something bulky on her way in.

22

8:17 p.m.

The property gate was closed, but that had never stopped Ian before. The gate was a halfhearted measure to keep folks out. The Aldridges owned too much of the surrounding land to enclose the entire property so he simply walked around, veering toward the woods where he'd found the shoe the day he'd first met Augusta.

Scrambling down the embankment, he slid onto the oyster gravel drive in front of the little cottage near the shore. Augusta's car was parked in front, along with another vehicle

It was dark. Peering into Augusta's car, he found it empty. So was the car beside it.

Lightning ripped the skies around him, illuminating the porch. The wind rattled the bottles on the little bottle tree. The front door was wide open, so despite the voice of caution, he walked inside to take a look.

The house was completely dark, but when he walked inside, he kicked an object on the floor and it lit up. He bent to pick it up, recognizing Augusta's cell phone.

His gaze took in the room as he clicked the ON button, turning on the screen. It was still logged into her text program and his last text to her was the last one he saw.

Where the hell did you go, Augusta?

Something had distracted her, but what?

He poked his head into the kitchen, where a cat was crouched on the kitchen counter. He could barely see the animal silhouetted against the window, black against the night sky.

No one else was here.

"Hello?" he called out.

No answer.

It was a tiny house—not much chance he wouldn't be able to hear someone skulking around, but he poked his head into the bedroom anyway—just in case.

He walked back outside, onto the front porch, a bad feeling settling hard in his gut, and he set out toward the main house on foot, calling Augusta's name.

AUGUSTA SAT SHIVERING beneath the rotten boat hull.

Underneath, it smelled of mold and old, wet wood —and something worse. She was sitting in the middle of sludge, soaked to her teeth, her hair caked with mud, but she didn't dare move from beneath the little shelter. Outside, the rain pelted the back side of the boat, dripping in where the wood had already rotted through. A persistent drip on her back, and another on the top of her head kept her on edge, feeling vulnerable and terrified of being discovered.

Who was he? Why was he in Sadie's house? Where was Sadie? And why wouldn't she answer her phone? She wondered if Caroline had come home yet. Would she spot her car at Sadie's? Or worse, would the man go after her sister?

Even the mere possibility made Augusta feel like a horrible person, because she was so frightened she couldn't move to save her own life. She felt paralyzed with fear. She had always thought she would be braver than this, but she was frozen with indecision, terrified to her core. She swallowed salty tears, her throat constricting as she held back a sob.

She couldn't think straight. Outside, lightning cracked again, illuminating her dubious shelter. It was more like the skeleton of a wooden boat, long forgotten in the tidal flats. Probably some fisherman got stuck at low tide and didn't bother to come back for the boat because it was too much trouble. From the looks of it, it had been here a long time.

Lightning flickered again, and this time, she spotted something red outside, near the boat—a bag maybe. She must have unearthed it as she'd trudged toward the boat.

Shuddering with fear or cold—which she couldn't tell—she stretched out a hand to grab the strap of material and pull it under the boat.

She had to tug hard, and nearly thumped her head on the roof of the boat, but the bag finally came up, and along with it, something else. Another flash of lightning revealed a small hand, decomposing still, and Augusta couldn't hold back a shriek of fear.

Her mouth opening to scream again, she slapped a hand over it, and shoved the bag away, scurrying out from under the boat. Suddenly, she became aware of things in the mud—solid things—things that felt terrifyingly familiar as she bumped her way through them. Her mind refused to identify them, but they were everywhere, touching her. She froze, standing outside in the rain, knee-deep in pluff mud, and focused suddenly on the sound of her name in the distance.

"Augusta!" Ian called again.

She wasn't up at the house, and all the doors were locked so he made his way out to the dock.

"Augusta!" he shouted.

The boathouse door was hanging, half of it collapsed into the water. Inside the boathouse, one of the bay doors was open and he assumed a boat was missing because the bay was empty.

There was no damned way she would have taken a boat out in this weather, he reassured himself—no damned way—and he retraced his steps, going back onto the dock. He walked to the end of it, which stretched out a little farther into the water than the boathouse did. From there, he could see nothing. The sky was pitch-black, the sliver of moon obscured by sheets of rain.

"Augusta!" he shouted.

Suddenly, he heard a voice in the distance, and he stopped to gain his bearings. She was screaming. Out there. Somewhere. The sound of terror sucked the air out of his lungs.

"Augusta!" he shouted, and started in the direction of her screams.

Augusta was in a panic now.

Now that she heard Ian's voice, she knew she would be safe, but she didn't think she would ever be okay after all that she had seen. Sobbing, she trudged through the mud, pushing past the horrors in the marsh, toward the sound of Ian's voice.

"Ian!" she cried, and kept walking, following the promise of his voice.

At last, when she reached firm land and could see his face, illuminated by a flash of lightning, she fell down and curled up into a fetal position to sob.

As the rain pummeled her, she was aware of Ian's body suddenly shielding her, lifting her up, carrying her. She clung to him, desperate for an anchor in the storm.

23

———

The ER at Roper was crowded, but they took Augusta immediately upon seeing her. In shock and shivering feverishly, she was given a bed and her wounds examined. Ian refused to leave her. She wouldn't stop sobbing so they gave her a sedative.

"There were bones everywhere," she kept saying. "All in the mud!"

They called the police. Ian called Jack Shaw, grateful now that he had a direct line to reach him. Jack came straight from Lockwood station.

"There were bones," Augusta repeated over and over, sobbing still. "Everywhere ... touching me ... there was a hand, Jack!" And then she began to sob uncontrollably again.

Jack placed a comforting hand on her shoulder, eyeing Ian. Judging by the look on his face, he was trying hard to keep his personal feelings out of his work, but clearly the story Augusta was telling disturbed him for more reasons than the obvious. He spoke to her with the patience of a father, gently but firmly. "Augusta, tell me again what you were doing in the marsh."

The sedatives were beginning to take effect and

she was having trouble focusing. She clung to Ian's hand. "I told you ... there was a man ... Sadie's house. He chased me. I fell in the boat." She shivered and her eyes sought Ian's, as though to gain strength from his presence. He sensed it and her trust moved him deeply. They were connected somehow. He felt it now more than ever.

"You *fell* in the boat?" Jack persisted.

"Jumped," she clarified and wiped her nose against Ian's sleeve. The fact that he thought it was endearing, not disgusting, was incredibly telling. "I didn't know where else to go!"

"There are contusions on her chest," the male nurse explained to Jack. "We're taking her back as soon as we can for X-rays to make sure there are no broken ribs."

Ian squeezed Augusta's hand, but said nothing, letting her talk directly to Jack, sensing she was about to pass out and knowing that what she had to say was important. He reached out to smooth the mud-encrusted hair from her bruised and cut face, flicking it away where it had dried to her skin. There was bloody mud all the way down the left side of her face and some caked on her lips ... lips that were now as familiar as his own.

"Where is Caroline?" she asked groggily.

Jack sighed, a heavy, burdened sigh. "With Sadie, Augusta. We're searching for Daniel."

"It wasn't Daniel," she offered, then hiccupped, and closed her eyes.

"I thought you said you didn't recognize the man?"

"I didn't," she said, without opening her eyes. "But it wasn't Daniel," she persisted. "He wore a mask."

Ian shrugged when Jack looked at him for answers. "I didn't see anyone," he told Jack. "I walked the entire property."

"Can you tell me where you saw the bodies?" Jack asked one more time, directing his question at Augusta.

"In the ... mud," Augusta replied with a whine that sounded so much like a child's, Ian wanted to scoop her up into his arms and hold her close. It was killing him to see her lying there, looking so vulnerable—nothing like the firebrand he knew she was. She was clearly shaken to the core. Whatever she had seen out there had done this to her.

What if he hadn't gotten there in time?

He refused to consider that for even a second.

"Augusta ... where exactly?" Jack persisted.

"... old boat," she replied, but didn't open her eyes.

The nurse returned and Jack asked him, "What did you give her?"

"Diprivan. It works very quickly but wears off fast."

All Ian wanted to know was that she wasn't seriously injured. "Can you tell if anything is broken?"

The nurse was checking her vitals. "Doesn't appear so, but we still need to make sure."

"What about the cut on her head?"

"Superficial. She shouldn't need stitches. We'll just clean that up and put a bit of surgical glue on it."

Ian bent to kiss Augusta on the forehead, right next to her cut. She whimpered in her sleep, dozing fitfully now.

"Did you see anything at all?" Jack asked, directing the question to Ian.

Ian shook his head. "But I know the direction she came from." Torn, because he didn't want to leave Augusta here alone, but knowing in his gut that whatever she had found out there in the salt marsh was pertinent to Jack's investigation—critical to the protection of others—he offered, "I can show you where."

Jack nodded, considering Augusta, too. She had released her hold on Ian's hand and lay there resting now. "She should be fine here in the meantime," he said. "I'll call her sister," he offered, and then pulled out his cell phone to dial her right there.

"Alright," Ian said, but his tone was full of conflict.

"Don't worry, she'll be fine," the nurse reassured. "She'll get a little rest and we'll take some X-rays and then you can probably come back and take her home after." Clearly he mistook Ian for her significant other.

Jack ended his call, then dialed another number. Ian heard him leave a message, and assumed he was talking to someone at the *Tribune's* offices.

"She's damned lucky you were looking out for her," Jack offered, as he ended the second call.

Ian brushed the hair from Augusta's lips, thinking of all the times she had come to his rescue, even when she hadn't known him all that well. With the same tenacity her sister had exercised to crucify him, Augusta had become his savior. "I'm the lucky one," he said, and meant it, and then he bent to whisper in her ear. "I love you, Augusta. I'll be back soon."

"She won't even know you're gone," the nurse assured him.

Ian nodded, and then before he could change his mind, he left her while she slept.

———

CODY THREW up a little after drinking the water that had accumulated in a puddle on the floor. But now he felt a little better. He focused on that feeling.

His grandma Rose always said a joyful heart was

good medicine. Cody thought it might be from her Bible, but he didn't know for sure. The only medicine he had right now was his brain so he was gonna use it.

Stay awake. Don't give up. Don't throw up in the butter beans.

He kept thinking about mind over matter, remembering the time he worried about throwing up in his dinner at Grandma Rose's house, but he'd ordered himself not to, and he didn't. He waited until he and his parents walked out of his Grandma Rose's house and the screen door closed behind him, then he threw up in Grandma Rose's azaleas.

Don't worry 'bout the snake. Stay awake. Keep your eye on the ball.

I'm watching, Daddy.

He worried the snake would slither down out of its wooden throne and try to bite him, but it stayed right there in its dark corner—under the boards—not sleeping exactly, 'cause its eyes were open and watching—resting, and keeping Cody company.

Somehow, he understood that if he let it be, it would leave him be, as well. It was like a silent pact they'd made, one he felt down to his aching bones.

It was still raining outside, and the night was foggy. He could barely see the train trestle through the mist. The steady pelting on the roof calmed him. It spoke to a distant memory of noises lulling him to sleep ... the sound of the ocean, the gentle song of spring rain, a gurgling brook ...

The bad man was never coming back again, he thought, and now that he felt a little better, he tried to figure out what he had to do. Gross as it might seem, he pretended to be a snake and used his tongue to lick up bugs that crawled past his face. He saw once in a

war movie that soldiers ate maggots to keep themselves alive.

He was a soldier here, fighting for his life. If he was
smart, maybe he would live long enough for someone
to find him and take him home.

His skin was on fire, but that didn't matter.

His eyes burned, but he focused harder.

His legs were numb, but he remembered the pain.

The snake coiled up on its bed of wood, idly
flicking its tongue out, showing Cody how to feed
himself.

Cody blinked, focusing on the ant crawling toward him on the floor, waiting ... like his friend the
snake.

10:56 p.m.

The Aldridge property comprised a great portion of
the salt marsh surrounding Oyster Point Plantation,
and whatever wasn't owned by the family had been
annexed by the City of Charleston. Despite the final
successful bid for township in 2012, large portions of
the island still belonged to the City instead of the
town of James Island. The result was spotty police protection as some areas were still policed by the City of
Charleston, while others were patrolled by the county
... and others, barely at all.

Fortunately for Jack, the area they were searching
belonged to both the Aldridges and to the City so he
didn't feel the need to wait for a search warrant,
knowing Caroline would give her permission without
question. The search party began on Aldridge property. They couldn't bring dogs out—impossible to

track within the marsh, but they found Augusta's boat grounded at the mouth of the creek.

In the pouring rain, they swept northeast, twenty men deep, from the point at which they discovered her boat to the point at which Ian had discovered Augusta stumbling through the spartina flats. Some of the men were forced to use boats, because the water was too deep to wade through. Others kept to the shallows. Overhead, choppers lit the night sky, spotters slicing through the heavy mist. SLED and FBI joined them with every available man in the area.

They found the small, wooden boat Augusta had told them about at approximately 10:32 P.M. It was wedged into a small sandbar surrounded by deeper waters. The boat had once been a small fishing skiff. Now all that remained were parts of a rotting hull, clinging to a wooden spine that was visible enough above the water at high tide not to require any warning markers for area boaters. It was entirely possible the boat had been there since Hugo. Since it didn't impose any real danger, it hadn't warranted much attention, but it apparently missed a recent cleanup of debris along the estuaries. Converging tides along with vegetation had created a natural earthwork of sorts. Behind it, semi-protected from the currents, they found the mass grave.

Some of the bodies had been there for years, judging by their state of decomposition—slower than it might seem possible because the marsh was a natural preservative. On some of the older bodies the skin was still intact and hair clung to the scalp. Working closely with the search team, the medical examiner led the efforts to make certain they salvaged every trace of evidence—mostly for identification purposes. The most recent bodies were still in a much-decelerated state of decomposition, but even so, the physical evidence would be compromised by time submersed in the water.

There was no way to move heavy equipment into the marsh, so wearing biohazard suits, and using whatever tools they could find—waders, nets, heavy gloves—the men worked by hand to unearth the most gruesome discovery in Charleston in nearly forty years. Within the first hour, they had exhumed more than six bodies.

ABOUT AN HOUR before Caroline left the office, Daniel was taken into custody. Wanting to be certain the breaking news surrounding his arrest was covered, and covered fairly, Caroline had worked late. It wasn't until she'd been about to leave the office that her receptionist finally gave her the message that Jack had called. Unfortunately, her cell phone had died around 6 P.M. and she had forgotten her charger in Jack's car, so she was completely incommunicado on the drive home. By the time she reached Oyster Point, the property was blanketed with flashing blue lights. Choppers roared overhead, spotlights swinging all over the night sky.

Caroline's first thought was of Augusta. Heart thumping painfully against her ribs, she ran into the house. Finding it still locked and empty, she came rushing back and ran toward the marsh. There were officers swarming the boathouse. More out on the water.

She tried to get information from one of the uniformed officers on the dock. Something momentous was happening here, but no one seemed inclined to share any information.

"This is my property!" she told one uniformed officer.

"You'll have to talk to Detective Shaw," the man insisted, and pointed out toward the lights on the marsh.

Unless she took one of the boats out, there was no way to reach Jack, and her cell phone was dead. Realizing the phone in Sadie's house was closer and easier to reach, she made the trek over to Sadie's. But Sadie wasn't home either, and there were more policemen guarding her front door. She asked to use the phone and was refused.

"I'm sorry, we can't let you in," the man insisted.

Frustrated, Caroline returned to the main house and hurried back to the office, where there was one of only two available landlines in the house. It crossed her mind that people were entirely too dependent on cell phones. Now that she needed one, there was none to be found. She tried Augusta's number first, but there was no answer. It went straight to her voice mail. Next she tried Jack, but his, too, went straight to voice mail. Sadie's, as well. Finally, she checked her messages and discovered the message from Jack. Thankfully, Augusta was at Roper with minor injuries. No word from Sadie, though she was certain she knew where Sadie must be.

Finally, she called Josh, and told him about Augusta and Daniel.

"I'll go see how she's doing," he offered. "You stick around and see what's going on. Call me back the instant you know something."

"Thank you, Josh," Caroline said, grateful he was so willing to help, despite all the trouble she had caused him with the paper's investigation, and despite the ordeal with his mother. Augusta in particular would appreciate his care. Unfortunately, she didn't have Ian's number, and wasn't quite ready to talk to him anyway. Apologies seemed in order—to Augusta, as well. But that was probably why she had asked Josh to go get Augusta. She didn't know what to say to her sister yet.

She stood on the dock, watching the police boats in the distance, and tried to muddle her way through confusion and guilt over her actions toward Ian Patterson.

She had been wrong.

So wrong.

She had decided Ian Patterson was guilty and set her sights on bringing him to justice. There was no rationalizing her way out of this one. She'd helped put an innocent man behind bars. He might have faced the electric chair, a man who had very likely saved her life. And still she had persecuted him while the guilty party ran around under their noses the entire time: Daniel Greene.

Jack had been right.

Augusta had been right.

She had been wrong.

Nothing was as it seemed.

24

Augusta awoke in the ER, groggy, though she remembered far more than she wished she did. Horrific images flashed through her brain—a tiny hand in the mud—that terrible sense of nudging her way through a nightmarish orgy of decomposing bodies.

A male nurse hovered over her. He smiled warmly when she met his gaze. "Do you know where you are?" he asked.

Augusta cleared her throat and nodded. Her usual sense of sarcasm failed her completely. She was grateful, remembering how he had helped her through X-rays, his disposition pleasant and far more patient than she could have ever mustered herself. He'd given her a sock for her foot, because it was cold. She wiggled it out of the covers as she stirred. The nurse came to check the rails on her gurney, as though to be sure she wouldn't roll out. "I guess they abandoned me?"

He winked. "They left you in good hands."

Augusta tried to smile and found her face hurt. She lifted fingers to her cheek.

"You're going to have a nasty bruise and a black

eye, but no broken bones, and the cut won't leave much of a scar."

Blinking, Augusta reached for her face, feeling tentatively. "Scar?"

"Just a little one," he reassured, and then winked. "It adds character."

She vaguely recalled smashing her face into the dory seat, but didn't realize she had done so much damage. In that moment, all she had thought about was getting away. "Has anyone called my sister?"

"Your husband must've. Your phone's been ringing off the hook." He picked up her cell phone from a table nearby and brought it to her, setting it down on the bed beside her.

"Thank you."

"You're welcome."

"For everything," she said, and tried to sit up, but swayed. He came to help again and once she was in a semi-upright position, she checked her messages. Several missed calls from Ian, but none from anyone else. She guessed Caroline must know by now and apparently wasn't very concerned. She tried Ian's number first. It rang until it went to voice mail.

It was only belatedly that she recalled the piece of paper she had shoved down her shirt and she patted her sore ribs.

"Looking for this?" The nurse held up a torn and waterlogged scrap of paper and walked over to hand it to her. "We peeled it off during your X-rays. Not much left of it."

Augusta tried to unfold it but it was stuck together, completely ruined. Faded gray spots were all that remained of the ink and it was ripped, as well. *But she knew what it was.*

Sadie didn't have a malicious bone in her body, but

there was a reason she had this codicil in her possession, and Augusta was going to find out why. "It's ruined," she said to no one in particular.

"What was it?"

Augusta shook her head, feeling disordered. "More lies."

At this point, the lies were adding up to epic proportions. Maybe Daniel had discovered the codicil and given it to Sadie? That was the only palatable explanation—unless her mother had written the thing and then changed her mind and given it to Sadie. But that would mean Sadie had lied about its existence. She didn't believe that scenario either. It seemed more credible to her that her mother had shown it to Daniel and that Daniel had kept it out of the will after her death. She decided he must have given it to Sadie after the fact, because, recalling Sadie's anger that day on the porch, Augusta didn't believe any of it was feigned. Whatever the truth, Daniel was obviously not the man they'd thought him to be.

"Are you going to keep me here?"

"Overnight?" The nurse shook his head. "We can release you any time, but I can't let you leave unless I know you have someone to drive you."

"I feel fine," Augusta lied.

Although she didn't have any broken bones, on the inside, she felt ravaged.

And a far more insidious thought was working its way through her brain—something she didn't want to believe. In trying to protect Sadie, could Daniel have staged his own burglary and later the attempted robbery at their house, as a means to retrieve the codicil? She knew it hadn't been Daniel at Sadie's house, but what if he'd hired some thug to do his dirty work—like last time? It was a kid who'd stolen her purse after leaving Daniel's office last month, but that person could have easily handed her phone to someone else to lure Caroline to the ruins. Only Daniel had known exactly where she was that afternoon because she had been at his office, and if it was true that Jennifer's car was registered to him and that he was Karen Hutto's attorney, as well, then he had a traceable connection to nearly every victim.

The nurse helped her sit the rest of the way up. "Do you have someone you can call?" he persisted. "The Diprivan wears off fast, but you're not supposed to drive within twenty-four hours of an administered dose. We can't release you unless you have someone to take you home."

"I can find someone," Augusta assured him, realizing it was a battle she wouldn't win.

"Good. Then if you'll wait a minute, I'll get your doctor."

"Thanks," Augusta said, and dialed Ian's number again as the nurse walked away, her thoughts centered on Daniel.

Worrying her fingers in her lap, Sadie sat waiting at the Lockwood station for someone to let her know she could see Daniel. She'd come straight from Queenie's after his phone call. Whatever it was they were doing back there—interrogating him, arresting him—it was taking forever. But now something else was going on. Uniformed men rushed by her.

She knew enough about the law to know that they could only hold him for a certain amount of time without filing charges, but she refrained from calling Josh to find out exactly how long, reminding herself that Daniel knew the law. And he was innocent. She knew that, but she was getting a bad feeling in her bones ...

Way down deep.

She didn't want to talk to Josh right now—nor to Augusta or Caroline—leastways not until she gathered her thoughts ...

There were bodies buried in the pluff mud ...

She heard them saying so as they rushed by, thinking no one could overhear their hushed conversations. But there was a room full of people waiting, and every one of them exchanged looks, putting pieces together.

Sadie was putting pieces together, too.

She remembered *that* day as though it were yesterday. He came runnin' to her, scared and uncertain what to do. It was hot that day, hadn't rained for nearly a month—since long before Sam went missing. The watermarks were low and even lower at low tide. She was cutting potatoes for a salad and he came in and said he knew where Sammy was.

Sadie hadn't really believed him, but she'd always had a strange feeling in her breast where her son was concerned, so she followed him out into the marsh at low tide. He led her to a place on the spartina flats where the tide had created a pocket in the marsh. That was where she'd found Sammy's body trussed up, covered by debris, like alligators did to save their meals for later. But the water was low now, and his body was exposed.

Josh admitted he'd found the body a few weeks earlier, said he stumbled over it by accident and was afraid they would think he'd hurt Sammy, so he kept it from everyone—including Sadie. She'd believed him ... back then.

Sammy's body was already badly decomposed and he was long gone, so telling everyone after all that time would have been both cruel and suspicious. They had already searched every nook and every crevice of every beach and every inlet. But they hadn't found Sam because he was hidden so well.

Only now she was beginning to understand why.

For the love of God—there were bodies in the mud.

A terrible feeling settled in her breast—and this time, it planted itself stubbornly and refused to go away—no matter how much she reasoned with herself. No matter how many excuses she made. No matter what she tried to tell herself.

This time she couldn't make it go away.

She sat there, thinking about all the times she had denied her suspicions and felt heartsick. But what sort of mother thought such horrible thoughts about her son?

She felt guilty, thinking maybe she'd put all those bad thoughts on him because of his father—because she never actually *saw* her son hurt anyone.

Not people.

He'd told her Sammy's drowned body had washed ashore—and it could have happened just exactly that way. Sadie had believed the worst was over. The poor baby was gone, and the funeral was long over with. No one could help that Sammy had drowned, but it was a different time, back in those days. She'd thought they would blame him, too—her little boy—so she had buried Sammy in a good place ... somewhere with shade and flowers and she had prayed every day for his soul ... and for the soul of her son ... and her own.

But deep down ... she knew ... some folks were born bad ... no matter how much you loved them ... no matter how much you did for them.

Josh had everything, but he always seemed to want more. Florence had loved him too well, doting on him, giving him everything her son should have had ... through the years, Sadie had compensated by giving him less, though she had given him the greatest mother's gift of all—blind faith.

The thought of it brought hot, stinging tears to her eyes.

A vision came into her head of the first dog they'd kept before Tango—a black Lab named Bear. She remembered Josh calling that dog out into the water where he was sitting in his fishing boat. He knew that cottonmouth was lying right there in the dog's path, but he called that poor animal even knowing Sadie had gone in to phone animal control. When he thought she was out of earshot, he insisted the dog come, his voice mean as a devil.

They couldn't save Bear. But it was something about the way her son had watched the animal die that had disturbed her down deep in her bones—that soulless look in his eyes as he'd watched the animal in its death throes. Josh swore he was simply trying to get the dog out of harm's way. But Sadie had had a bad feeling that day—a bad feeling she ignored.

She ignored it again the day Josh showed up with Sam in his arms, covered in ant bites. He said the baby had gone and sat in an ant pile.

But Sadie wondered. She hated herself for wondering, but she wondered as she dabbed at every one of his angry bites with bleach to stop the itching.

Josh had never done anyone real harm. It was simply an odd feeling she always had that something wasn't right—the feeling that somehow her son orchestrated very bad things—like a conductor in a symphony.

She'd had that feeling again the morning they'd found Florence. He'd come over to her house very early in the morning, even though he never visited on Saturdays. That morning he insisted they go visit Flo to make pancakes ... for old times' sake ... as though he knew what they would find in that house.

He had watched Sadie's reaction with a detached calm as they found poor Florence lying there at the bottom of the stairs, as though she'd fallen down. He'd even helped Sadie turn over the big mirror so Florence's body wouldn't be reflected in the glass. He chastened her about silly superstitions, but he had helped her turn it nevertheless, and then he had kissed her on the cheek and asked her if she needed him to stay ... because he had to go.

It felt bad then ... but now it felt worse.

There were too many lies, too many secrets.

And they were getting harder and harder to keep.

"Excuse me!" she said to a police officer who passed by her seat. "Where exactly did they say they found those bodies?"

He knew who she was, and looked at her apologetically. "You know I really can't say exactly, ma'am, somewhere near Clark Sound."

Sadie nodded woodenly and sat back down, but only for a moment to gather her courage. This was the hardest thing she would ever have to do.

But it was long past time.

Long past time.

If her son was innocent, the law would discover the truth. She had to believe that with all her heart. And if he was guilty ... then she had raised a monster and he had to be stopped.

Choking back a wave of guilt for all her ugly suspicions about her own flesh and blood, she got up from her chair in the hall and set out to make a long overdue confession.

11:26 p.m.

After speaking briefly with Caroline, Augusta understood why no one was answering their phones. As it turned out, her sister's cell was simply charging and she spoke to Augusta long enough to say the police had taken a search team into the salt marsh where Augusta had discovered the bodies. Apparently, Ian was out there, as well, working with Jack, although Caroline had only heard bits of information through one of Jack's men, because she had yet to speak with Jack directly. Sadie was at the police station, but Caroline hadn't spoken to her either, and Josh was on his way to pick Augusta up from the hospital.

"I would have come to get you myself, but Josh was closer," she said. And then she paused a moment, adding, "Thank God he went looking for you."

The effects of the sedation were wearing off, but Augusta was momentarily confused, certain Caroline wouldn't have meant to praise Ian. "Josh?" she asked.

"No," Caroline said, and waited another moment to clarify, as though it pained her somehow to say it. "Ian."

Augusta refrained from pointing out that it was the second time Ian had saved one of them from harm. But it was enough that Caroline had acknowledged his part in Augusta's rescue. She knew her sister well enough to know it was a start. Pushing her now wouldn't get them any further. They had that in common—that same, stubborn quality they had both inherited from their mother.

"He should be there soon," Caroline promised.

They hung up, and Augusta sat on the bed, waiting for her discharge, feeling strangely disconnected.

It was probably partly the sedation. But it was something more, as well. Caroline was there at home, waiting for her, and she felt as though they were making progress, but with Savannah gone, Sadie's revelations and Josh avoiding her lately, she felt as though their lives were unraveling.

Josh might be her brother, but she didn't feel close to him anymore. In fact, she had never felt further removed from the child she had grown up with.

And Sadie ... all the lies ...

The last time she'd felt so morose, it was after Sammy's death ... when her father abandoned them and her mother shut down emotionally. Sadie had been the glue that had kept them together, but it felt like that glue was decaying before her eyes.

What the hell was she supposed to say to Josh?

Their entire life was a lie.

Obviously, he shared her feelings. When he arrived, he didn't bother to come in to retrieve her. He called to say he was outside. The nurse wheeled her out—probably to make sure she wasn't getting into the driver's seat alone.

So much for chivalry. Whatever Josh had felt for her once upon a time, he obviously didn't anymore. By the look on his face, he seemed annoyed by the thought of coming to help her. Augusta didn't pay much attention to the car he was driving; it was dark and the nurse was chatting endlessly. Anxious to get home, she practically ran to get into the passenger's side, sparing Josh the effort of getting out to help. Apparently, he wasn't in a hurry to do that anyway, because he sat behind the driver's seat, with the window rolled halfway down, waiting. It wasn't until Augusta was in the car that she realized it wasn't his.

It was Sadie's.

Her shoulders tensed immediately.

Sadie's car had been parked in her driveway while Augusta was sitting in her house. How had Josh ended up with it? "Thanks for coming to get me," she said, though suddenly a little uncertain.

"No problem," he replied tersely and then he said nothing more as he navigated the parking lot. They pulled onto the road and the hospital parking lot disappeared behind them.

Although he kept his eyes on the road, Augusta had the feeling he was watching her in his peripheral vision. She settled back into the seat, sore, but thankful that most of the effects of the sedative were wearing off. She didn't like feeling out of control.

It was raining still. Drops beaded on the windshield as quickly as the wiper blade could sweep them away. Silence was a third occupant in the car, its presence as palpable as the growing pain in her chest—getting more intense with every passing minute as the medication wore off. The insistent sound of the wipers worked her nerves.

"It's awful about Daniel," she said, forcing conversation.

"Yeah."

"Are they going to charge him?

He shrugged, barely lifting a shoulder, a grudging response.

"What about your mom ... she okay?"

He wouldn't look at her. "Haven't talked to her."

They were heading over the expressway now, toward home. She could see the choppers in the sky over James Island, their spotlights honed in on an area behind the tree line.

Beside her, Josh seemed tense, his gaze following the choppers in the air.

She wanted to say something about Sadie's confession—wanted to ask him if he felt as strange as she did about their sudden sibling relationship, but couldn't broach the subject. She wanted to bring up the will, but again something stopped her. It sat like a bomb in her purse. She couldn't have been more aware of it, but the tension was already high enough and she had never felt the breach between them so acutely.

Her gaze fell upon the phone in the console—a small red flip phone that looked like a cheap prepaid. Josh's phone was an iPhone—like hers, only white and newer. Reaching out for the flip phone, she commented, half-jokingly, "You got a new phone?"

His hand snaked out at once, stopping her, pinning her wrist to the seat at her side, giving her a look that made the tiny hairs on her nape stand on end. Brushing his hand off, she shrugged away. "Jesus, why so touchy?"

He didn't respond.

They drove the remainder of the way over the bridge in silence. Augusta laid her head back on the seat, staring out the passenger side window. She could see Josh's reflection on the window, his jaw taut and his eyes in the air as much as on the road.

Her gaze reverted to the phone on the console ... she wanted to pick it up again, but didn't dare. Josh wasn't the type to keep old technology around.

So whose was it?

She stared at the phone, and Josh began to tap his fingers impatiently on the steering wheel...

25

Knee-deep in pluff mud, Jack felt his cell phone vibrate in his pocket. At this point, he was a little surprised it worked. Although he hadn't actually submerged it, his clothes were about as wet as they could get without having gone swimming.

Peeling off the thick gloves he was wearing, he fought the urge to toss up his guts now that he had a second to think about what they had discovered here. The fact that it was so close to Oyster Point almost made him retch.

The phone stopped ringing long before he had his hand free to shove down into his pocket. He fished it out and walked away from the rest of the crew to talk privately. Recognizing the number, he dialed the station, identified himself and waited for the dispatcher to determine who had called him. A message beeped through while he waited, and he cast a glance at the dredge nets stretched across the water. So far, they had unearthed eight bodies. The net was there to filter out personal belongings—rings, jewelry, clothing—anything that would help identify the victims. After being submerged in the water and mud, there wasn't much chance they would salvage any physical evidence that might lead them to a killer, but they'd called in a forensic anthropologist to assist with the identification process.

"Jack..." It was Don Garrison on the line. Don was back at the station booking Greene.

"Whatcha got?"

"It's the housekeeper," he said, and paused. "She just came forward with a helluva tale."

"And?"

"Uh ... she's coming out to show where to locate a body."

"We've got them," Jack said, not wanting Sadie in the way. Hearing the ruckus behind him, as they unearthed yet another, he said, "Nine so far."

"No," Garrison said, his voice sounding somber. "This one's ... in another location."

Jack pulled the phone back for an instant, bracing himself to hear what Garrison had to say. Anything involving Sadie would directly affect Caroline. He put the phone back to his ear, a new sense of dread settling in his gut.

Around him, men waded through the mire, some pushing inflatable rafts laden with body parts and bones. They had spotlights trained on the area from nearby boats. Standing in the middle of the shallows, he couldn't see out beyond the glare, but he knew Caroline was back there, watching from the Aldridge dock. One of his men had spoken to her, securing permission to search the area—permission he'd known she wouldn't deny them.

But where she was concerned, there was still a little hesitation on his part. He knew better than to talk to her about the unfolding investigation. Not only did he feel the need to protect her, but he also felt the need to insulate himself, because Caroline was bound to think in terms of breaking stories.

"Spit it out, Garrison."

"It's Sam Aldridge," he said. "Childres and her son buried the kid out in the marsh ... Jack ... I think Josh Childres is our man."

11:46 p.m.

The closer they got to Oyster Point, the more tense Josh seemed to become. Augusta couldn't help it; her suspicions were roused. After all the lies, she couldn't blindly ignore the thoughts that were racing through her brain.

The phone.

Sadie's car.

Josh's demeanor.

It was all a little unnerving.

She tried to roll down the passenger side window and found it locked. Josh didn't make a habit of riding around town with kids in his car, so why would he use the child lock? Neither did Sadie, for that matter. Just to be sure, she pressed the button again, sliding Josh a nervous glance. "So ... what are you doing driving Sadie's car?" she asked, trying to sound casual. "Just wanted a change?"

Her fingers began to tingle. She thought maybe it was because she was breathing a little too fast.

They were close enough to hear the choppers now, and his attention was centered overhead. The simple fact that neither of them had bothered to mention the aircraft left Augusta all the more on edge.

"I needed the cargo space ... I'm moving."

He was lying, she sensed.

Augusta turned to look at the backseat. There were no boxes, no tape, nothing that would indicate he had been moving all day. "You could have asked for help," she suggested. "I would've been happy to ..." Her sentence caught on a swallow. "Help."

Sadie's car had been parked at her house.

She stared at him, remembering.

Josh had the same build as the man in Sadie's house.

Why would Josh break into his own mother's house?

It didn't make sense.

She tried to keep the tremor out of her voice. "So ... have you been driving Sadie's car all day?"

She knew he hadn't been. It was a test. He slid her a look, one that said far more than words could have revealed, and her heart skipped a beat. For an instant, his blue eyes held her transfixed, and then he turned back to the road. The hairs on her arm stood on end. He knew what she was thinking. He made a sudden turn on Riverland Drive—away from home.

A sense of panic infused her. "Hey! I'm tired, Josh. Where are we going?"

"I want to show you something," he said.

"It's late. I'd rather go home."

He kept driving, and the car sped up, racing through back roads. She tried the lock again. The choppers disappeared above a canopy of ancient oaks, though she could still hear them.

"Please," she begged.

"It'll just take a minute," he said calmly, and kept driving. Faster now.

Augusta's heartbeat quickened painfully. Her gaze

turned to the phone in his console and then to her own, lying in her lap.

The slight fuzziness that had lingered in her head disappeared entirely. She could suddenly see every-thing with startling clarity. The beat of her heart played like drums in a symphony, and her breathing grew heavy enough to hurt. Minutes stretched by ... moments of indecision and confusion that hindered her ability to react.

She thought she smelled the scent of blood, but it was probably her own ... her shirt was stained with it.

"Josh?" she said, testing the name, because he suddenly seemed like a stranger. "Where are we going?"

She clicked on her cell phone to call her sister and he reached over to seize it from her, tossing it out his window. Without missing a beat, he reached over to grab her by the hair and slammed her face into the dash. The last thing Augusta remembered was the warm, thick trickle that seeped into her mouth.

JACK HUNG up and his gaze sought Ian Patterson.

Standing waist-deep in the muck, Patterson was taking direction from one of his men. He had promised to stay out of the way, but in the end, they'd needed all the willing hands they could rally.

Right now, he had a cold feeling down in his gut that was chilling him in a way the steady rainfall hadn't been able to accomplish.

He'd yet to return any of Caroline's calls, and he was far less inclined to call her now because he didn't know what to say to her—not yet. He didn't want to tell her anything, but he couldn't lie.

If what Don Garrison had said was true, they were

about to exhume her four-year-old brother after twenty-nine years. The thought of it made his head spin.

Sadie knew where Sam was buried.

She was bringing the police to exhume his body.

And somehow, Josh was involved.

Augusta, was his next immediate thought.

Before riling Patterson, or Caroline, he placed a call to the hospital, waiting with a sick feeling in his gut for the nurse who had treated Augusta to get on the line.

"She left about thirty-five to forty minutes ago," he said. "No broken bones. No concussion. There was really no reason to keep her."

Jack peered down at his watch: It was 12:10. He knew Caroline had decided to remain on the property and Sadie was on her way from the police station, which left only one logical conclusion. "Did she say who was picking her up?"

"No. But one of the other nurses wheeled her out after the discharge. Hang on, let me see what she knows." He set the phone down. Jack heard it clink softly on the desk. After an excruciatingly long two minutes, with Jack staring at his watch, the nurse returned. "She left in a silver SUV," he said. "But she couldn't remember what kind."

Jack dialed Caroline's number, his chest constricting painfully. "Where is Augusta?" he asked the moment she answered her phone.

"Jack!" she exclaimed. "Finally! I've been calling you nonstop all night! You can't just leave me in the dark here!"

"Caroline," he interrupted. "Where is Augusta?"

"She's on the way home," Caroline said, sounding

annoyed, but her tone softened at the urgency in his voice. "Josh offered to pick her up."

Jack felt as though a cannonball dropped in his belly at the disclosure.

"What's wrong, Jack?"

"Call me immediately if you hear from Augusta. I need to call you back," he said, and hung up, icy cold fingers ripping down his spine.

He had no proof, he reminded himself, but he knew ...

Augusta was with Josh.

If they'd left the hospital forty minutes ago, they would already be home by now. It was a short drive over the James Island Expressway.

He looked at his watch again: 12:12. He called the station back, instructing Garrison to call Sadie's escort to find out which car she had driven to the station. While he waited for the return call, he made a decision he might live to regret, and trudged toward Patterson through the mud. There was no proof, just gut feelings, but if it were Caroline whose life were in danger, he would want to know.

His phone rang as he struggled through the mud and he answered without hesitating to look at the ID.

"She came in Josh's Z4, said he needed her car to haul things to the house on Tradd Street. Apparently, he's moving."

"Fuck!" Jack said. "Put a BOLO on Sadie Childres's car right now. Silver 2014 model X3. Check the house on Tradd Street, and put a track on Augusta Aldridge's cell phone!"

26

Augusta awoke on a hard floor, dazed and sopping wet. She caught a sickly sweet smell—like rotten magnolias—and her head was pounding.

She heard voices.

No, just one.

Josh.

"Everything's fucking ruined!" he muttered beneath his breath.

Even as her brain honed in on the sound, her mind rejected the knowledge. There was a cloth covering her mouth. She reached for it, flicking it off, rolling toward the sound of his voice.

He hadn't noticed her yet. He was talking to a dark form in the corner, struggling with something. She blinked, focusing, and her breath caught at the sight of the child huddled on the floor. It was Cody Simmons. She hadn't seen him since he was in a hospital bassinet, but his picture had been plastered in every paper.

He was alive.

The boy met her gaze across the puddled floor, his eyes feverish but coherent.

Don't talk, Cody said to the lady in his head. *Be still.*

He was smart enough to know it wasn't good the man wasn't wearing a mask. He lay quietly while the man muttered to himself, like his dad did whenever his parents got into a fight. He'd brought a lady with him. She turned and met his gaze, and Cody warned her with his eyes not to speak.

The man was taking off Cody's cuffs, freeing him. He was standing close to the snake but he couldn't see it. It wiggled its tail silently in warning, and then cocked its head back, exposing fangs and a white stain in the shadows.

"Josh," the lady said.

She knew the man's name.

The bad man ignored her, unhitching Cody's cuff, pulling the metal brace apart before he turned to look at her.

Keeping his eye on the snake, Cody tested his freedom, wiggling his arms a bit. They didn't respond well, but he kept wiggling them, wincing as pain shot through his arms.

"You don't have to do this," the lady pleaded.

The man got up and walked over to the woman, away from the snake, looking down at her. "I'm not stupid, Augusta. I know what I have to do."

The lady sat up, holding her ribs. "They'll realize it was you, Josh. You're the one who picked me up from the hospital."

She was hurt, Cody thought.

"I can't control you, Augusta. Everyone knows how pigheaded you are. I'll say I dropped you off at Patterson's and that's the last I saw of you."

"What about Sadie's car?" she snapped.

"What about it?" he answered. "Did you bother to tell anyone it was parked at her house?"

The lady remained silent, rubbing her chest.

"That's what I thought," the man scoffed, but he sounded relieved. "I dropped you off at Patterson's and haven't talked to anyone since, so how could I possibly know he would be out with Jack, minding other people's business? And that you would be left all alone? Poor Augusta—always in the middle of things she shouldn't be."

The lady grimaced and tried to rise, but the man walked over and kicked her back on her butt and she let out a whimper. "Ian saw her car, too," she argued.

Cody thought she was brave.

The man said nothing for a minute, and then, "Ian's brain is full of shit, largely because of you. He was getting close, but all it took to get him off Jennifer's trail was for you to come into the picture. No one knows shit," he insisted. "Everyone sees exactly what they want to, no more."

"You killed her, too, didn't you?"

The man shrugged, Cody's handcuff dangling from his hand, and Cody knew he intended to put the cuffs on the lady's wrists ... unless Cody could do something to stop him. But he knew he couldn't fight the man alone. He was weak, and his feet were still tied with rope ... but he still had a brain ... and a friend.

His gaze slid to the snake.

"They're going to find you, Josh."

The man's pant leg was hitched around a knife holster that was strapped to his leg. In it was the biggest knife Cody had ever seen. The blade winked in a spear of moonlight that penetrated the window.

"No, they won't. There's not a shred of evidence pointing to me."

Cody peered back at the snake, its body black as coal, blending with the darkness.

"You can bet *someone* saw *something*. They *are* going to find out."

"I don't think so," the man argued. "But if they do, you won't be anywhere around to tell any tales."

Augusta peered around, examining her surroundings more closely.

She didn't recognize this place.

It was an old building in the middle of nowhere. The windows were all boarded up, except one. Outside she could see a train trestle through a blanket of mist. She didn't recognize it, but there were many of them around—old defunct bridges that had carried coal-powered trains.

"Do you know how many bodies Gaskins tossed into the swamp?"

"What is he now? Your idol?" Augusta countered angrily.

"He was stupid," he spat. "The point I'm trying to make is that I'm not." He swung the metal cuffs between them, almost as though he intended to swing them at her. Augusta watched the shiny metal rings move to and fro, her brain searching for options.

The rain had stopped, but the entire floor on one side was wet. Cody was lying in a puddle on one side of the floor, with his hands still stretched above his head as though he didn't realize his wrists were free. The kid was barely aware. Augusta's heart ached for him. "Where are we?" she asked.

Josh smiled coldly. "You've seen too many movies, Augusta. This isn't the part where I tell you where you are and why I did it. Sorry to disappoint you."

Even the sight of the swinging cuffs couldn't silence her. "No, I know why you did it, Josh. You did it because you're crazy!" Her gaze reverted to Cody.

"Why don't you at least let him go? What do you want him for?"

His grip tightened on the cuffs, but his anger wasn't apparent in his face. "Sure, Augusta. Why don't I set him free so he can run all the way home—and now, thanks to you, he even knows my name. No. That's not the way this is gonna go. I promise, no one will find you here. No one has a clue where this place is, and those who do forget about it five minutes after they see it. They're blind to it, just like people are blind to all the shit they don't want to see!"

His blue eyes glittered, cold as diamonds. "Flo was a stupid bitch. She thought my mother would be happier with the house on Tradd Street. She was doing it for you, you know? Giving away all that land to please a little girl who didn't know enough to appreciate what she had. Well, I wasn't about to let her expose my little secret!"

A little piece of Augusta died with that revelation—that until her last breath her mother had been trying to mend fences Augusta was so determined to reinforce. For years she had begged her mother to donate the slaves' quarters and the overseer's house to the city—a compromise for Caroline, who valued their history. Augusta had simply wished to wash her hands of all things that brought her shame.

"So what are you doing to do?"

He smiled thinly. "Maybe I'll cut you into pieces and feed you to the gators. That ought to appeal nicely to your inner conservationist."

"Is that what you did with the rest of them?"

He shook his head. "Not exactly. But don't worry, we'll give you a better funeral than Sammy had—and then maybe I'll find a way to reunite you with Savannah and Caroline, too." He stooped, cuffs in hand, ready to put them on her, and Augusta kicked him away a little desperately.

"I am not going to just let you put those on me!"

Very calmly, he unsheathed a knife from his boot, holding the gleaming blade between them. "Maybe this will persuade you?"

"Fuck you!" she screamed, and kicked again when he came close, landing a blow near his groin. His face contorted. "I'm not going to make this easy for you, Josh! If you're going to slice my throat, they are going to find your flesh beneath my nails." She scrambled backward as he straightened.

The look on his face changed to one of pure fury. "You always were a fucking bitch," he said. "I don't know what I ever saw in you!"

Augusta thought she might puke at his declaration. "Even knowing the truth, that's all you can think about?" she asked. "You're my fucking brother—not that I can ever be proud of that fact. You're a monster!"

He smiled coldly.

"All those bodies out in the marsh," she said. "They're all yours, aren't they?"

"Yep," he said, without remorse. "And every single one of them looked at me like I was God in the end— and so will you, *sister.*" He made another lunge for her, and Augusta scrambled away from him, her ribs burning. "You're crazy!" she spat. He went after her once more, knife extended, and Augusta kicked his hand. The knife flew out of his grasp and slid across the floor, skipping through the puddles like a stone.

"Fucking bitch!" he groused.

The knife gleamed under a shaft of moonlight.

Cody realized he could reach it.

Instinctively—like the time he caught the grounder and got that mouthy kid out at second—he dove after it, willing his hands to work as he dove as far as the ropes would let him go. The pain in his right ankle sharpened as the ropes caught his feet. With floppy hands, he slapped the knife toward the wood-pile in the corner. The cottonmouth hinged its mouth back farther, warning everyone to stay away, but the man couldn't see it in his upright position. The knife landed beneath the woodpile, its handle winking from the shadows.

"Goddamned brat!" he shouted as he lunged to-ward the knife, glaring at Cody. "I should've killed you as soon as I brought you here!"

Cody recoiled at once, away from the man, away from the woodpile. His eyes sought the lady's. For an instant, the two of them locked gazes. Her eyes were wide with fear, but Cody wasn't afraid. She tried to get up, clutching her ribs, and Cody shook his head no, telling her without words to stay. His gaze skidded to the corner where the knife had landed beneath a board, its gleaming blade reflecting the moonlight.

It happened fast.

The cottonmouth struck as the man reached down to grab his knife. With the force of a hammer, it sank its fangs into the man's arm, gnawing to embed its poison deeper. The knife slid over to Cody. Shrieking in pain, the man pulled his arm away with the snake still attached, swinging wildly as the cottonmouth clung to his arm. He finally flung the snake off. It fell to the floor, then propelled itself after him again, its fangs sinking once more into the flesh of the man's calf. The man shouted again, trying to flip the snake off his leg.

The woman scrambled to Cody's side, taking the knife and quickly cutting the rest of Cody's ropes, then scooped him up while the man fought with the snake. The heavy knife fell to the floor with a clatter.

"Over there!" Cody pointed and the lady ran with him toward the hole in the floor. The metal grate was still pushed away from the opening where the man had dragged the woman through with him. She dropped Cody down into the water. He sank like a rock and held his breath. Like in a dream, he heard the splash of water as she came into the water after him.

27

Realizing she had mere seconds before Josh pulled himself together and came after them, Augusta dragged Cody beneath the building toward safety. The water was deep here—deep enough that she couldn't feel the muddy bottom. There was a narrow space of air between the floor and the river. But she wasn't strong enough to keep Cody afloat and still get them far enough away from Josh. Grateful Cody wasn't struggling, she pulled his weight along behind her, praying he was holding his breath.

She had no idea where they were.

Even less where they were going.

She just knew she had to get away.

Resurfacing for a moment to get her bearings, she dragged the child up for a breath and could hear Josh cursing somewhere in the building. It sounded as though he was running toward the trapdoor in the floor, his footsteps clumsy, and then he stumbled and fell again, cursing profanely.

"You're going to be fine," she assured Cody.

"I know," the boy whispered, shivering. But she knew he must be terrified.

"Hold your breath," she ordered and pulled him

back beneath the water. Ignoring the pain that shot through her ribs, she swam with every bit of strength she possessed.

It was impossible to see where they were going. The water was black. But Augusta kept swimming. When she resurfaced, she had never been happier to see open sky, and even happier to hear the sound of choppers in the air. She knew instinctively they were searching for her, and they were coming closer.

All she had to do was get Cody to shore, she told herself, and kept swimming, pulling the boy behind her. Though his upper body felt like dead weight, he kicked his feet, helping her stay afloat.

In the darkness, the bank seemed so far away.

Cody sputtered as she dunked him and came back up, gasping for breath. Augusta didn't think she would make it, but she couldn't stop now, knowing Cody was counting on her.

Dear God, she prayed. *Let me get Cody to safety.*

The Ashley River was nearly thirty miles long and wider than the Cooper. On the other side of Folly, the Stono River cut its way through more swampy terrain, wrapping around John's Island and separating it from James Island. Augusta had no idea which river they were on, but instinct told her they were somewhere on the Stono. She had no memory of the drive to this place and realized Josh had probably kept her out cold by giving her a dose of chloroform. They could be anywhere.

Above them, one of two choppers swept by and then suddenly turned around. The other followed, spotlights swinging toward the water. In their light, she could see Josh appear from beneath the building. He swam toward them, closing the distance faster than Augusta could manage with the burden of a child in her arms.

The bank was too far.

Keep swimming, Augusta.

Josh was a better long-distance swimmer than she was, but she had determination on her side.

Watch this, Augusta! she heard in her mind—a long-buried memory. Josh dove out of the boat with more than five hundred yards left to go through rough waters to get to shore. By dint of sheer determination, with Augusta motoring beside him, he'd made it without any problem.

The memory alone was enough to make her sink beneath the surface, but she propelled herself back up and kept going.

The choppers were circling now, searching for a safe place to land.

In the distance, she heard police sirens approaching. But not fast enough. Josh kept swimming, faster, closer. It felt as though she had swum miles already. The pain in her chest threatened to blacken her senses.

From nowhere, her sister Savannah's voice whispered in her ear. *There might come a moment when you will ask yourself, "What should I do?" Do what Augusta Aldridge would never do.*

Her arms were tired now.

Don't give up.

Her sister knew things.

The last time she had followed Savannah's advice, she had avoided a mugging in a dark alley—maybe worse—because *now* she realized how close they had lived for so long to something vile.

What should she do?

Josh was closer—close enough that she saw the

brilliant blue of his eyes gleaming beneath the spot-lights. Suddenly, the choppers spun their lights away and disappeared behind the tree line.

"Can you swim?" she asked Cody.

"Yes!" he said, and she shoved him toward shore, but he sank like a rock. She grabbed him by the hair, dragging him back up.

What could she do?

Do what Augusta Aldridge would never do, her sister's voice insisted.

Josh knew her better than anyone. He knew her secrets. He knew everything. What would Josh expect her to do?

He was so close now.

His head momentarily bobbed beneath the sur-face, but reemerged at once and he took a clumsy stroke.

Augusta turned to peer at the shoreline. It was get-ting closer now, but that was what anyone would be expected to do. *Swim toward shore.*

On land, Josh could easily overtake her. A single snakebite probably wouldn't kill a grown man, but the snake was large, its body thick and black. She knew it had bitten him more than once.

Her ribs burned, her arms hurt, but Cody was helping her as best he could.

When their dog Bear died, his body had swollen to twice its normal size within fifteen minutes. It hap-pened quickly. They'd learned later the cottonmouth's venom was a hemotoxin and caused paralysis. The dog had probably drowned before he was pulled ashore.

Josh's head sank beneath the water again, and Au-gusta didn't hesitate. She didn't wait to see if he would resurface this time. Making a sudden decision, she turned away from shore, swimming back into the middle of the river, toward the brightest part of the night sky.

She held Cody around his neck. "Swim, Cody!" she encouraged and she didn't have to ask again. He moved his feet like little flippers and the two of them swam blindly toward the city lights. The sirens grew closer, but Augusta kept going, swimming parallel to the shore.

Josh tried to follow, swimming clumsily now. "Augusta!" she heard him scream, but her name was a slurred sound coming out of his mouth. She didn't stop. The boy in her arms was all she cared about right now.

Behind them, Josh began to fall farther and farther behind.

Another chopper flew by, swinging its spotlight into the river.

That was the last time Augusta spied Josh's head above water. He took a last awkward stroke, slapping the water and then his head went down and didn't reappear.

Augusta swam until she couldn't anymore, pulling Cody by his neck. They ran aground on the tidal flats, and she dragged him through the spartina grass to his feet, scooping him immediately into her arms. Finding strength she didn't know she possessed, she trudged through the mire. The child's grip tightened, his little arms squeezing her tighter. Despite the pain in her ribs, Augusta welcomed the feel of it.

"Thank you," he cried, burying his face against her neck.

Too out of breath to respond, Augusta held him close, and made her way toward the sirens.

In TOTAL, sixteen bodies were unearthed from the pluff mud.

Sam's bones were not among them, but they had been nearby all along, buried along a stretch of their own property near the ruins ... where an ancient magnolia tree vied for survival among the more aggressive natural flora. Covered by vines, and pressed between overgrown oaks and blackgum trees, the tree was diseased and dying.

The leaves had formed purplish-black spots with white centers and powdery mildew. Infected leaves fell prematurely from the tree—a blanket of disease covered Sam's unmarked grave—like the lies and deceit that had cloaked their lives.

So they moved him to a spot nestled within reach of their mother's loving arms, beneath a gorgeous live oak, its branches thick and leaden with age. Silver moss clung to the boughs like hoary curtains. After twenty-nine long years they finally had closure.

Coming to grips with everything would become their journey now—a journey the three of them had agreed to embark upon together. If there was one thing this ordeal had done for them ... it was to bring them closer together.

Savannah booked a flight home the minute she heard. She would finish her book here, unfettered from her life in D.C. Caroline set a date to marry Jack and arranged to empty her storage units in Dallas. Augusta formally quit her job in New York and planned to finish the renovations before making a decision about what she would to do with the rest of her life.

As for Sadie, they were trying hard to forgive her. After all, she was the woman who had raised them ...

and she hadn't actually known about Josh's secret life —nor had she consciously suspected until they had begun to unearth the horrors in the marsh. It was only then that she had dared to see her son with different eyes and had come forward to confess.

But she had lied. She had kept Sam's body a secret from them—and it didn't matter whom she was protecting. She had lied about Josh, as well. Understanding her reasons didn't excuse her, but she was only human ... and none of them could claim to be perfect.

Still, Augusta couldn't bear to see her grieve for a monster. Josh might have been her son, and their brother, but she could not separate the good from the evil. All their memories now were tarnished beyond repair.

Cody Simmons remained in the hospital, but he would recover. Six days without food or water had taken a toll on his little body. His ankle was broken, and it was possible he would lose the use of his left hand. The pressure of leaning on one side of his body had constricted blood flow to that limb, but he was a lucky little boy and didn't seem to care. The Charleston police department planned to award him the medal of valor, for acts of bravery and endurance. Without him, Augusta knew neither of them would have survived.

If any one thing had been different, Cody—and Augusta—might be exactly where Sam was right now.

As a matter of courtesy, Sadie had stayed away from the private ceremony, leaving these moments for Augusta, Caroline and Savannah alone. It didn't seem appropriate for her to be there.

Augusta couldn't have borne a crowd. This moment was private, painful and long overdue. All the tears she had not been able to shed at her mother's funeral now flowed from her eyes in an endless stream.

At her side, Ian held her by the arm, as though to keep her upright. Jack stood by Caroline's side, and Savannah stood stoically at Augusta's left, leaning close, but standing alone.

There was no way to determine Sammy's cause of death precisely, but there were no fractures in his skeleton—nothing to indicate his death had been violent. Sadie claimed his body had washed ashore long after the fact, and that she had buried him. But knowing what they knew now about Josh, Sam's death broke Augusta's heart all over again.

The rest of her brother's story remained shrouded in mystery because Josh's body was never found. They dredged the shore for miles, searching for his corpse to no avail. Augusta decided it was poetic justice.

"Give us light to guide us out of our darkness into the assurance of your love, in Jesus Christ our Lord," the pastor intoned—words she'd heard far too often in such a short time.

"Amen," all three sisters said in return.

Caroline was the first to step forward to toss her white lily into the grave. Augusta and Savannah followed. And then it was done. At long last, her baby brother's little patch of empty earth was empty no longer.

The last rays of sun glinted off the boathouse roof in the distance. Ian and Augusta sat on the joggling board on the porch, staring out at the marsh.

At one time, the idea of enjoying the sounds of the marsh from this front porch had been a nightmare.

Suddenly, it didn't seem such a bad thing. After the year was up, they might sell the property, but they hadn't decided as yet. She still had to restore it, Caroline had to continue to revive the newspaper ... and Savannah would have to write her book. With eight months left to go, anything could happen ... and if Savannah was brave enough to write it ... there was a story to tell ...

Her sisters and Jack were now inside with Sadie.

Punishing her for Josh's sins seemed wrong, but it would be difficult to put the past entirely behind them. She and Daniel had come by to let them know that she was giving her property to the city in accordance with Florence's will. Daniel had asked her to marry him. Sadie had agreed, and planned to move in with him in his house downtown. For Sadie, leaving her home was as much a matter of healing as repairing the main house was for Augusta.

The police were not pursuing charges against her, although they could have. Sadie hadn't known about Josh's crimes. Her greatest sin was in trying to protect those she loved.

On the porch, she and Ian lapsed into an easy silence and Augusta sucked in a breath of sulfur-tinged air, trying to feel differently about the place she'd once called home ... could she do it again?

"This is straight out of a painting," Ian said at her side.

"Yeah," Augusta agreed, and nodded. For certain, the marsh was beautiful, but she wasn't sure she could live here once the house was restored.

Beside her, Ian pulled something out of his shirt pocket, and held it in a closed fist.

"I hear people say all the time that if you wait until

the right time to have a baby, there would be no kids born on this planet."

Augusta looked at him, wondering at the random remark.

"I've never been much for doing things the way other folks feel is right ..." He slid to one knee beside her. "But you're right ... asking the woman I love—the only woman I've ever loved—to marry me in a text is lame." He opened his hand to reveal a beautiful silver ring set with at least a two-karat emerald. "So ... will you marry me, Augusta?" he asked, his heart shining like a light in his bright blue eyes.

Augusta stared at the ring, tears forming in her eyes. Moonlight shone off the silver band with a twinkle that mirrored the one in Ian's eyes.

"Yes," she said, and in that instant, a flicker of light lit the air between them. For an instant, the glitter took Augusta aback. Fireflies were becoming rare in this area, but here one was, its light a symbol of hope. It lit again, flying up above their heads like a tiny electric bulb, and then flittered into the night.

She and her sister had once sat right here on this porch counting fireflies ... looking for hope in the rare glow of their bodies. They'd sat here all night, waiting, hoping ... and they'd seen nothing, going back inside, disheartened and hopeless.

Ian couldn't have truly understood the magic this insect's appearance held for her, but he sensed the pent-up emotion she couldn't share, and kissed her gently.

"I love you," he said, and pulled her back to lay her head upon his shoulder. Then they sat there, under the veranda, staring out at spartina grass ... where, if you looked hard enough, a symphony of glow lights accompanied the musical sounds of the marsh.

SPEAK NO EVIL

Did you read book 1 in this series?

Lifting the veil of secrecy on a grand Southern family in decline. New York Times bestselling author Tanya Anne Crosby explores the lives of Caroline, Augusta, and Savannah Aldridge, three sisters who share a dark past and an uncertain future...

After the death of their mother, a newspaper heiress, Caroline Aldridge steps up to head the paper. But a killer is making headlines, and Caroline may have unwittingly stepped into the crosshairs. Even as she mends the tattered bonds of sisterhood, a sinister force beyond their control may tear them apart forever...

Get Speak No Evil Now

"Crosby easily paints an eerie setting that on the outside seems beautiful, but lurking beneath the shadows is something sinister. Reminiscent of an old Hitchcock film."

— A READER

THE GIRL WHO STAYED

EXCLUSIVE PREVIEW

TANYA ANNE CROSBY

FOREWORD

Dearest reader

My very first hardcover release, The Girl Who Stayed, is a book of the heart. Set in Sullivan's Island, South Carolina, this book takes me home and is both deeply personal and intensely satisfying. It's not a romance, not a historical, but you'll find my same voice here, with the same connection to the characters.

These are some of the things people are saying about The Girl Who Stayed... and then keep reading for an excerpt...

A beautifully written, page-turning novel packed with emotion.

— #1 NEW YORK TIMES BESTSELLING AUTHOR
BARBARA FREETHY

THE GIRL WHO STAYED is a deeply moving story. I am fascinated by the concept and by Tanya Crosby's stunning storytelling.

— STELLA CAMERON, NEW YORK TIMES
BESTSELLING AUTHOR

THE GIRL WHO STAYED defies type. Crosby's tale is honest and sensitive, eerie and tragic. It's a homecoming tale of a past ever with us and irrevocably lost forever. A haunting vision of that chasm between life and death we call 'missing.'

— PAMELA MORSI, BESTSELLING AUTHOR OF SIMPLE JESS

An intense, mesmerizing Southern drama about a young woman who returns to her coastal home to put to rest the haunting ghost of her sister's tragic past. Told in the rich, lyrical style of Siddons and Conroy, THE GIRL WHO STAYED is a woman's story of discovery and acceptance, redefined by Tanya Anne Crosby's dramatic storytelling, sharp characters, and well-defined plot. A must read for any woman who believes she can never go back home. Fabulous, rich and evocative!

— NEW YORK TIMES BESTSELLING AUTHOR JILL BARNETT

Crosby tugs heartstrings in a spellbinding story of a woman trying to move beyond her past.

— NEW YORK TIMES BESTSELLING AUTHOR SUSAN ANDERSEN

1

EXCERPT

The cell phone on the passenger seat gave a rude squawk. It rang on and on but Zoe ignored it, as though the act of doing so might buy her more time.

Compelled to look at every blond head she passed by—inside cars, along the bike ramp—it crossed her mind that Hannah would have loved biking over the new bridge—the third bridge to span the Cooper since the island's colonization. Originally, there had been two, standing side by side.

Zoe dated a guy once who'd claimed his grandfather helped build the first Cooper River Bridge. He was an oddball, talking incessantly about an ex-girlfriend, who just happened to look a lot like Zoe. Hearing this had made Zoe look at him differently, not the hunky guy he'd appeared to be, but the obsessive stalker beneath, who'd rather kill and stuff an ex-girlfriend than lose her. Regrettably, this image was further reinforced by his other favorite topic, which happened to be the family business, a mortuary. Not taxidermy, but close enough.

So one night, while crossing the Cooper—about three miles worth of mindless chatter—he'd gone back and forth between telling Zoe about this look-alike ex, explaining the process of embalming, and regaling her with tales of his grandfather's escapades during the building of the first bridge. Of course, at the time, both bridges had been past their prime, and even without stories about cadavers and look-alike exes, it was creepy enough driving over a swaying expanse of groaning, creaking metal—in the dark, mind you. Suffice it to say, the date hadn't turned into a second and even now, Zoe couldn't remember his name.

Bart, maybe.

The bridge Bart's grandfather had worked on was built around 1929, the second in 1966. The Silas Pearman Bridge was constructed to relieve load limits on the Grace Memorial Bridge, but both had been narrow enough to make driving over them harrowing, especially after the lanes were opened to two-way traffic.

It wasn't like that anymore. The first two bridges were demolished and a third went up—the Arthur Ravenel Jr. Bridge, a cable-stayed, eight-lane overpass that included pedestrian and bike lanes. This bridge was named after a retired US Congressman, although if you asked anyone the name of any one of these three bridges, they'd give you the same answer: it was the Cooper River Bridge.

The point being: on that old bridge, especially at night, you drove all the way across, shoulders tense, black skies overhead, black river below, ignoring the headlights that appeared as though they were coming straight into your lane. There was nowhere to swerve off to, nowhere to escape—unless you wanted to ram through thick sheets of metal and off into the river below.

Once on the bridge, you were at the mercy of oncoming drivers and your choice—the only choice—was to stay the course, fists gripping the steering wheel, holding your breath, hoping today wasn't your day to end up in the grill of an oncoming vehicle. And all the while, you could feel the bridge shuddering beneath you.

That's how Zoe felt right now: Tense. Expectant. No choice but to move forward. Hoping to avert impending disaster.

Back when Zoe's great-grandparents first purchased the house on Sullivan's, they'd had to take a ferry. It was a short hop from the peninsula in plain view of Fort Sumter. Edgar Allan Poe once wrote that the island, little more than a splinter of land, was "separated from the mainland by a scarcely perceptible creek, oozing its way through a wilderness of reeds and slime." Zoe loved his description, unflattering as it was, because it was the way she saw the island too—full of secrets whispered through dense tangles of sweet myrtle . . . secrets kept, no matter how long or hard you searched.

Leaving the bridge, shoulders tight, Zoe passed repurposed buildings and shopping centers that appeared as though they'd already lived out one commercial lifetime during her absence and now were preparing for a dubious rebirth, with freshly painted facades and empty parking spaces out in front. The hamburger joint she and her friends had satisfied munchies at was gone, converted into a ratty tire shop. But the Page's Thieves Market was still there, with the vintage street clock still guarding the porch, like a shiny silver sentinel.

They sold houses now as well—at least that's what her brother said. Maybe she could enlist their help.

The last few times Zoe had come to Charleston

she'd stayed with her brother Nick, never bothering to check on the house. She left Sullivan's on the day she turned eighteen and never looked back, except to return long enough to bury her mom. Her dad was already gone before she moved away, puffing on unfiltered cigarettes every minute of his miserable life, until the smoke cleared and he was no more. Throat cancer. But like she told Nick, Rob Rutherford was dead to her long before that.

Of course, Nick led a Hallmark life, like the one they'd always believed they'd shared . . . back before that day in December, back when all the neighbors crowed about their perfect family. Beautiful children. Beautiful parents. A house with a foundation as old as Charleston. How lucky they were.

How lucky they were.

That house. It had weathered Hugo, withstood the sea, but never made it past Hannah Rutherford's disappearance—or, more to the point, her family hadn't survived. The house on the feral lot on Atlantic Avenue, with the screened-in porch was standing still . . .

Zoe pulled into the familiar driveway, stopping the car where she remembered parking Hannah's bike all those years before. The engine idled like an old man with hiccoughs. She pulled out the keys and palmed them, clutching the metal so hard the teeth cut into her skin. The scar on her forehead itched, but she tried to put it out of her mind. Seated in the driver's seat, Zoe took a moment to survey the dirty white bungalow.

It was older now, not so old as some. The wood and cinderblock siding needed a good coat of paint. The yard had returned to scrub. The native sweet myrtle had overtaken the lot. It clambered toward the house, clawing desperately at the siding. In one spot, it managed to stab meanly through the porch screen.

Fifteen feet high in some places, the shrubbery on the right side of the lot obscured the neighbors' house from Zoe's vantage in the drive. On the other side, a six-foot-high row of red azaleas were in full bloom—blood-red blossoms dripping from every branch.

On the front side of the screened-in porch remained a baseball-sized hole in the mesh. Zoe remembered when it happened. She and Nick had been throwing the baseball out in the yard, just the two of them. Wearing her dad's stiff glove, she'd made a sad attempt to help her brother improve his game.

Standing in the front yard, her brother had looked sullen, ready to give up. "Come on," Zoe had said. "You're so much better than me."

The comparison hadn't cheered him. He was better than Zoe, but Zoe rather sucked. "I'm no good, Nicky. Why don't you ask Kevin to come throw with you?"

Kevin was Nick's friend who'd lived over on Goldbug Avenue—a kid whose family still ate dinner together and who sometimes went fishing with his dad.

Her baby brother had given a half shake of his head, as though the effort might be more than he cared to make. He'd dropped the ball into his glove, then picked it up again, dropping it yet again, probably wondering why their dad was inside yelling at their mom. Again. Or maybe he'd simply been wishing he had a brother instead of a sister—one sister. That was key. By that time, Hannah was already gone, her twin bed donated to a new mom from church, whose three-year-old had outgrown his crib.

There was something about the look in Nicky's

eyes that had made Zoe feel his life—all that he could be—hung in the balance.

It had been hot and humid that day, not unlike today. The hair had stuck to the back of Zoe's neck. The inside door shut tight to keep the argument contained within, probably hadn't improved either of her parents' moods.

Staring into his glove, Nicky had continued dropping the ball, picking it up again, decisions being made...

"It's my fault," Zoe had reasoned. "I'm not very good, Nicky. Let's just do it again."

Her brother had seemed to consider this. His wavy, blond hair was sweaty at the ends, dark—as dark as his somber brown eyes. At nine years old, he was already becoming a crusty old man. Shifting uneasily from foot to foot, Zoe had pounded her fist into the oversized glove the way she'd watched them do on TV.

"Come on," she'd coaxed. "I'm ready now. Come on, Nicky Boy!"

Nicky Boy. That was the name her dad would have used—mostly when he was in a good mood. But good moods had become few and far between.

A half smile had turned her brother's lips then, a little gleam in his eyes that brought to mind Casey at the bat. He'd taken a ready stance, thinking, thinking, aiming...

Rearing back, he'd set the ball loose. It flew over Zoe's head, powered by all the anger he'd had mustered up inside, ripping through the flimsy screen, and crashing into the inside window, shattering glass.

No longer contained, her parents' voices had risen to a crescendo. Zoe's brain had refused to recognize coherent words and phrases. She and Nicky had given each other wary glances, and then their father had exploded onto the screened porch—red face, tan khakis, silver keys. He'd flown out the screened door, toward his pickup, mouthing obscenities, and Zoe had pretended to be a statue until Robert Rutherford was safely inside his truck. And then, just to be certain, she hadn't moved until after he'd peeled out of the driveway, kicking up gravel and shells in his wake.

And now, seated in her own car, with the windows rolled up, Zoe stared at the hole in the porch screen. The mesh was curled with age, never repaired. One month after Nick ripped the screen with his baseball, Hurricane Hugo had thrown more than baseballs at the house. It managed to stave off that assault as well, but as far as the will to set things right went, it pushed any remaining resolve over the edge, never to return.

Across the street, a brand-new triple-story house on stilts had gone up since Zoe left the island. Only because she was checking the housing market, she knew it was now in foreclosure. Sitting empty, with its lovely peach facade, it was a million-dollar oops for somebody. Somewhere near two dozen homes remained of the original dwellings that once complemented the old military base. A few of the island houses were as ancient as Fort Moultrie, but not included in the registry as original base housing.

Fort Moultrie was where Edgar Allan Poe was once stationed. All these years later, the man had a street, a library, and a pub named after him. In return, he had immortalized the island in his story "The Gold-Bug"—not Goldbug, as some dummy had named one of the back streets on the island. Only a writer would get the difference. And there, behind Goldbug Avenue, up against the salt marsh, was Raven Drive. Here, you see, was a going theme. Probably not because of it, though certainly not in spite of it, this pinprick of land on a splinter of sand was worth more than Zoe could walk away from. So here she was, at their "Kingdom by the Sea," appropriately named by her great-grandmother in honor of Poe's Annabel Lee. Clever.

Very clever, indeed.

The wooden sign out on the porch hung stock-still, despite the proximity to the beach, as though the world itself held its breath to see what Zoe would do.

Breathe in.

Breathe out.

It's just a house.

Zoe opened the car door, stepping out. Heavy and oppressive, the island heat smacked her full in the face. She moved through it, stepping through a time warp...

Keep reading, buy the Girl Who Stayed

Download the FREE prequel short story, The Things We Leave Behind

ABOUT THE AUTHOR

Tanya Anne Crosby's novels have graced numerous bestseller lists including the New York Times and USA Today. Best known for stories charged with emotion and humor, and filled with flawed characters, her novels have garnered reader praise and glowing critical reviews. She lives with her husband, two dogs and two moody cats in northern Michigan.

For more information
www.tanyaannecrosby.com
tanya@tanyaannecrosby.com

9 78

9 781947 204249